■ ■ ■

Triads

■ ■ ■

Triads

■ ■ ■

Poppy Z. Brite

and

Christa Faust

Subterranean Press ▪ 2004

FIRST EDITION

ISBN
1931081-40-9

Subterranean Press
P.O. Box 190106
Burton, MI 48519

email:
subpress@earthlink.net

website:
www.subterraneanpress.com

To Su Wei

■ ■ ■

PART ONE

■ ■ ■

Hong Kong, 1937

■ ■ ■

Backstage at the Lucky Dragon Theater, the air was thick with the smell of greasepaint and incense and the sweat of young boys. Small warriors in richly embroidered red and gold jackets crowded before fragments of cracked mirror, painting lips and smooth-lidded eyes with long brushes. Pairs of boys took turns stretching each other's muscles in the complex and painful positions that prepared their bodies for the rigors of Peking Opera. Thighs made fluid 360-degree rotations in hip sockets; spines bent backward like grasses in a wind. An older boy, fourteen or so, tied a long white beard around his feral young jaw and struck an arthritic pose, his pleated sleeves quivering.

Against the far wall, a boy in an iridescent green-and-silver tunic squatted with his arms crossed. He was tall for his age and broad-shouldered, with bony wrists and wide, expressive hands. The angles of his painted face were strong and lean, and might have been considered harsh if not for a pair of comically large ears that stuck out like the handles on a jug.

He tipped his head back against the splintery wall and drew in a slow breath. His body felt tight as a finely tuned string waiting to be plucked. The wet ribbon tied across his forehead was beginning to dry beneath his peaked cap, tightening the skin above his eyes until it was impossible to blink. This gave his red-shaded eyebrows a classical arch. After an hour or two, it also dried out his eyeballs to the point of agony.

But the burning of his eyes and the hot itch of his skin beneath the makeup were familiar torments. After eight years, these were no more noticeable than the ache in his empty belly or the pain inflicted by his daily exercise routine.

"Ji Fung."

The soft voice pulled him from the well of mindless contemplation. He looked up into the wide painted eyes of his best friend, Lin Bai, in the white-and-silver robes of the seductive White Snake.

In full dress, Lin Bai was transformed from an unusually pretty boy to a vision of beauty that disturbed Ji Fung every time he saw it. His friend's familiar face eclipsed by fantasy made Ji Fung's belly boil with a stew of contradictory emotions. He would recall the long hungry nights when he and Lin Bai had huddled close under their thin blankets, whispering small dreams and secrets in the cavernous silence of the dormitory hall.

Master Lau was old-fashioned and still believed that real women were bad luck onstage. He had given Lin Bai his name, which meant *hidden lotus*, more like a girl's name. And Lin Bai was brilliant in the roles of pretend women. He played female warriors like Mu Lan and tragic heroines like Chu Ying-tai with equal finesse. Ji Fung's own broad chest and natural acrobatic dexterity conspired with his mediocre singing voice to keep him in the grueling roles of soldiers and other sword fodder.

Lin Bai was born to play the leads. He possessed the grace of a swallow, the flagrant lushness of a full-blown orchid, the cool beauty of white jade. His voice was plangent and full of color. He had already struck sparks of competition in stars ten years his senior. His fellow students despised him as a cosseted lapdog, the Master's favorite, who had a mouthful of hot rice even when everyone else went hungry. Ji Fung was his only friend.

"Help me with my banners." Lin Bai's cherry mouth turned up slightly at one corner.

Ji Fung took the padded harness with its four white banners, motioning for Lin Bai to turn around. Lin Bai obeyed silently, head down; he knew how to take an order. Ji Fung pulled the straps across his friend's narrow chest and knotted them tight, tugging lightly to make certain they would hold. Lin Bai shook his upper body, testing. The silver embroidery flashed as the four banners fluttered like wings. Lin Bai smiled, and Ji Fung felt suddenly hot and cold at once. He turned away.

Dusty purple curtains at the far end of the dressing room parted, and Master Lau strode into the midst of the bright chaos. The boys' musical chatter died.

"Enough playing around!" The Master's heavy eyebrows dipped low over his eyes, then shot up alarmingly. He was a tall man, heavily muscled, with a sensuous mouth that seemed misplaced beneath his blade of a nose and sharp stony eyes. Displeasure in those eyes was every boy's nightmare, for the Master's punishments were dispensed often and without warning. Ji Fung had known them all: forced to dance and somersault until his ligaments screamed in agony; made to bend over and count off the strokes as his tender bottom was caned raw; ordered to balance on his hands so long that he could not unbend his wrists for hours afterward. The Master was their teacher, their father, and their god. They longed for his rare praise and lived in terror of his disapproval. Many could not imagine their lives without him.

"The performance is beginning," said the Master. "No mistakes."

The boys lined up for inspection. Master Lau walked down the row, critical eye burning through his young charges. Here, a crooked pompon on a headdress earned a cruel ear-twist; there, an imperfectly painted face brought a stinging slap to the back of a neck. The Master passed over Ji Fung and the other bit players with little more than a nod, but he stood before Lin Bai for nearly a full minute, glaring at him as if he could see through cloth and flesh and into the ruby depths of the boy's beating heart. Lin Bai would not meet his master's gaze. His female garb and the demure cast of his eyes made him seem coy. Only Ji Fung knew him well enough to read the hatred in his stiff spine and taut jaw.

Lin Bai loathed Master Lau with a vehemence Ji Fung had never fully fathomed. Ji Fung knew what it was to curse the Master in his heart while he bit back tears under the sting of the rattan cane, or during the long hours spent motionless in a single excruci-ating position. But Lin Bai's hate was different, deeper, a thing he hid inside himself like a dark pupa whose final shape could not be guessed. There was a peculiar intensity in the air between the Mas-ter and his star pupil that made Ji Fung feel weak and sick, yet fiercely protective of his friend.

"Good," Master Lau said suddenly, and then the music began to wail and it was time to slip into that other world.

The auditorium was nearly empty. Nothing but small clusters of gray heads and fidgeting children. As Ji Fung stood in the wings, he found himself wishing he were one of those children. A small boy whose mother and father sat on either side of him in the stuffy red-and-gold theater. A boy who would go home to sweets and a soft bed, not a small bowl of rice and a crowded dormitory.

He had been a boy like that, in another life. Somewhere in him was a barely remembered dream of a fine house and a smiling *amah*. Of silver toys that wound up and a little black dog with the softest fur. Of family, uncles and aunts and cousins; rich noisy banquets full of laughter and strange tales.

But Ji Fung was too old to long for the comforts of childhood. And if he let his mind wander too far down those old paths, he would end up at the terrible crossroads of the night he had been taken from his home forever. Back then he had just been called Ji, or son. He had another name that was much longer and finer, but at home it was Ji; sometimes Siu Ji, or little son. But on that night everything had been taken from him, even his true name.

His mother's desperate hands had dragged him up from uneasy sleep. She had put him to bed a few hours earlier with no supper, ignoring his cries for his *amah* and the steamed lotus buns he loved. Now she was shaking him awake and buttoning him into a plain cotton jacket. She was dressed that way too, dull blue tunic and loose trousers, her shining hair coiled at the nape of her neck, her pale face scrubbed clean of makeup. She looked like a servant, not the first wife of a rich and powerful man.

Ji had known, in the way children know without understand-ing, that something was terribly wrong. He felt sick to the bone and was sure the world was ending. His mother had not spoken more than a handful of words to him in his seven years of life. Now she was calling him *good boy* and *little man* while she stared past him into nothing. Her eyes shone in the darkness like moonlight on treacherous water.

When he was able to speak, he cried softly for his father. Father always had time for him, brought him presents from Macao and Shanghai, would make important business associates wait while thoughtfully considering a scraped knee or a broken toy. Yes, Father spoiled his only son, but never to the point of helplessness, for sons must grow strong and brilliant. Ji would sit behind that desk one day, would understand the mysterious transactions his father engineered, would engineer them himself. Already Father had presented him with his own name chop, a carved seal of jade Ji kept with him always. It was in his sweating hand now, snatched from under his pillow as he woke, its cool curves and tiny characters as familiar and soothing as his father's voice. If he could only see his father now, the night would lose this skewed sense of menace.

But when he called out, his mother turned away. Her spine was stiff and strange.

"Never speak of your father again," she said.

The hatred in her voice paralyzed him like spider's venom. Ji knew then that the world had already ended.

She led him through the still house, moving wraithlike through the long silent hallways. Their cloth slippers made no sound on the heavy rugs and polished marble floors. He asked where they were going, but she did not answer. He asked for Second Mother and his little half-sisters. For Third Mother with her big round belly and placid eyes. For his *amah*. For the houseboy with the broad chest and strong arms. For anyone who might be able to stop Siu Ji sliding out of control down a slick incline, toward some unfathomable future. But his mother would not answer any of his cries. She only twisted his arm and made him walk faster.

Moving through the dark kitchen, he saw the forms of his *amah* and the cook curled on the floor by the stove. His *amah*'s head was haloed with black fluid on the clean while tile. The air was stale with old food and smelled faintly of vomit.

"*Amah*," he called, straining toward the crumpled body.

His mother shushed him. "*Amah* is sleeping. She is very tired."
She looked away. "Everyone is very tired. We must be quiet, and
not wake them."

Ji tried to look back as she dragged him through the servants'
entrance, but it was too dark and the door swung shut too quickly
behind them.

They walked all night, taking a twisted, nonsensical route
through the streets, down dark alleys reeking of fish guts and urine.
They slipped unnoticed through staggering battalions of foreign
sailors with yellow hair and red faces and foul drunken breath. When
they passed an open noodle shop, bright and crowded behind glass
windows opaque with steam, Ji tried to pull his mother toward the
good doughy smell. He was faint with hunger now, but she would
not turn aside.

The Hong Kong night was a collage of images horrific and fantastic. He saw hollow-eyed prostitutes flaunting shrunken breasts,
and diseased beggar children licking the blood of slaughtered chickens from the filthy pavement outside a charnelhouse. He saw lurid
neon reflected in the glossy black skins of long automobiles carrying millionaire tai-pans and their exotic red-haired women. Glamour and squalor lay belly to back, intimate as lovers.

For Ji, seven years old and exhausted, it was brutal sensory over-
load. He clutched his jade chop until its edges dug into his palm,
resolving not to cry, not to *see*, to blindly put one foot in front of the
other until this incomprehensible journey was over. Perhaps he was
still dreaming in his own bed, and his *amah* would soon wake him
with a bowl of hot rice porridge.

Foul toothless mouths muttered close to him, but he would not
look up to see their owners. Glittering light danced temptingly in
the corners of his eyes, but he would not turn to see its source. He
saw only his own feet, clad in rough-stitched peasant shoes. Black
cloth shoes, worn around the edges, shuffling over greasy cobblestones. One step after the other and his mother's hand like a mouthful of sharp teeth around his own, never letting him slow down. His
room, his bed seemed impossibly far away now. Perhaps there had
never been anything but this endless walking. Perhaps his whole
life had been a dream, the invention of a wandering mind while his

14

body plodded on. He began to gray out, his consciousness coming slowly untethered, and he might have gone forever if his toe had not struck something stiff but yielding. His vision snapped back to razor clarity.

There was a dead girl in the alley before him, half-hidden behind stinking bins of garbage. She was almost pretty, her little hands curled like seashells. Her long graceful neck parted in a wet red smile. Her bloodstained Western-style dress was rucked up over her hips. To Ji's childish eyes, the pink folds of her exposed and battered labia looked like some dreadful mutilation, a wound far worse than the one in her throat, a deep cut that could never heal. He hitched in a great shuddering sob.

If his mother had slapped him or ordered him to be quiet, he might have been able to keep loving her. But she only stared at him without seeing, lost in some private hell where the terror and sorrow of her only child was no more important than the buzzing of the flies in the garbage bins. The blankness in her face was so terrible, so unforgivable that Ji's tears died inside him, leaving a coldness so deep that it would never quite thaw again.

They arrived at the Hong Kong Opera School as dawn was bleeding into the deep blue sky. At the gate, his mother paused and laid her hands on his trembling shoulders. Since she had pulled him up from sleep, Ji had been wishing for her to look at him, to acknowledge him in some way. But when she fixed her burning eyes on his, he was more afraid than he had ever been.

"Your new name is Wang Ji Fung," she said. Her voice was a monotone, devoid of emotion. "Your father was Wang Sau. He pulled a rickshaw, but he died. Say it."

He repeated the lie, not understanding but terrified of making a mistake. *Fung* was *phoenix*. His new name meant *phoenix sun*.

"If you ever tell anyone your real name, bad men will come and cut out your tongue. Do you understand, Wang Ji Fung?"

He pictured hard-faced men in dark suits coming after him with oily black guns and knives as sharp and cruel as their eyes. He nodded. His terror was huge and pure.

The sun broke red over the horizon. With it came an eerie lilting keen, high and strong, echoing off the mossy stone walls of the main school building. It was a sound that would define his life for the next eight years. It was the sound of young boys singing their morning exercises. It gave him a sick precognitive chill that brought cold sweat to his skin.

In a shadowy office, he stood still and silent beside his mother as Master Lau read the contract aloud. Slowly Ji came to understand that he would belong to this man for the next ten years, a raw bit of property the Master would endeavor to polish and make valuable. The newly born Wang Ji Fung felt nothing but coldness as his mother pressed her thumb into the sticky black ink and set her mark on the bottom of the page. She knew how to write perfectly well, but he supposed she was pretending to be the illiterate widow of a poor rickshaw puller.

She bowed her head and turned to her son. Ji Fung felt those bleak, hot eyes settle on him again.

"Never forget what you have been told," she said.

He watched her as she walked away, her shoulders set beneath the cheap blue tunic. He tried to memorize the wisps of ebony hair against her pale neck, her delicate wrists, the proud set of her spine. He thought of running after her, of hurling himself onto her back and smashing her fragile skull against the cold stone floor. Instead, he looked away. That was the last time he ever saw her.

■ ■ ■

"Dreaming of your dinner?"

Lin Bai tweaked Ji Fung's earlobe. "Pay attention. If you miss your cue, Master will take it out of you later."

Ji Fung was about to answer, but Lin Bai heard his own cue, bowed quickly to the opera gods, and swirled away, small feminine steps carrying him onstage. Ji Fung and the other boys in White Snake's army of sea creatures poured out behind him in tight formation, and the battle began.

Ji Fung tried to lose himself in routine. He knew the moments and motions of this story so well. Forward and back, tassel shake and spear flash, flip in the air and land on his feet, mirroring his three partners. But in his mind he saw himself truly fighting for the honor of his love, Lin Bai in White Snake's garb. He imagined slitting open the bellies of the rival soldiers, slashing off the head of White Snake's unworthy husband who rejected her love and conspired to destroy her. He imagined bringing the severed head to White Snake and being rewarded with a kiss.

This thought coiled around his spine, hot and distracting. As his opponent struck a wide, dramatic death blow, Ji Fung's balance wavered, skewing his backward somersault, making him land badly. Pain shot through his left arm, but he recovered flawlessly, following through with a series of flips that carried him offstage.

Leaning against the splintery wall, Ji Fung rubbed his sore shoulder and watched Lin Bai battle the others. Spears flew and twirled like so many straws. The deep tragedy in the curve of Lin Bai's shoulders and graceful hands always broke Ji Fung's heart a little. You could see that White Snake didn't want to fight, that she still loved her husband in spite of his betrayal, and that this futile love only increased her pain.

Ji Fung felt that strange protectiveness welling up in him again, as if it were not an ancient female character but Lin Bai himself who had been so betrayed. He tried to push it down inside himself, as always. But each time it was a little harder to push down.

■ ■ ■

Later, Ji Fung knelt before a basin of greasy water rinsing the paint from his stinging skin. Around him, naked boys gathered up armfuls of discarded costumes and carefully folded them into trunks of scented wood. Weapons were gathered and wrapped in soft cotton, pots of paint stacked in lacquer boxes. When everyone was scrubbed and dressed in plain gray uniforms, they lined up and waited for their Master.

It was an hour before he finally arrived, his jaw tight, his eyes squeezed down to thin slits. He stood for a long time staring at the line of boys. Then he turned away.

"Tonight's performance was our last here at the Lucky Dragon." Master Lau spoke to the wall, his body still as stone. "Mr. Sung tells me he will have no more Peking Opera." His chin trembled, barely perceptible. "From now on, jazz music only."

The students were silent, eyes down. Ji Fung felt as if he had taken a blow to the sternum. He wondered what would become of him now. His ten years were nearly up, and the Opera was all he knew. He had always assumed he would join a troupe and spend the rest of his life performing. What other choice did he have, and if this was no longer a choice, had his body and soul been sold to a dying art?

But this thought was too vast and slippery to hold. It was much easier to walk the familiar streets that led back to the school, Lin Bai in step before him and another boy behind, all helping to carry their prop trunks like ants with a heavy load. Ji Fung calmed himself by staring at the back of Lin Bai's neck, at the silky blue-black stubble hugging the vulnerable curve of the skull. He tried to make his mind as blank as the sky.

Back in the darkened dormitory, the two lay on their narrow cots, close but barely touching. All around them, boys were rustling, sighing, settling into sleep. Lin Bai's and Ji Fung's cots were pushed together in one corner of the big common room, up against the stone wall. This spot was cold and dank, but afforded them a small measure of privacy.

"No more performances at the Lucky Dragon Theater," Ji Fung whispered. He still could not get used to the idea. "It's hard to believe."

Lin Bai nodded. "People would rather go to the cinema." His voice grew soft and dreamy. "See films made in America. In Hollywood."

The name meant nothing to Ji Fung. It was simply a foreign-sounding word.

Lin Bai reached under the thin pad of his mattress and pulled out a tattered magazine. His delicate fingers were reverent on the slick sweat-stained cover. Ji Fung could barely make out the image of a pale-haired woman in a tight dress that pushed her breasts up under her chin and nipped her waist down to the size of a spider's.

He wondered how she could breathe. The words on the cover were loopy and incomprehensible.

"One day I'll go there," Lin Bai said. "To Hollywood. I'm tired of boring old Chinese operas. The same stories over and over. I'll go to America and become a famous film star."

He slid down in the bed and pulled Ji Fung after him, yanking the covers up over their heads. Ji Fung was acutely conscious of Lin Bai's warmth mingling with his own, of Lin Bai's shoulder and hip touching his.

"We'll go together," Lin Bai whispered. "We'll be action heroes. Partners. We'll fight cowboys and gangsters and ride in automobiles and drink fine champagne."

"Sham-peh-yin? What's that?"

"I'm not sure," Lin Bai admitted, "but all the film stars drink it. It must be very sweet."

"Yes, yes," Ji Fung said, warming to the fantasy. "We'll wear leather shoes and grow our hair long. We'll lie in bed all morning, and a servant will bring us champagne and cakes."

"People will cry when they see us perform," Lin Bai giggled. "We'll hide in the theater and watch our faces ten feet high on the silver screen."

"And Master Lau will be sorry to have lost such fine actors."

There was a short, loaded silence. When Lin Bai spoke, his voice was full of a dark poison, a hatred as lethal as ground glass.

"Master Lau will be dead."

The silence grew, hot with unspoken truths and the boys' breath beneath the covers.

"The Master has not called you tonight." Ji Fung's voice was soft, on the verge of breaking. He was terrified to speak of this. Never before had he mentioned Lin Bai's nightly lessons alone in the Master's room. It was the source of much speculation and cruel innuendo among the other boys: since Lin Bai was so good at playing a woman onstage, perhaps he also played one in the Master's bed.

More silence. Ji Fung expected Lin Bai to turn away angrily, lost in his secret hurt. He wished for a way to call back his thoughtless words, to offer Lin Bai some meager comfort, some shelter from his internal storms.

Then, there in the dark, came the softest sound. A sound that obliterated the gulf between them, made the scant space separating their bodies crawl with strange heat. It was the low, broken whisper of tears.

Ji Fung hardly dared to breathe. His wrist lay against the curve of Lin Bai's shoulder, and he was excruciatingly aware of this tiny contact. He felt Lin Bai's body shudder with stifled weeping and thought of White Snake weeping for the death of her heartless husband. Ji Fung realized that what he really wanted was to take Lin Bai in his arms and kiss the tears from his face, to protect him from the Master and Hollywood and all the world, but most of all from the fierce pain devouring him from the inside out. This realization brought hot blood rushing to Ji Fung's cheeks and his stiffening penis.

He pulled his wrist away, rolled his body away. His heart hammered wildly. He wanted to jump up and run outside, bathe his body in the cool wet nighttime air, anything to escape this hot cave of blankets and shame and the intoxicating odor of Lin Bai's sweat. He felt as if he might drown in the heady hormonal stew raging inside.

He almost broke loose, almost got up. Then Lin Bai's bony little hand curled itself around his, and Lin Bai whispered, "Don't go."

And then he brought Ji Fung's fingers to his lips, those sweet cynical lips still stained cherry-red at the corners. Ji Fung let himself be drawn down into an awkward embrace that felt like falling off a mountain, like stepping into a languorous dream. Like coming home.

Lin Bai's skin beneath the coarse cloth of his pajamas was so fine and soft that Ji Fung felt sure he must be bruising it with his rough hands, but he could not stop himself. He was no longer aware of the other boys in the room around them, no longer cared whether anyone was watching. He wanted to press harder into that silken smoothness, to feel the warm half-painful friction of Lin Bai's nakedness against his own. He wanted to crush Lin Bai's ivory bones, to tear into the vulnerable flesh of his mouth with savage starved teeth. The intensity of his desire frightened and ignited him.

Then the cocoon of blankets was ripped away like the fragile layer of skin covering a newly healed wound. Ji Fung felt hard fingers dig into the back of his neck. Before he knew what was happening he had been hauled out of bed and thrown against the wall. His skull hit hard, and the inside of his head shimmered with stars: red, blue, silver, like New Year's fireworks.

He barely had time to slide to the floor before he was yanked up again. As his vision cleared, Master Lau's face appeared inches from his own, disfigured with fury. Behind the Master were the rows of cots, the other boys pulling their covers over their heads, pretending not to see. Ji Fung's desire curdled in his belly, giving way to sick guilt and sharp-edged fear.

Master slammed Ji Fung against the wall again, sending tremors of agony down his spine. Then the unthinkable happened: Master's fist came looping down into Ji Fung's upturned face. His head filled with more glitter and a sound like a glass bowl of fruit being smashed with a padded club. He knew then that he was going to die. The Master had beaten Ji Fung and every other boy more times and more ways than they could count. But never did he hit a student in the face. *Your face must be as clean and pure as blank paper waiting for the ink.* This was one of the Master's countless rules, the ones he would make them recite as he burned the tender skin at the insides of their elbows with a hot iron or whipped their naked asses bloody with a bundle of twigs. Master Lau was a man of unshakable rules and routines. This was what made him a brilliant teacher. This was what terrified Ji Fung now: if the Master broke one rule, he could break any of them.

As Master Lau's grip tightened, Ji Fung's throat began to fill with thick, choking blood. His fists clenched, aching to break the hold and fight back. But an immovable block inside him forbade any resistance to the Master. His mother had handed him over to this man. He was Master Lau's property, to keep or kill. Ji Fung felt his consciousness receding into grayness as the Master dragged him across the room and shoved him into a closet full of dirty laundry. He lay curled on his side vomiting sticky gouts of blood and rice, clutching fistfuls of rough sweat-stenched cloth. The door slammed, the lock clicked home, and Ji Fung's darkness was complete.

■ ■ ■

Lin Bai crouched against the wall, feeling the heat of a hundred eyes peering out from under blankets, crawling over him like shiny black insects, judging him with gutter words. He spread his hands over his face, knowing how weak this gesture would make him appear, but unable to bear the scourge of so many cruel eyes. He wanted to unleash all his rage upon them, to destroy them.

But he had no power, no flammable source of anger. He had nothing but his agility and his beauty, nothing but his grace and his wiles. These were the things that had made Ji Fung love him. His hands smelled of Ji Fung's body. Silently Lin Bai sentenced himself to a thousand torments for pulling his friend down into his own private nightmare. Master Lau's nightly ministrations were a burden he had always borne alone, a secret tattooed on the meat of his soul. Anyone who ate of that tainted meat would suffer, just as he had suffered. Just as his parents had suffered, burned to death in their tiny tea shop for the crime of bearing him. Just as the small son of his auntie had suffered, choking to death on a bit of sweet beef jerky four days after Lin Bai had come to live with them.

The day his auntie brought him to the opera school, she had called him a bad-luck child, cursed to bring pain and death upon anyone close to him. He had never wanted that to happen to Ji Fung, so he had kept his friend at arm's length, all the while aching to pull him close. Tonight his need had overwhelmed him. Now both he and Ji Fung would pay the price.

Master Lau tore Lin Bai's hands from his face, gripped the boy's jaw hard enough to abrade the skin. "Whore," he whispered through clenched teeth.

Lin Bai's whole body trembled in anger and shame. The air around them was gravid with silent listening. Dreams of death and murder unspooled behind his eyelids, but he offered no resistance when Master dragged him away into the privacy of his studio. From these rooms the other boys might catch an odd whimper or shriek, but they would not really know what was going on behind the heavy door.

Lin Bai's thoughts beat against each other liked caged birds. His body remained passive as always, as it had been trained to do since he was barely old enough to walk: feet together, head bowed, alone and motionless in the void of the studio, facing the man he had hated and serviced for years. His body remained passive as Master Lau bound his wrists above his head with a red silk cord, passive as Master tore away his threadbare pajamas and laid into his bare flesh with a length of soaked rattan. The pain was as familiar as breathing.

"How dare you give yourself to another man?" Master demanded. His breath was hot and harsh against the downy hairs at the back of Lin Bai's neck, right at the juncture of his skull. He imagined Master Lau sinking his teeth into that spot and barely managed to suppress a shudder.

"Worthless gutterslut. Stinking little whore."

These insults were familiar too, though not as comforting as the sting of the cane. On other nights, in this same scene, Lin Bai had played his role just as he played all the other roles he had learned flawlessly. *Forgive me, Master. I am not worthy of your hands' wisdom, of your cock's power.* Like a song to stretch his voice, an exercise, sounds with no meaning.

But tonight his anger burned hotter than his terror, hotter even than his shame at his reluctant desires. In his blackest moments he had to admit to himself that, sometime in the last two years, he had begun to like the way the Master touched him. Not tonight, though, not after feeling Ji Fung's hands on his body, not after seeing Ji Fung's face beaten bloody. Lin Bai bit back his anger as the Master's fingers skittered over his rattan-striped flesh, down into the cleft of his lacerated ass. He gnawed on his fury as the Master thrust a long blood-greased finger up into his anus.

"Did you let him inside you?" the Master hissed, his voice crawling with contempt. "Did you accept his puny little noodle? I doubt you could even feel it after mine."

Acid boiled up over Lin Bai's tongue.

"I'm not your wife," he said.

The finger slid out of his asshole too fast, a sickly scraping sensation. This weak pain was quickly eclipsed by the sharp one of a slap to the face. He could smell himself on the Master's hand.

"I own you," the Master spat, Lin Bai's face squeezed between thumb and ass-pungent forefinger. "I created you. I carved the womanhood out of the scrawny peasant boy your aunt sold me nine years ago. You are more than my wife. You are my *possession*."

Lin Bai heard the Master hawk deep in his throat and spit into a rough palm. Then, though he had known the sensation many times, he shrieked as the thick length of the Master's erection slid up inside him. It felt like a fist punching at his intestines, like a tree trying to grow in his gut. Lost in a vortex of pain and guilty pleasure, Lin Bai groped for some solid emotion, something to keep him from drowning in shame and fear. He thought at once of Ji Fung, the taste of his skin, the silken-muscle feel of his hard cock pulsing between Lin Bai's palms, the sound of his skin splitting under the Master's blows.

He was certain that, afire with sex, the Master would go back to the closet and kill Ji Fung. A dark part of Lin Bai's mind even wanted to embrace this brutal logic. He was bad luck, poison, and anyone foolish enough to get close to him would die.

No. He would not give in to that. An icy wash of clarity drained away the last of his confusion, and Lin Bai knew what he had to do.

He arched his spine, melted his insides around the Master's thrusting penis, and moaned as if he had found himself back in Ji Fung's arms. He threw himself into the performance with every bit of strength he had. Somewhere along the way, as always, he lost himself in the role. The pleasure he pretended became real, and he let his body work with the Master's as he would with a fellow actor. Speaking with words and without, he told the Master everything he needed to hear. Soon the Master's orgasm erupted inside him.

When the red cord was undone, Lin Bai crumpled to the floor, seeming to swoon. His senses were clearer than they had ever been, and he was very aware of where they had tumbled in their passion. The Master, half-drunk on the nectar of Lin Bai's submission, noticed nothing. But a few feet away, with the other props, was a rack of battle spears. These were richly ornamented with silk and inlay, designed as stage props, not weapons. Still, they had some heft, and the tips were sharp enough to puncture skin. Lin Bai had seen boys pricked with them more than once during practice.

As always, he kept his face averted until Master had wiped off and stuffed himself back into his trousers. At last Master's voice came, gruff but no longer as angry as before. "Get up, woman."

Lin Bai could not see the Master, but sensed him standing close. If his judgment was even the tiniest bit off, he would die before Ji Fung tonight.

"Master," he whispered, "I am too weak to stand."

His finger crept ever so slowly toward the lowest spear, red and gold, adorned with silk pompons and a horse's tail tied on with a black ribbon.

"Help me, my husband." The word was sour bile in his mouth. He turned what he hoped were helpless, flirtatious eyes up to the Master.

The Master made a hoarse, throaty sound, the closest he ever came to smiling. He took a step closer and bent to help his star pupil, his woman.

Lin Bai heaved out a long breath. He was filled with the ecstatic terror he always felt before trying a difficult trick onstage for the first time. This time there had been no rehearsal, and error meant his life. He knew he could carry out the necessary motion. But this was the man who had taught it to him.

The Master grabbed his wrist and yanked. Lin Bai came up fast, using the other man's motion to propel his own. His arm shot out—he had the spear—it was slicing forward, forward, toward Master Lau's shocked face. He saw the Master's hand coming up to stop it, fast as a stroke of lightning but not fast enough, reflexes dulled by sex and sadism. The tip of the spear was at Master Lau's throat, punching into the V of his collarbone and through the wattled skin there.

Lin Bai twisted the spear, then pulled up. The blade caught on something hard in Master's throat and snapped off. Master's hands clawed at it, pulled it out and sent it clattering away. The wound came open like a fruit or flower, edges parting cleanly, bloodless for an instant. Then there was blood everywhere, streaming down the front of Master's body, raining on Lin Bai's face. He tasted it on his lips, salty as the man's sperm.

Master Lau staggered backward, trying to hold the two halves of his neck together, failing. A wet choking sound forced its way out of his crushed larynx. The look of surprise on his face was exquisite.

Lin Bai sprang to his feet as the Master fell. He caught sight of himself in the small looking glass the Master kept over his basin. In the blue moonlight, blood glittered black on his pale face, symmetrical as makeup around his wide eyes. He struck a pose with the spear held close.

"The sun rules all heavenly beings," he sang, *"but the moon can deceive it by patience and reflection."*

He tossed the spear high, spinning, and twisted his bare body to catch it. The blade glittered and the horsetail swished wildly. Lin Bai laid the spear on the floor at his feet and bowed before the corpse of his Master.

■ ■ ■

Ji Fung lay curled into himself, entombed in blackness and roaring pain. A voice twisted through his head, through his gut, whispering the same words over and over.

It's happening again.

The mindless routine of his life had been blown wide open. Beneath its sundered skin was his childhood demon of raging chaos, of huge horrible events he could not control or understand, events that swept him along in their wake.

When the closet door swung open, he almost screamed. Hands clutched at him, tried to drag him out. He flailed at them, certain Master Lau had returned to beat him to death.

"Ji Fung!"

A spitting whisper close to his face, and a rich coppery scent. Ji Fung opened his eyes and saw Lin Bai with dark blood splashed across his high cheekbones, streaking his pale forehead, dripping off his chin. There was a sheen of madness in Lin Bai's gore-rimmed eyes that froze Ji Fung's heart. It was as if his mother's lunatic passion had returned to haunt the familiar face of his only friend, his almost-lover. He was paralyzed before this madness; it threatened to pluck him from this life and send him spinning into the past.

"We need to get out of here! *Now!*"

Ji Fung squeezed his eyes shut and shook his head. He felt his arm being yanked, but he could not move. "I want to see my father," he heard himself saying in a child's voice.

"Ji Fung..." Lin Bai's voice was suddenly softer, saner. He cupped his friend's face between bloody hands. "I can't leave you behind. If you stay here, I will stay too and die with you."

Ji Fung opened his eyes. He saw tears making crystal tracks through the congealing blood on Lin Bai's face. His body went limp and unresisting as Lin Bai slid warm arms around him and whispered the words he needed to hear more than any others.

"I love you," Lin Bai said.

The ancient armor around Ji Fung's heart shattered. He was still half-sick with terror, but he could do this. He could escape the prison of the opera school with Lin Bai at his side, could look for a new life where he had thought there was none.

He hugged back fiercely for a long moment, incapable of anything else. Then he remembered. "Wait," he said, pulling away.

Under the curious eyes of the other students, who had watched the entire scene without moving to interfere, Ji Fung raced across the dormitory to his cot. The blankets still held traces of warmth from their bodies. Ji Fung reached beneath the thin cotton mattress and closed his fist around the jade chop. He pocketed it and ran back to Lin Bai, who was staring at his hands and smiling strangely.

"Come on. You said we had to hurry."

Lin Bai looked up, and his eyes cleared. "Yes. Let's go."

Hand in hand, urging one another through the dark passages and haunted halls, they fled the school that had been their world for more than half their lives.

■ ■ ■

The streets were alive with people. Westerners with bulbous noses and fearful pale eyes. Merchants proclaiming in song the perfection of their pears or crabs or shoes. Tough-looking boys lounging in doorways, their pockmarked faces lit orange by the glow of foreign cigarettes. Hard-eyed women offering, for a few pennies, to do things the boys had never even heard of. They ran and ran, dodging bicycles and pedicabs, becoming drunk on the night wind and freedom. Lin Bai stopped briefly to wash the blood from his face in a marble fountain filled with carp, the big orange-gold fish that would someday grow into dragons.

Soon they found themselves down by the waterfront. The harbor swarmed with life. The junks with their strabismic eyes and the flat-bottomed sampans ranged far out into the pea-green bay. The people who lived on the boats comprised their own lantern-lit, floating village. They cooked sizzling fish on small stoves of charcoal, hung tattered laundry out to dry as best it could in the humid air. A girl sat on the prow of a much-repaired sampan combing long hair that fluttered in the sea breeze. Her little brother pissed into the black water, laughing.

"Where can we go?" asked Ji Fung, looking out across the water to the distant lights of Kowloon. "We know no one. We have no money."

Lin Bai smiled, struck a wide-armed pose, and sang out. His strong, clear voice carried far out over the harbor.

"It's sooooo cold!"

"Shhh," Ji Fung hushed, waving his hands. A perfect sequence from *Twice a Bride* might have gained Master Lau's approval, back in that other life, but it would do them no good here.

"The icy wind cuts like a dagger," Lin Bai chanted, eyes wide. *"With stomach empty, I'm forced to be a beggar."*

"Have you gone crazy?" Ji Fung glanced wildly around. "Stop singing! Someone will take you back to the school!"

"For a poor scholar, little the future holds in store. I am starved and cold. How can I endure any more?"

The boys had gained a small audience of curious faces. Ji Fung grabbed Lin Bai's hand and bowed his head.

"Sorry to be disturbing you. Suddenly my brother thinks he is an opera star!" Ji Fung tried to force a laugh, but Master Lau had squeezed his throat raw. Their little crowd soon vanished, and they were alone with the sound of water lapping at the wooden flanks of a hundred boats.

"Why did you do that?" Lin Bai hissed. "They were going to give me some money."

"Stupid! They don't have any money."

"Food, then."

Ji Fung smelled the cooking odors from the sampans: sliced ginger, bubbling oil, fish so fresh and tender it would melt in the mouth. His stomach rumbled, and he wondered whether he should have let Lin Bai sing after all.

"That was very pretty," said a new voice, raspy and sneering, directly behind them.

They turned to face a boy two or three years their senior. He was thin as a dog, with long filthy hair and a smile like a saber cut.

"Tell me," said the boy, taking a step closer. "What other tricks can you do?"

The back of Ji Fung's neck prickled. He moved in front of Lin Bai and tried to stare the boy down, hoping he looked tougher than he felt. "Piss off," he said. "You don't want any trouble with us."

"Ai, don't scare me so." The boy's narrow smile grew wider. From the darkness behind him materialized four others, even thinner and more ragged than their leader. "Did you hear this bald-headed faggot try to threaten me?" he asked them.

Ji Fung and Lin Bai started backing away, but found themselves flanked on either side by grinning boys with broken teeth and missing fingers, closing in. Ji Fung's nerves were screaming, ready to fight. When two of the boys made a grab for him, he lashed out madly, loving the sensation of skin splitting beneath his knuckles. He flipped out of their reach and came back with both legs extended, catching a boy in the abdomen, feeling ribs crack as his feet connected.

For a few moments he thought he could beat them all. Then an arm slid round his neck, and the icy bite of a blade under his chin froze him. He heard the leader's raspy voice again. "Get the pretty one."

Lin Bai clawed the eyes of one scrawny boy, landed a flying kick in another's testicles. But there were too many, and he was dragged before the leader, whose face he spat in. The leader trailed a filthy finger through the spit, licked away a stray drop near the corner of his mouth. He smiled, and in that instant Ji Fung believed this boy would kill them both.

Then suddenly there came a series of sharp pops like a string of New Year's firecrackers going off. Ji Fung felt something buzz past his shoulder, barely grazing his collarbone. The boy holding him dropped the knife and ran. A second later the others scattered too, quick as a nest of insects frightened by footfalls. The leader threw one last evil glance over his shoulder at them as he disappeared into an alleyway.

Ji Fung swayed on his feet, nauseous and dizzy. He had been struck again in the face, on top of the blows Master Lau had given him, and his skull felt full of metal shavings. Lin Bai was beside him, and Ji Fung leaned into his friend's bony shoulder, trembling like an old man.

But Lin Bai was nudging him, gesturing at something. As Ji Fung managed to raise his head, a new voice called out. "Get in if you want to live!"

A long, sleek, dove-gray sedan had pulled up in the lane ten feet away. A shadow-shrouded figure sat in the back, beckoning to them with one hand, holding a gun as small and shiny as a toy in the other.

Lin Bai and Ji Fung didn't even have to look at each other. Sick and exhausted and utterly out of options, they headed for the long gray automobile.

■ ■ ■

The marksman wore a white Western-style suit and shiny black shoes. *Leather* shoes, Ji Fung noted. He was alarmingly pale, though his long black hair was glossy and neatly styled. His clothes, his skin, the inside of his car smelled at once sweet and stinging. But the strangest thing about him was his eyes. They were Chinese in shape, with lashes as long and black as Lin Bai's, but their color was a milky jade like the eyes of some predatory animal.

After ordering his chauffeur to drive on, he tucked the gun away and offered them a slim silver flask from some inner pocket. "Here, have a nip."

The boys stared at him, uncomprehending.

The young man sighed. "You *do* speak Cantonese? You didn't just tumble off a passing boat, by any chance?"

Ji Fung found his voice. "Yes, we speak Cantonese." *More clearly than you,* he thought, but did not say it. Their savior's accent was mainland, maybe Shanghaiese. And it was tinged with something even stranger, something Ji Fung could not begin to guess at.

He felt those milk-jade eyes on him and bowed his head. "In ten thousand lifetimes we could never repay you for saving our worthless lives. For this, we are forever indebted to you."

The man smirked. "A small thing, not even worth mentioning. I would not have wanted the world to lose such a talented singer."

A flush crept into Lin Bai's smooth cheeks. Ji Fung was unsure whether to smile or feel jealous.

"But," the man continued, "since you *are* forever indebted to me, you might at least grant me the favor of trying my refreshment."

Again he offered the flask. Ji Fung was afraid to sully the gleaming surface with his grimy, bloody fingers. But Lin Bai reached out and grabbed it. He drank deep, then smiled, licked his lips, and passed the flask to Ji Fung. Emboldened by the flavor of Lin Bai's mouth on the metal, Ji Fung took a swig.

The taste went blazing down his throat, seared his stomach like a branding iron, filled his skull with translucent amber fire. He choked, coughed out a spray of saliva and stinging liquor, clapped his hands to his face in consternation and dropped the flask. Lin Bai caught it neatly in midair.

Their savior was laughing. "Not your poison, eh?"

"Poison?" Ji Fung's stomach clenched in horror, and even Lin Bai looked alarmed.

"No, no, don't be so stupid. It's only a saying, a ridiculous American saying. That's Jack Daniel's whiskey you just drank."

Lin Bai was unable to hide the excitement in his voice. "Are you American? From Hollywood?"

"God, no." The man rolled his eyes. "Americans make good whiskey and good music, but they don't know how to live. *Especially* not in Hollywood. I am French."

Manners did not allow any show of curiosity about the obvious tinge of Chinese blood in the veins of this exotic being. The boys remained silent. Lin Bai's disappointment was almost tangible.

At last Ji Fung asked, "What can we call you?"

"My name is Pierre Jean-Luc LeBon. My friends call me Perique."

Lin Bai frowned. "Pei-week?"

Perique's laughter was low and, Ji Fung thought, ever so slightly cruel. "If you intend to go to Hollywood," he said, "you're going to have to work on that accent."

■ ■ ■

Perique took them to a hotel that was more like a fantasy, the corridors all blue and silver, brightly lit, ultramodern. He smuggled them through a back entrance, down hallways with carpet so lush the boys could barely keep their footing, and into a suite bigger than the Lucky Dragon's auditorium. The baroque furniture was draped with clothing of the latest cuts and fabrics, soft trousers and thin shirts and silk neckties in deep, brilliant jewel tones.

Ji Fung tried to remain aloof, suspicious of all this wealth and casual generosity. But Perique had saved their lives, and there was no way to leave without shaming him and themselves. Besides, Lin Bai was utterly seduced. The glamour had sucked him in deep, the bright clothes everywhere, the novels with gilt-edged pages, the box of French chocolates Perique offered. Ji Fung could not swallow the jealousy in his throat each time Lin Bai's face lit up over some new luxury.

Perique ordered food for them, Western delicacies that were both disgusting and fantastic. Everything seemed too sweet, too soft. Ji Fung found himself longing for some noodles fried in hot oil, a meal Master Lau had always given them as a New Year's treat. But thinking of the Master reminded him of Lin Bai's crime, such a monstrous thing. Killing one's Master was as bad as murdering one's father. Ji Fung felt suddenly hunted, terrified, unable to forget. For an instant, the chocolate smeared across Lin Bai's mouth looked like blood.

But it was so difficult to remember that they were fugitives, murderers. So difficult, when Perique was constantly offering a taste of this, a sip of that, and encouraging him to feel the lining of this jacket, real silk, and wouldn't he like to try it on? They drank champagne, which was not sweet after all, but a sharp bubbling drink that stung the roof of Ji Fung's mouth and slowed time to a languid crawl.

Soon Perique was pushing the furniture against the walls and begging the boys to perform. Ji Fung was reluctant at first, but Lin Bai needed no convincing. The sound of that clear, rich voice banished the ache in Ji Fung's throat, and he plunged in. They sang to each other, battled with curtain rods, died in each other's arms. Perique's rapt smile urged them on, and the champagne wet their throats until it seemed they could go on for hours.

As they grew more and more tipsy, the boys began to forget the words that had once seemed branded on their tongues. Perique suggested making up new words, a concept so shocking that it had them first giggling self-consciously, then trying to outdo each other in vulgarity and silliness. *"Your balls are succulent as ripe kumquats— let me suck their juice,"* Lin Bai sang in flawless operatic tones, and Ji Fung collapsed laughing. Perique played the part of a Hollywood director, making them kiss like long-separated lovers, pretending they hadn't gotten it right, making them do it again and again. Then they were naked together on Perique's bed, a cloudlike fantasy of white linens and goosedown pillows, their limbs tangled and their mouths joined, just as if they knew how to make love.

Perique was still murmuring directions, but Ji Fung scarcely heard him, scarcely heard anything but Lin Bai's breath and heartbeat. Under those watchful eyes that were somehow at once Chinese and foreign, in this place that was like nothing they had ever imagined, Ji Fung and Lin Bai finally found each other.

■ ■ ■

Ji Fung awoke to shrouded sunlight. His first thought was *It's late, the Master will kill us for sleeping so long...*

Then his head began to pound and a slick nausea twisted in his guts, and he remembered everything. His muscles ached; his cock felt hot and raw. Lin Bai curled asleep beside him, one familiar thing in this terrifying new world. Perique was gone, leaving behind the sweetish miasma of his various grooming products. Ji Fung slid his arm around Lin Bai's waist, hid his face in the silken curve of Lin Bai's shoulder.

Lin Bai stirred, groaned low in his throat, then shot bolt upright and stared wildly around the darkened room. His eyes met Ji Fung's, and Ji Fung saw memory seeping back in.

"Ai-yaa," said Lin Bai at last. "My head feels ready to burst."

"My *bladder* feels ready to burst. I wonder what the toilet looks like here."

"Probably carved out of jade."

"With gold fittings."

"And squares of fine silk to wipe your ass."

Laughing blearily through their pain, the boys stumbled around the room opening door after door. They found several enormous closets crammed full of Perique's clothes and shoes—Ji Fung had assumed their host's entire wardrobe was strewn about the room, but that was hardly a fraction of all he had to wear. Everything was scented with sandalwood and sharp cologne. One door swung open to reveal a claw-footed tub; behind another was a gleaming porcelain toilet.

"Almost a shame to piss in there," Ji Fung said. But the boys stood hip to hip and did so anyway, streams of urine crossing before they splashed into the clear water.

Perique returned in a rush of sugar smells and fresh sea air. He tossed his jacket across the bed and pulled the boys to him. "It seems you've been very naughty," he said.

Ji Fung stiffened in Perique's perfumed embrace. "What do you mean?"

Perique retrieved a much-folded sheet of newspaper from his jacket and smoothed it out on the bedspread. "Look."

Triads

Ji frowned at the paper. He could feel the blood rushing to his cheeks. "Bad eyesight," he said. "You read it."

Perique looked up, realization dawning in his eyes. "You can't read, can you?"

"Of course I can." Ji Fung waved a dismissive hand. "Too much drinking last night gave me a headache. That's all."

Perique smiled and shrugged to show that he knew Ji Fung was lying, but that he was not entirely without manners.

"It says that Lau Tung Ho, master of the Hong Kong Opera School, was murdered last night. Stabbed to death. Two pupils are missing, wanted in the murder. Their names are Lin Bai and Wang Ji Fung."

Perique turned the page and laid the paper out flat. Lin Bai sat up and leaned over Ji Fung's shoulder to look.

"Here is their picture."

It was a portrait of their class, taken a year ago by the owner of the Lucky Dragon Theater. The fugitives' heads were circled. Ji Fung stood in the back row with the tallest boys, his face a nondescript pale blur. But Master Lau had posed his star pupil at the front, and Lin Bai's fine features were instantly recognizable.

Ji Fung felt a helpless surge of anger. Lin Bai had destroyed his safe, complacent world and dragged him into this incomprehensible whirlwind of a new one. He had killed their guardian, and now they were at the mercy of this new one, Perique, who was fascinating but surely insane.

At once he realized the pettiness of his feelings. *He* was not the one who had endured nightly humiliation and rape at the hands of Master Lau. *He* was not the one who had faced the torment of all the other boys for doing something he hated. Those dubious honors belonged to Lin Bai alone. Lin Bai had had to kill Master Lau, had done it to save Ji Fung's life as well as his own. And Lin Bai had had to run. Ji Fung had chosen to run with him, and now they were bound to each other for all time. If rotting in prison was part of their destiny, then they would rot together.

He looked up at Perique. "Are you going to turn us in?"

Perique burst out laughing. Ji Fung thought again that their new friend's laughter was not entirely kind, but now it came as a relief. "And miss more of your command performances? Don't be stupid!" He swept the newspaper away and gripped the boys' hands tightly. "I have my own habits that are, how shall we say, outside the law."

Lin Bai shrugged. His eyes were brimming, about to spill over. Ji Fung wanted to embrace him, but if Lin Bai felt sorrow for his murdered Master, he must face it alone. It should not be diluted by meaningless words of comfort.

"He must have been very cruel to you," Perique said. "I only want to help."

Ji couldn't restrain himself. "You don't know us—you like our looks, true, but we're nobody in your world. Why be so generous to us? Why risk trouble for yourself by helping two criminals?"

"I enjoy trouble."

"Well, but…" Ji Fung struggled for a way to say what he meant without robbing Perique of face. "Perhaps you are of noble birth, or an important international businessman. We are only poor actors unused to such a life. It is not right that you should endanger yourself for our sake."

"In other words," smiled Perique, "you're not going to trust me until I've told you something about myself."

Ji Fung and Lin Bai stared. Surely Perique was not, could not be Chinese. No Chinese would dream of slicing so neatly through a veil of polite obfuscation.

"I don't mind. I speak five languages and I like talking about myself in all of them. Let's have a pot of coffee, shall we?" Perique ordered it, then pulled up a gilt armchair next to the bed. "Where to begin? I was born in Shanghai. My father was an artist from Paris, an adventuresome madman whose talent greatly exceeded his wealth. My mother was the daughter of a rich coastal trader who owned a fleet of opium junks. I have five brothers and sisters, three living in France, two in London. I often spend summer overseas, so you're lucky to find me here now."

The coffee arrived, rich black brew that smelled delicious but tasted bitter and strange.

"My parents are dead now. My Chinese mother left me a fortune; my French father, a dream. I was like him, he said. If the world ever ceased to amuse me, I would die. And I believed him. So I travel the world filling my brain with the newest ideas, my stomach with the finest delicacies, and my bed with the loveliest creatures I can find."

Ji Fung looked at Lin Bai, then back at Perique. "Why *both* of us?"

A tinge of crimson flushed Perique's pale cheeks, but he was smiling. "I like to watch," he said.

■ ■ ■

Perique ushered the boys from the silver car into an alley that smelled of joss sticks and oyster shells. A woman with powder-white skin and red lips stood by an unpainted metal door. Perique spoke rapidly to her in an unfamiliar language. Hearing the word *jazz*, Ji Fung guessed it was English. The woman pushed the door open and ushered them in.

The interior was dimly lit, thick with the smoke of tobacco and opium. Onstage, an exotic beauty in a white satin dress sang strange quick notes. Her voice was nimble and light, sparkling like champagne. Her skin was dark as strong tea, her brown eyes heavy-lidded, her mouth impossibly full and lush. Perique winked at her, and she smiled.

Perique led them backstage, into a tiny dressing room filled with cut flowers. The sweet, humid scent was at once refreshing and overwhelming. Soon the singer came sailing in, followed by waves of applause and shouts for an encore. She kissed Perique lightly on the mouth and began speaking in that same unfamiliar language, slurred and slow.

Perique gestured at the boys as he replied. The singer nodded thoughtfully. "Boys," Perique said, "this is Clarice. She is going to help you prepare for the most important roles of your acting career—the roles that will save your lives."

With a slow smile, Clarice unfastened her dress and let it fall. The soft points of her breasts fell with it, for they were sewn into the bra-cups of the dress. Beneath it her chest was flat, small brown nipples above a tightly laced corset.

"You see?" she said in Cantonese, her accent thick and lisping. "I am a boy like you."

She caressed the bulge in her silk panties.

"But it is my own secret. And now it will be your secret too."

Ji Fung shook his head, horrified at the sight of the cruel corset, the manhood swathed in lace and silk, the idea that he could ever look like this creature. "Lin Bai plays the woman," he said. "Not me."

Perique grinned at his distress. "If the police catch you, you will both be executed. What choice do you have?"

"But who will believe that I am a woman? It's impossible." Ji Fung grabbed his ears, tugged them out like jug handles. "Look at these! I would be the homeliest woman in China."

Perique shrugged. "Do you have a better idea?"

Ji Fung turned to Lin Bai. "Tell him! You know it isn't possible!"

Lin Bai turned his head, smiling behind his fingers.

Ji Fung jumped up. The scent of blossoms nearly sent him reeling. "You're all against me!"

"Stop fighting it," Clarice scolded softly. "You fight it, you see, no one will believe in you."

He felt Lin Bai's hand on his arm. "Don't be so upset, Ji. I'd love to see you as a girl." Ji Fung let his head drop and his shoulders sag. He knew when he was defeated.

"Undress," Clarice told them. "Before you can be a woman, you must let go of the man." She held up a gleaming straight razor.

Ji Fung was halfway through the door before Perique stopped laughing long enough to gasp, "Shaving, my dear. Only shaving."

■ ■ ■

Clarice brought a basin of water, soaped the boys' forearms, legs, and armpits, and scraped away the lather with her shiny blade. Afterward, they could not stop stroking their own skin, marveling at the newly silky texture.

Perique's eyebrows lifted as Clarice opened her makeup kit. "They're both so pretty. Surely they don't need that."

Clarice snorted. "Shows how much you know about being pretty." Perique looked hurt until Clarice leaned over and gave him another kiss on the mouth, not so light or quick this time.

"We can do our own makeup," Lin Bai volunteered. "We know how."

They dove into the kit, outlining their eyes, accenting their eyebrows and the hollows of their cheekbones, painting their lips and powdering their skin. Even Clarice's stage makeup felt light and dry compared to the sludgy greasepaint they knew from school. Still, the act of decorating their features was a small comfort, something familiar in this sea of strangeness.

Lin Bai appeared to enjoy being laced into a complex corset of elastic and whalebone, but Ji Fung refused the frightening contraption. Clarice clucked her disapproval and said he would have a flapper's figure. Ji Fung didn't know what a flapper was, but he insisted on being able to breathe.

Next came brassieres with cotton padding sewn in, just a hint of swelling for Ji Fung, fuller cups for Lin Bai. The heavy false breasts looked incongruous on his slight frame, but Perique pronounced them sexy. Then slippery stockings held up by elastic bands, and Western-style dresses of bright silk, summer sky and shimmering jade. And leather shoes, high-heeled pumps that hurt to walk on, but felt wonderful when sitting still.

Finally, the crowning touch: their wigs. Clarice fussed over the possibilities, holding up one glossy shell of hair, tucking it back in its box and pulling out another, holding the boys' chins and turning their faces this way and that. Lin Bai's face lit up when she brought out a blonde bob, but Perique called it implausible. Lin Bai sulked until Perique chose him another wig in the same style, this one brown with brilliant reddish highlights.

For Ji Fung, the selection was harder. Clarice finally settled on a tumble of shiny black waves that fell past his shoulders and easily covered his offending ears.

When Clarice led them before a full-length mirror, Ji Fung could not believe he was looking at himself. Lin Bai was stunning, of course, as flawlessly feminine as any of his roles. But Ji Fung could not stop staring at the woman he himself had become. She was not half as beautiful as Lin Bai, but she was undoubtedly female. A little on the plain side, taller and broader in the shoulders than she ought to be. A girl who would have to settle for marriage to an older man—a widower, maybe

—but a girl nonetheless. It was frightening. He felt as if part of himself, the wholly masculine part, had died back at the school with Master Lau. For the second time in his life, his identity had been erased and recreated. It made him feel lost and dizzy. He reached for Lin Bai's hand.

"Brand-new girls must have brand-new names," Perique told them. "American names, suitable for American movie stars."

He cupped Lin Bai's chin. "You will be Betty Lee."

"Betty," Lin Bai repeated as if hypnotized.

With his other hand, Perique stroked Ji Fung's powdered cheekbone. "And you will be Jenny Lee. Betty's sister."

If you ever tell anyone your real name, bad men will come and cut out your tongue. Do you understand?

"Jenny Lee," said Ji Fung, feeling the slow fear of a dream. He would not forget. He would never tell.

■ ■ ■

Two months passed. Ji Fung began learning to move like a woman, like Lin Bai. They were used to spending hours each week practicing and performing together. In lieu of that, their bodies exchanged information in every other way, all the time—side by side on a crowded street, hips swaying in tandem; in the marvelous bathtub all slippery with soap and sweat; making love under Perique's hungry gaze.

Perique scarcely touched the boys in private, but made a great show of pawing them in public. Like his style of gesture and dress, like his ostentatious displays of wealth, it was as if he were saying to the world, *Look what I have. Look what I can get away with.* He was teaching them English, drilling them on their pronunciation until they could say "I'm very pleased to meet you" just like proper ladies. They spent hours in the cinema and hours afterward imitating their favorite stars, struggling to pronounce incomprehensible names like *Greta Garbo* and *Marlene Dietrich*.

Perique was proud of his students, who drank information like thirsty sponges. When they wanted something, he would make them ask in English. He had even taught them to read and write it a little; Ji Fung found that he had an aptitude for the magic of words on paper. Perique was like an angel compared with the harsh master they had known before, but still there were times when Ji Fung wondered if their savior was a bit too fond of his superiority.

There were also times when he wished he had never learned English. He was standing at the bar of a Western jazz club one night, getting a drink for Lin Bai while Perique danced with him, when a slick-haired American sneered at them and asked his stylish but homely companion, "Who brought the little Chinks?"

The woman's grin seemed to split her sharp face like a hatchet cut. "Perique LeBon, I'm sure."

"That boy likes to pass himself off as white, but the yellow is starting to show through."

"At least they're *girls*. You should have seen the creature he dragged in here last month…"

Ji Fung got Lin Bai's drink and another one for himself, hoping to quench the insult's subtle sting. He returned to Perique's table, took a compact from the silver mesh bag in his lap, and examined his face, rubbing at an imaginary smudge of eyeliner, applying an unnecessary dash of lipstick. He still could not believe the face he saw in the mirror was really his. Lin Bai saw Ji Fung gazing at himself, smirked, and poked him in the ribs with a long red-lacquered nail.

As he tucked the compact away, he felt something smooth and round in the bottom of the purse. His jade name chop. He'd kept it with him since the night of their escape, but had scarcely thought of it in recent days. Now he pulled it out and turned it over and over in his hand. His head was swimming with alcohol fumes and clubland glitter, and he suddenly felt as if this small relic was the only thing linking him to his previous lives, a seed from which he might someday regrow his true identity.

Ji Fung pressed the cool jade to his lips. Glancing around the club, he noticed the bartender serving a pair of Chinese men in suits and black fedoras. They exuded a predatory nonchalance, and Ji Fung wondered if anyone would dare to call them Chinks.

Perique planted a liquor-scented kiss near the corner of his mouth and mumbled something about going to spend a penny, but Ji Fung could not take his eyes off the pair by the bar. Lin Bai soon noticed the focus of Ji Fung's attention. "Who are they?"

"I don't know," Ji Fung said. Part of him wanted to forget about them, leave this club, take Lin Bai home and spend the night devouring his smooth, skinny body. But he could not look away. There was something familiar about these men, about the curious stiff way they held their fingers as they raised cigarettes to their lips.

One of the men spoke to the bartender, a few short explosive syllables. The bartender nodded, brought out a thick envelope from beneath the bar, and handed it over. Slipping it into an inner pocket, the man turned his head and caught Ji Fung's gaze.

Ji Fung turned away, heart rocketing, but it was too late. The man was coming over, was at their table.

"Good evening, ladies." His smile showed off a mouthful of perfect teeth, but never touched his eyes. It vanished altogether when he saw the jade chop in Ji Fung's hand. Ji Fung tried to slip the chop back into his purse, but it was too late. The man grabbed his wrist and yanked him to his feet. "Where did you get this?"

Blank terror flooded Ji Fung's vision. He knew now who these men must be. They were the gangsters his mother had warned him about, the ones who would cut out his tongue if he ever told. His mind was spinning out of control, dizzy with panic. He knew he was going to lose his tongue. He could not remember what he must never tell. His name—what was that? Wang Ji Fung? Jenny Lee? Or something else entirely?

The man twisted his hand, caught the chop as it fell. "Answer me, bitch!"

But Ji Fung could not. When he felt the cold kiss of a gun against his ribs, he closed his eyes and waited to die. Instead, the two men gripped his elbows and hustled him toward the door. Dimly he heard Lin Bai shrieking syllables that might have been his name.

Triads

In a fetid alley behind the club, the man with the perfect teeth examined Ji Fung's jade chop in the meager light. His friend held Ji Fung against a slimy wooden gate, murmuring vile endearments that were more like threats of torture.

"Thief," said the first man softly, as if speaking to a lover. "Tell us how it is you came to have a precious item belonging to Gong Wa Toi."

His father's name. Ji Fung had not heard it spoken in years. He saw his mother's mad eyes on that long-ago dawn, felt her hot breath as she ordered him, "Never speak of your father again."

The other man loosened his grip on Ji Fung's throat. The pearl choker Perique had bought just this afternoon broke, scattering the pale spheres across the stinking mud of the alley. Ji Fung could not speak, only shake his head.

The man made a spitting sound, twined his fingers in Ji Fung's hair and yanked. When the long black tresses came off in his hand, the expression on his face was almost comical. He tore the front of Ji Fung's dress open and cursed at the sight of the naked, boyish chest.

Of course they beat him then. Ji Fung offered no resistance, giving in to the blows just as he had once given in to Master Lau's rattan cane. When consciousness receded, he welcomed the blackness and prayed that he would never wake up.

■ ■ ■

The gods did not answer his prayer. Awareness descended bit by painful bit: a wrenching pain in his elbow, a throbbing in his kidneys, a dull ache in his right eye. He awoke to find his sore cheek pressed against the weave of a fine rug, its rich red and gold pattern writhing in the blurred vortex of his vision. He felt cool air on his back and thighs and realized that he was nearly naked, the expensive dress reduced to rags.

Ji Fung closed his eyes, seeking the comfort of oblivion. But suddenly rough hands were touching him, shaking him. He looked up into the face of his attacker.

The man was white as a ghost, his eyes bright with panic. He showed his perfect teeth in a desperate smile that was more like a rictus. "Drink this," he said, holding out a translucent blue cup. "It will make you feel better."

Ji Fung sat up, wincing and baffled. He took the cup, since the man's hands were shaking so badly that the liquid inside threatened to slop onto the rug. It was tea, strong and honey-smooth. He drained it in three swallows. The man was there at once to refill the cup. "I am Chi Gwai, your servant. I have brewed you a pot of Cloud Mist, which grows only on the highest mountain peaks where men cannot climb. Monkeys have been trained to pluck the tea and bring it down in baskets. A very special infusion. Please tell me at once if there is anything else you require."

Ji Fung's mind was all jagged edges, unable to grasp the puzzle of his attacker's behavior. He sipped the tea and inventoried his body. Nothing was broken, but his flesh felt bruised and torn, low aches punctuated by clusters of pins and needles. His lower lip was split, though not badly, and several teeth wiggled in their sockets when he poked them with his tongue. His head rattled with half-formed questions.

"I humbly offer you these clothes," said Chi Gwai, bowing his head. "Poor quality, but the best I own."

He held up a Western-style suit, charcoal-gray with thin white stripes, and a black silk shirt. The clothes were exquisitely made. Ji Fung took them, feeling as if the world had completely ceased to make sense.

"Please accept these shoes also." Chi Gwai handed him a box. The shoes were black-and-white leather, shiny as glass. They fit his feet perfectly.

Chi Gwai brought him hot water to wash the crust of blood and lipstick from his face, and a comb to slick back his growing mop of hair. Dressing himself in the suit, Ji Fung found his jade name chop tucked discreetly into a vest pocket. At last he looked into the mirror—and saw yet another brand-new person. He was stylish, almost handsome. The bruises and split lip lent him a sinister air. He looked like the gangsters of whom his mother had warned him.

Chi Gwai led him along a hallway and into a great room half-filled with a carved table and rows of inlaid chairs. A niche in the wall held a statue of Kwan Ti, the fierce general-god of loyalty and brotherhood, with three sticks of incense burning before him. On the far wall hung an enormous painting of a village in winter, full of tiny people performing a thousand busy tasks. Ji Fung recognized the painting an instant before he saw the man sitting at the head of the table.

"Hello, Siu Ji."

The name of his childhood. The first name he had ever known, the one he had almost forgotten.

Ji Fung remembered eating meals at this table, staring at the painting and wishing for a way to step into that perfect miniature world. He and his parents had always been welcome at this man's table. His uncle's face was heavier now, his hair beginning to thin. But his eyes had not changed. They were like Father's, high-lidded and clear brown—but cold where Father's had been warm, cruel where Father's had been lit with humor. A thin American cigarette was pinched tightly between nicotined fingers, smoldering. Ji Fung remembered the constant smell of tobacco smoke that had pervaded all their meals.

"Uncle," Ji Fung murmured, bowing his head to cover his confusion.

Gong Sut Fo took his nephew by the shoulders. "At first I did not believe my eyes. The ghost of my brother's son, come back from the grave as a woman."

Ji Fung's face burned with shame, but he did not understand. Had his mother told his family he was dead? He took a deep breath and forced himself to speak the name his mother had told him never to think of again.

"Where is Gong Wa Toi?" he asked. "Why is my father not here to greet me?"

His uncle's face went blank as still water. Silence spooled out for an endless moment, and Ji Fung thought his heartbeat must surely be the loudest thing in the room. Then Gong Sut Fo took a cautious slurp of tea.

"You must be hungry." He stared for a moment into the depths of the painting, then clapped his hands. In a few seconds a servant girl appeared.

"Bring my nephew some soup and steamed dumplings." He held up his cup. "And some more tea."

"No, please," said Ji Fung, struggling with long-rusted manners. "It is too much trouble."

In truth he was not very hungry; his belly was full of acid from the fear and the drinks he'd had earlier. But he knew better than to refuse outright.

"It is no trouble," Gong Sut Fo said, his face creased with a peculiar sunless smile. "Only leftovers."

When the food arrived, it was twice what he'd expected, each dish fresh and hot: a spicy pork filling in the dumplings, succulent bits of shark's fin in the soup, little sweet cakes and pickled vegetables and a big bowl of steaming, sticky white rice. Ji Fung's appetite came back in a nostalgic rush. He was tired of Western food with its stodgy lumps of meat and thick bland sauces. The fragrant Cantonese dishes arrayed before him brought back memories of huge banquets at this table, of himself and his two small sisters running back and forth like little playful dogs, snatching a morsel of fish, a sticky rice cake, a slice of candied lotus root.

He ate hugely under his uncle's watchful gaze and waited for the answer to his question. But it was not until Ji Fung had finished every dish that Gong Sut Fo spoke.

"Your mother was from Soochow, a middle-class girl whose family made musical instruments. She was known for her sweet voice and beautiful face, and her father was ambitious, refusing offers from respectable men. He was holding out for a wealthy man from Hong Kong, a man with power. A man mentioned to him by a local fortuneteller."

Ji Fung refilled his cup and drank, listening intently.

"I met your mother, Miao-Ying, in Shanghai." Gong Sut Fo paused. "We fell in love."

Ji Fung frowned, but his uncle's eyes looked right past him.

"Foolish," he said. "We had not been introduced. But it was true. I adored her odd little ways, the faraway look in her eyes. How

46

bad we were—she allowed me to hold her hand, and even to kiss her fingers! But she was a strange girl. She said she didn't want to depend on men all her life, and everyone knows a woman must depend on men.

"Miao-Ying went home and told her father that she had met the husband of her dreams. She told him I was from a powerful Hong Kong family, just as the fortuneteller promised, and she begged him to let us marry. Her father was pleased, but being ambitious, he investigated my family and found out that my older brother was also unmarried. He thought, *Why give my daughter to the second son of the Gong family when she could be the first wife of the first son?* And he offered Miao-Ying to Wa Toi instead of to me.

"At the time I thought I would die, seeing her every day, knowing she slept with my brother every night. Now I realize that losing her may be the only reason I am still alive. Her odd ways—that faraway look—I believe they were signs of her madness."

Ji Fung's hands twisted together in his lap. The delicious meal lay uneasy in his belly.

"After the wedding, Miao-Ying became like a ghost in the house, never speaking to me or my brother, and to the servants only when she had no choice. In my youthful arrogance, I imagined she was pining for me. She was ill all through her pregnancy. When you were born, she didn't seem to recognize you as her son. When you cried for her, she would hand you to a nurse, but then she would disappear, and the servants would find her staring at you while you slept.

"Wa Toi tried to love her, I think. And he worshiped you. But when she returned none of his affections, he took a second wife, the mother of your sisters, and later a third who was carrying a child that spring. Miao-Ying withdrew further, as if she thought nothing more was required of her.

"Even though by that time I had wives and children of my own, I was still tormented by thoughts of Miao-Ying. I imagined us running away together, foolish dreams that haunted me endlessly. I imagined that I would save her. I wish we had run away—I could not have saved her from herself, but I might have saved my brother.

"It was early that spring, during the season of the vernal equinox, when she took you away. I had been out drinking all night and

47

well into the morning, and I came to the decision that I could not live without her. I went to my brother's house and banged on the door, demanding that he divorce Miao-Ying without further delay. When there was no answer, I pushed the door open and walked inside. What I found in there I will never forget.

"First, the smell. Awful, like a sick person who has not washed in months, like an overflowing toilet. I came upon poisoned servants lying where they had fallen. I ran upstairs to look for my brother, only to find him tangled in stinking bedclothes, stiff and dead with his second wife beside him.

"As I continued my search, I found nothing but death throughout the house. I was enraged in my drunkenness, swearing vengeance upon the man-headed demon that had poisoned my brother's family. I had left Miao-Ying's chambers for last, dreading the sight of her poor poison-wracked body, but needing to know. I stood at the door with tears on my face, and as I took a deep breath to ready myself, I detected a new odor. Kerosene. I pressed my ear to the door and was able to make out the faintest of sounds, like muffled weeping.

"Enthralled by the idea that Miao-Ying might still be alive, I pushed open the door and saw her kneeling in the center of the room. Her pale arms encircled a small child swathed in a blanket. I could not see his face—I assumed it was you. The stink of kerosene was overwhelming; I could see that her hair and clothes were soaked with it, as was the blanket wrapped around the child. I realized it was he who was crying, his sobs muffled in the thick cotton that covered his head.

"When Miao-Ying turned to look at me, I knew it was she who had poisoned my brother. Her face was as composed and lovely as always, but her eyes were hot like a mad dog's, full of sickness and loathing. I watched in horror as she struck the match and gave herself to the flames.

"The child screamed and struggled in her arms, trying to cast off the burning blanket, then writhing as the fire took his flesh. Miao-Ying held him tight, her face beneath the flames at once serene and ecstatic. I could only stand and watch the fire eat away the face that had haunted me for so many years.

"To this day I am ashamed to admit I made no move to save her, or the child I thought was you."

Gong Sut Fo turned his gaze to Ji Fung, though he did not seem to see his nephew.

"Now that I have told you a story, you must tell me one. The story of how you came to be here in my house eight years after your mother murdered you."

At first, no words would come. Ji Fung could only think of questions. What depths of emotion had curdled in his mother to make her capable of such an act? Her heart must have been like a thousand-year-old egg, preserved in ash and lime, buried until it was black as a millennium of midnights. And what child had died in his place? Too easily he could imagine her leaving him at the opera school, then luring some starving waif back to the house of corpses, promising him food, giving him death. He imagined the boy's dirty face blackening and shriveling in the flames. It seemed more real than the face of his uncle before him, more real than the memory of his mother's face.

Ji Fung was sick to the bone, sure that he would never speak again. But eventually he did. Once he had begun the process of unburdening after so many years, the story took on momentum beyond his control, pouring forth like blood from a wound he had thought healed. Of course he said nothing of Lin Bai or Perique; he said only that he and a friend had killed their Master and run away from the opera school to escape being beaten, and implied that he and the friend had gone their separate ways.

His uncle listened intently, always pulling at his cigarette, pock-marked face empty of emotion. When Ji Fung trailed off into helpless silence, Gong Sut Fo clapped for more tea.

"I have already taken care of the trouble with your Master Lau," he said, refilling Ji Fung's cup. "The police are no longer interested in you as a suspect."

"Uncle, you are too generous." *But what about Lin Bai?*

Gong Sut Fo's mouth turned up in the chilly grimace that passed as his smile. "It is the least I can do for the only son of my only brother."

Ji Fung knew could not ask reprieve for his friend. If he knew what sort of friends they were, his uncle would probably have them both killed. Could Lin Bai remain a woman forever? Ji Fung felt as if the favor were a weight settling onto his heart. He could not imagine what he would be asked to pay in return.

For an hour they spoke of ordinary things, like any nephew and uncle visiting after a long absence. Gong Sut Fo showed photographic portraits of his five daughters, all well-married or promised to good families, and Ji Fung remarked on what lovely young women they had become. They spoke of a granduncle who had died, a cousin Ji Fung barely remembered. Of mah-jongg and the weather and a trip Gong Sut Fo had recently made to Peking. Ji Fung was beginning to feel he had truly returned home.

Gong Sut Fo pushed his chair back. "Well, and it is late, nearly morning."

"Yes, it is," Ji Fung answered. He was exhausted, as if the evening's chaos had drained every drop of vitality from him.

"There is only one small thing I must ask of you before we retire."

Ji Fung's breath caught. This was it. He nodded, wary.

"It is a small favor, but one that would be much appreciated."

"Anything, Uncle."

"It is like this." Gong Sut Fo put a match to the latest of what seemed a hundred cigarettes. "I have a very important new business associate in Shanghai. An American. He is considering doing business with us, but would first like a sample of our product."

"What product is that?"

His uncle beckoned to the serving girl, who brought an intricately carved jade box to the table. Gong Sut Fo opened the lid, took out a bundle tied in red cloth, unfolded the cloth to reveal a sticky-looking black pellet as long as a man's finger. A rich, sweet odor emanated from it, strong enough to make Ji Fung's head swim.

"Opium?" he whispered.

"Does this shock you?"

Ji Fung could not speak. He stared down at his shiny new shoes. The gangsters, the murdering men his murdering mother had warned him of—they were his own family. But surely his father had not been an evil man...?

Ji Fung realized he knew nothing about his father save that the man had given him sweets and spoken kindly to him. Outside of his role as father, Gong Wa Toi could have been any sort of man at all. Was it even barely possible that something—a life of festering corruption, perhaps—might have justified Miao-Ying's murdering him and stealing his son?

It was not possible. And even if it were, nothing could justify the wanton murder of the other wives, the faithful servants, the children. And the boy who had died for him, who had suffered the ultimate loss of face for him, his features burned beyond recognition.

Seeming to read the confusion in his nephew's face, Gong Sut Fo spoke. "We are not criminals. We are revolutionaries, acquiring capital by any means necessary. Capital gives us power to fight the imperialist cowards who would drive China into the ground to satisfy their own greed. The Triad brotherhood is like a family, and a family must bind together in times of strife and sorrow." His voice grew tense with emotion. "It is a family you were born into, and from whose arms your mother tore you. Your rightful place is here with us. I thank the gods that you are with us again. You are the first son of my father's first son. I have no sons of my own, only daughters. It would be an honor to consider you my son."

All the long cold nights at the opera school came rushing back, all the times Ji Fung had dreamed of running away to find his lost family. The memories filled him with hope and gratitude, so much so that tears stung his eyes. He blinked them away and waited, knowing his uncle was not finished.

"But first there is one thing," said Gong Sut Fo, his eyebrows low and grim. "I must know beyond a doubt that you are the son of my brother, not of Miao-Ying. If my family's blood runs in your veins, then you will not disappoint me. Do this favor for your uncle as a demonstration of loyalty to your father's memory."

Ji Fung bowed his head.

"Tell me what to do, Uncle, and I will do it gladly."

"In three days it will be Yue Lan, the Festival of Hungry Ghosts. At that time, take the ferry to Kowloon and walk up Tung Tau Tsuen Road to the Walled City. Enter the City by way of Fui Sing Street where the illicit dentists practice their trade. A hundred steps in you will see a butcher's shop, and beyond it an alleyway where an old man sells shoes. Ask to see some woven grass sandals. When he tells you he has only one left, you say, *I only need one for the journey I must make.* Hand him the money like this."

Gong Sut Fo held a folded note in his left hand between the first and second fingers, the other fingers tucked into the palm, the thumb trapping them. Ji Fung took the money and mimicked his uncle's motion. Gong Sut Fo nodded, slipping the note back into his pocket.

"The old man will give you a box. Take this box to Shanghai by train. On the Bund, the main street that runs along the Whangpoo River, you will find an establishment called the Shanghai Club where our new friend dines daily with his French associates. You will meet him there and give him the box. He already has the key. The man's name is Herbert Hinchcliffe."

Ji Fung repeated the difficult name twice, softly.

"Your English pronunciation is excellent," Gong Sut Fo said. "Did they teach you that in the opera school?"

Ji Fung smiled, just a little, and his uncle returned it with more genuine feeling than he had yet shown.

"You are a good boy." He stood and patted Ji Fung's shoulder. "I have one more thing for you."

Gong Sut Fo motioned to the girl, who vanished. Seconds later, the two men from the alley sidled in.

"Nephew, you have already met Chi Gwai. This is Lam Bao, his associate." The two men bowed. Both looked pale and nervous. "They have come to apologize for causing you injury."

Ji Fung stood stiff and uncomfortable through the excruciatingly formal apologies. He could see that both men were terrified of his uncle. When the second man stumbled to a halt at the end of his ill-prepared speech, Gong Sut Fo reached into a drawer and took out a small silver-plated revolver. He handed the gun to Ji Fung, who took it with great reluctance.

Triads

"Do you forgive them?" Gong Sut Fo asked.

Ji Fung balanced the gun's cool weight in his right hand. The two men before him were silent and wild-eyed, their faces slick with sweat. Ji Fung realized there was a part of him that wanted to shoot them both, to make them feel the fear and pain he had felt when they dragged him away from Lin Bai.

Thinking of Lin Bai brought its own pain. Where was he right now? Was he mourning Ji Fung for dead, just as Gong Sut Fo had done for so many years?

Ji Fung bit the inside of his lip. He had to concentrate. This was not a question of revenge. It was a test. He closed his eyes for a long moment, then looked his uncle full in the face.

"I do forgive them," said Ji Fung. "They were only protecting the memory of my father. And I would not have found my family without them."

Gong Sut Fo nodded. He clearly approved of this answer. "My nephew's generous nature has spared your lives," he told the men. "But in my eyes, the road to forgiveness is long and painful."

He took the gun from Ji Fung and fired two shots. Blood exploded across the floor, spattering Ji Fung's black and white shoes. The two men fell screaming, each clutching a wounded leg.

Gong Sut Fo replaced the gun in its drawer and laid his hand on Ji Fung's shoulder again. This time Ji Fung struggled not to flinch.

"By the time their wounds have healed, you will have returned from Shanghai. From that day on, they will be your personal bodyguards. They will protect you with their lives and perform any other services you require."

Ji Fung forced himself to look away from the blood pooling on the beautiful rug. His eyes fell on the statue of Kwan Ti brandishing his sword, and he remembered that this was also a Triad god, one of three generals known as the Three Brothers because of their great loyalty to one another. He noticed that Kwan Ti's left hand was curled in the same way that his uncle had shown him to hand over the money.

It was all too much. Like a tired child, Ji Fung let his uncle lead him around the writhing men and out into the long hallway.

"It has been a long night for you," said Gong Sut Fo. "Today you will sleep undisturbed. You begin your journey at the next night-fall."

■ ■ ■

Lin Bai lay naked on his belly, head spinning, mouth dry as sand. His cheeks were scaly with tears that had flowed and dried, flowed and dried. Perique had gone out hours ago, desperately optimistic, certain that with money and what he called his "connections," he would be able to find Ji Fung.

Lin Bai had no such hope. He understood what was happening here. Everyone who tried to love him died, so Ji Fung must be dead. Lin Bai had not thwarted his ill luck by murdering Master Lau; he had only sent it astray for a bit. Now it had found him.

He knew he should leave this hotel before his poison luck spilled over onto Perique, who was rather weak and silly, but who had saved his unlucky life and Ji Fung's. But perhaps the poison had already touched Perique. Inevitably, it would touch anyone he cared for. He could go far away, deep into the mountains, become a hermit. But he knew he would not survive two moons. He had an actor's heart. He would wither and die without an audience. Perhaps he should.

How to do it? The window was not high enough. Perique had taken his gun with him. There were razors, but the blood would remind him of Master Lau. He did not want to die as Master Lau had died.

He looked desperately around the room, seeking the instrument of his own demise. His eye fell upon the bedside table, where Perique had set half a plate of little baked cakes full of red bean paste and sweet opium. Yesterday Perique had warned him and Ji Fung not to eat more than one at a time, for they were very strong.

He reached for the bottle of American whiskey beside him only to find the coverlet sodden with its reeking contents. No matter; he could do without it. Lin Bai began to eat the cakes, their brash flavor clenching the dry tissues of his mouth. When he had finished four, the plate fell away from his hands. He lay back and waited for death to claim him.

■ ■ ■

Ji Fung paused a moment before the door to Perique's suite, suddenly apprehensive. He straightened his new tie and ran his palms over his slicked-back hair, nervous and unsure of himself. He had come so far, changed so much in the course of one night. He was no longer an orphan on the run. He was a man with a powerful family, the long-lost first son welcomed back home. Was it even possible to return to this nightside world, this sex-scented opium dream of a life?

He shook his head. He had no choice. He owed Perique for saving his life, and that life would be meaningless if he could not share it with Lin Bai.

He had to fit together these two halves of his life. There must be some way. He could introduce Lin Bai to his family as Betty Lee—or better yet, Betty LeBon, Perique's cousin. His uncle would never believe Perique was from a good family, but perhaps a rich one would do. What had he said about the strange brotherhood, the shadowy gangster/revolutionaries whose true purpose Ji Fung had not even begun to fathom? *We gain capital any way we can.*

Perhaps Perique would even know where to buy him children. Then he could have sons, and replenish the family his mother had devastated. He imagined street urchins saved from lives of wretched hunger, from miserable deaths like that of the boy who had taken his place. Perhaps he could atone for that boy's agony, placate his burning ghost.

He was smiling and full of the future as he opened the door and strode through the suite to the bedroom. Lin Bai's naked body lay limp and accusatory on the bed, surrounded by the sticky remains of half-eaten opium cakes.

Ji Fung ran to the bed, yanked Lin Bai up by the shoulders, slapped his face lightly, then harder. Lin Bai's head lolled on his neck. His skin was cold and clammy, his eyes slitted silver-white.

"Lin Bai, wake up! Don't be dead now! I beg you, my brother, my lover!"

Lin Bai made a soft noise like a sleeper disturbed. A faint pulse jumped in his neck. Ji Fung hauled him to his feet, struggling to support the slight but inert bulk.

"Walk with me," Ji Fung commanded. "Dance with me! Come on, graceful feet, stand up."

Perique burst through the door, cursing in French.

"Ji, you're alive!" He rushed to help support Lin Bai. "What's happened?"

Ji Fung gestured with his chin at the half-eaten cakes.

"*Mon Dieu!* I should never have left him alone. But he's not too far gone yet. I've seen worse." Perique rushed into the bathroom and began to fill the tub. "Bring him in, quickly."

They laid Lin Bai in the cool water and splashed his face, slapping him lightly, rubbing his hands and his feet.

"Lin Bai," Ji Fung called. "My love, can you hear me?"

He began to sing. "*Since ancient times, how few lovers have remained constant to the end?*"

Lin Bai's eyelids fluttered. He rolled his head back and forth, groaned softly. Perique pursed his lips in approval.

"That's right, sing with me. *But those who were true have come together at last. Even though thousands of miles apart. Even though torn from each other by death.*"

Lin Bai's lips were moving, his voice a soft whisper, barely audible.

"How does the rest go?" Ji Fung asked. "You know I always forget the words. Help me remember."

Lin Bai's mouth turned up at the corners, faintest ghost of a smile. His voice was high and wandering, but now there was a hint of strength behind it. "*And all those who curse their unhappy fate are simply those lacking in love.*"

There were tears on Ji Fung's cheeks, and his voice cracked as he and Lin Bai sang together.

"*True love moves heaven and earth. Metal and stone shine like the sun and light the pages of old histories.*"

Triads

Lin Bai rested his head against the shoulder of Ji Fung's new suit, now damp with bathwater. "You never remember the words," he scolded. "Daydreaming instead of practicing. How will you become a star in Hollywood?"

Ji Fung pressed his lips to the crown of Lin Bai's head, remembering the feel of stubble where silky hair now grew. "I need you there to remind me," he said.

Lin Bai opened his eyes and looked at Ji Fung, fully aware now. "You're alive."

Ji Fung nodded.

"And so am I."

"Yes, you are."

"I didn't bring you bad luck."

Ji Fung smiled. "Definitely not."

■ ■ ■

None of them had ever been inside Kowloon Walled City, but they had all heard frightful tales. The place was a teeming nest of villains, where decay and dissolution throve. A man who entered at night was unlikely to see morning, and a woman would be foolish to enter at all, particularly if she were beautiful. Perique told them of squalid rooms where women were kept, drugged and shackled, forced to perform any abomination a customer's mind could dream up.

Even so, Lin Bai insisted on coming along. He could not spend another night waiting at the hotel; he said he would go mad. Remembering the image of his lover's limp body sprawled on the bed, Ji Fung gave in. He reasoned that anyone attempting to interfere with Betty Lee would get more than he bargained for; no one would expect such a demure young lady to be capable of turning a somersault in midair or delivering a double-footed flying kick strong enough to shatter a skull.

The Walled City met none of their expectations. Its claustrophobic mass of masonry and wood was nearly deserted. Once this place had been the Manchu stronghold against the British, fortified with walls fifteen feet thick, ruled by the iron hand of the *yamen*.

After the British takeover the place had become a no-man's-land governed only by the law of a razor across the throat.

In Hong Kong and the rest of Kowloon, the Festival of Hungry Ghosts was in full swing. Ji Fung and Lin Bai knew this celebration well, since it included special performances of operas to entertain the dead. Small bonfires dotted every lane and alleyway, every pavement and courtyard. The smoke from spiraling coils of incense mingled with that from the fires. The damp air smelled sweet, faintly singed. Paper replicas of necessities and luxuries—furniture, automobiles, clothes—were burned on this night to protect one's dead ancestors from want. Ji Fung thought again of the boy who had died in his place, fed to the flames so that his father would not lack a son in the afterlife.

Inside these walls, though, the festival itself was like a ghost—and an exceedingly hungry one at that. Most of the ramshackle structures were dark and empty. Some sagged and swayed, ruins ready to fall but held upright by buildings on either side, like a corpse supported by two cripples. Here and there, tiny fires were fueled by chips of bone and dried human shit, tended by crouching souls who occasionally fed them spirit-gifts fashioned out of cheap newsprint. The streets were so narrow that the boys had to edge past these mean celebrations in single file to avoid scorching their feet. The inhabitants of the city paid them no mind. Most did not even look up when they passed, and those who did looked quickly away again.

"It's almost as if they're scared of us," Lin Bai whispered as a rope-muscled young man peered at them from the doorway of a filthy shop, then ducked inside.

"They think we're Triad," said Perique.

Ji Fung glanced at him. "We are."

"*You* are. I'm on vacation. Ha." Perique neatly avoided a puddle of foul, oily mud. "Shanghai is going to look damned good after this."

They came to the butcher's shop Gong Sut Fo had mentioned. Roast pigs' heads were displayed in the window, eyes popped in their sockets, skin brittle and translucent, lower jaws split down the middle to reveal two rows of razor-sharp teeth. Above them hung a phalanx of badly preserved ducks, moldy and flyblown. A single taper burned in the shop, and by its light a small boy was skinning a dog. The colorful mass of its guts lay on the floor beside him. His naked body was greased with blood, his hair stiff with it.

They hurried past the shop and turned into the narrow alley just beyond it. The old shoeseller's stall and household were set up in a slight recess in the wall of the butcher's building. His territory was marked by a heap of cloth slippers and rough hide sandals. Beyond that were his cookpot and sleeping mat.

He put aside his bowl of noodles as Ji Fung entered the alley. His dark face was as desiccated as the hide of his sandals, but his eyes were sharp and bright.

"Shoes for the young gentleman?" he asked.

"I would like to buy some of your grass sandals," said Ji Fung, feeling as if he were onstage again.

The old man smiled, revealing a single tooth.

"Ah," he said. "I am ashamed to admit that I have only one left."

He reached into the pile of shoes and pulled out a single old-fashioned woven sandal, like those worn by monks.

"Best quality, though. Hand-woven from fine reeds."

Ji Fung looked over his shoulder at Perique and Lin Bai hovering at the mouth of the alley. Perique shrugged. But Lin Bai gave him a slight nod and frown, as he had always done when Ji Fung needed prompting.

He took a deep breath and delivered his line. "I need only one for the journey I must make." Then he fished out the note he had carefully folded on the ferry and handed it over as he had been instructed.

The old man's gnarled fingers snatched the money and made it disappear more quickly than Ji Fung's eye could follow. He lifted his cooking pot to reveal a deep hollow, removed a red lacquer box, brushed away some dirt and ashes, and placed it in Ji Fung's hands.

It was larger than he had expected. Big enough to require two hands to hold, with an ornate brass lock. This he must carry safely to Shanghai. Weighing it in his hands, he could barely conceive of the value this simple box represented. Not only the cash value, but the amount of trust his uncle had placed in him. Ji Fung silently promised his father's spirit that the brotherhood would not be disappointed.

■ ■ ■

The train had stopped again. This was the seventh time, and they had not even reached Soochow.

Perique rolled his eyes and shook his head, but the boys ignored him, hanging out the window surrounded by hordes of itinerant vendors. In recent days, these people had become so used to seeing the train stopped on the tracks that they loitered about with their wares, waiting for it to happen. When it did, they rushed up with trays of snacks and clay cups of tea, curious baubles and playthings. It disgusted Perique to see the way these yokels swarmed, like flies or some other sort of minor but annoying vermin. He wished the boys would not encourage them.

When Ji Fung and Lin Bai finally sat back down, their arms were full of junk. Brown pears and rice balls steamed in lotus leaves. Greasy paper cones full of fried noodles. A little mirror with a red-and-gold dragon on the back. A bamboo crab with waving eyestalks and moving legs. A painted tin monkey on a stick.

They began sharing out the food, unwrapping the limp gray-green leaves amid clouds of steam, dipping into the paper cones with fancy chopsticks. Perique wrinkled his nose. "How can you eat that?"

"It's good!" Lin Bai said. His lipstick was almost entirely gone. Only the corners of his mouth were still bright red.

"Here." Ji Fung offered him a pear, but Perique shook his head violently.

"Don't you know anything? These country people use human shit to fertilize their crops. Their food is filled with all sorts of disease. Cholera. Dysentery."

Lin Bai laughed. "No diseases can live with these." He held up a wrinkled red chili between his silver chopsticks, then popped it into his mouth.

"Besides," added Ji Fung, "that food in the dining car is terrible. Tastes like pale meat boiled in baby's vomit."

Perique hissed in exasperation. His hopes of turning these wild animals into civilized young men receded further each day.

■ ■ ■

Later, over supper, the dining car was abuzz with talk of war. Shots had been exchanged by Chinese and Japanese troops on the Marco Polo Bridge near Peking. A Japanese lieutenant and his driver had gone missing, their bodies eventually found near the Hungjao aerodrome.

"Sexually mutilated," a red-faced Brit elaborated with no little relish. "Cut off their willies. Appalling what these Chinee get up to."

His companion, a pale wisp of a woman with ashy blonde hair and faded blue eyes, spoke up. "D'you suppose there's any sort of danger?"

The Brit's enormous white moustache quivered. "Don't be so bloody thick, Enid! These things go on all the time in China. It isn't going to affect any civilized human beings."

At sundown, the train still hadn't moved. Perique sat in the stifling compartment with a tumbler full of whiskey and ice, Lin Bai's head pillowed on his lap. The boy was so beautiful, with his long bangs falling over his pale forehead, with those nymphet's eyes and that lush pink mouth. His hair had grown into a short bob, so he could leave off the wig, a blessing in these summer months. And his features were so fine and well-trained that he scarcely needed makeup to look like a girl.

Across from them, Ji Fung sat looking stylish and perhaps even a little dangerous in his new suit and two-toned shoes. He was the yang to Lin Bai's yin, just as beautiful, but in a hard-edged, masculine fashion. They looked ever so good together.

Ji Fung noticed Perique's attention and smiled, cocking his head in a way that displayed the fine muscles of his throat. "Tell us more about Shanghai," he said.

Lin Bai chimed in without opening his eyes. "Yes, tell us."

"Well...I remember the library at the Shanghai Club." Perique laughed softly. "The club is famous for its bar, which is the longest in the world—one hundred fifty yards, and I will buy you both a drink there, I promise—but when I was a boy, I cared nothing for bars. I remember the old men playing chess in the library, the scent of their pipe smoke. I remember the books, shelves and shelves of them rising up as far as the eye could see, with long ladders you climbed to reach the high ones. I would spend long summer days reading there, breathing the dust of leather and paper, the effluvia of imagination. I had few friends, so I comforted myself with those I found in books."

"Surely you must have had some friends," Ji Fung said.

"Who? I didn't know any other half-breeds my age. The Chinese children thought I was a snob, and the white children called me—"

"What?" Lin Bai propped himself up on one elbow. "What did they call you?"

Perique stared out the window at the motionless landscape. "A yellow bastard," he said finally.

Ji Fung leaned over and patted Perique's knee. "Then they were stupid and you didn't need to know them."

Perique nodded, but even to this day he remembered how lonely he had felt for the company of other boys, so lonely that he would gladly have siphoned out either his Chinese or his white blood if he had been able to do so. To be pure white in Shanghai's French Concession would have been heavenly. All the city's pleasures and opportunities would have been open to him. But even to be pure Chinese—to fully belong *anywhere*—

Ji Fung's voice jolted him out of his reverie. "What about your brothers and sisters?"

Christ. "Oh yes," he said lamely, "I often played with them."

He remembered once commanding the children of some servants to play with him. The two boys had done so with cold politeness, waiting patiently for this new duty to be finished so they could go back to plucking ducks in the kitchen. Agonized and enraged, Perique had dragged them to a vine-swathed pagoda at the back of the family compound and made them pleasure each other with their mouths while he watched. They exhibited signs of excitement, but after it was over, they had looked at Perique with such hatred that he never dared speak to them again.

He reached across the compartment and pulled Ji Fung over to his side, slipped his arm around the boy's waist, ran his other hand through Lin Bai's hair. "But now I have you, my boys. And when we get to Shanghai, I will show you the Paris of the Orient, or the Whore of the Orient if you like. Only a few years ago a visiting Christian missionary claimed the city was so decadent as to call for an apology by God to Sodom and Gomorrah."

Both boys frowned in confusion.

"Never mind. I'll take you walking on the Bund, by the river, where the Shanghai Club and all the grand buildings are. We'll go shopping at Sincere's and Wing On, where you can buy absolutely anything your pretty hearts desire. We will go to the Great World Theatre and see the Shanghai Ballet, or the Russian Opera. Would you like that?"

He received a pair of emphatic yeses. Just then the train lurched to a start, and cheers resounded along the car.

It was the middle of the night when they finally pulled into Shanghai's railway station. In spite of the late hour, the station was packed with people. There were elegant blonde mothers surrounded by matching suitcases, gossiping to each other about the "Oriental troubles" while Chinese nurses tried to soothe whining children kept up far too late. There were old European dandies and their handsome young companions of both sexes. There were Shanghai natives: well-dressed young couples, businessmen, wealthy women with painted eyebrows and severe rice-powdered faces.

All were fighting to get on a train and out of Shanghai. The tension was beginning to wear thin the mask of civilized manners. Ji Fung was shocked to see a pretty young mother push an old woman aside to get her children on the departing train. The old woman tottered and almost fell onto the tracks.

"Why is everyone in such a hurry?" Ji Fung asked, hefting three of their seven suitcases.

"How should I know?" Perique muttered, looking around for a porter. The last leg of the journey had wilted him, and he was annoyed at the prospect of carrying his own luggage.

"Is it because of the fighting?" Lin Bai asked, toeing a small case with the tip of his high-heeled pump.

"*Fuck* the fighting!" Perique barked. He raised an imperious hand. "Porter!" But the few uniformed porters they could spot were already laden with far too many bags.

"Listen," Perique said. "This isn't a bunch of ignorant country people squabbling over worthless bits of land. This is the civilized world. If we ran away every time these people started shooting at their enemies, there would be no Shanghai."

"*These people?*" Ji Fung dropped the bags he was holding. "You mean Chinese people?"

Perique rolled his eyes. "Are you suddenly a patriot? I'm talking about uncivilized people."

Lin Bai tried to push between them. "Here. I'll take two suitcases and Perique take two and Ji Fung take the rest. If we wait for a porter, we'll be here all night."

Ji Fung spat on the floor beside Perique's shoes. "If it weren't for all those uncivilized people, who would clean your fancy porcelain toilets and cook your food and spoonfeed it to you like the baby you are?"

"How dare you speak to me in that way?" Perique's face was flushed, his green eyes blazing. "Without me, your precious *people* would have cut your throat and left you dead on the Hong Kong waterfront."

"Yes, and you can turn a philosopher into a biting dog if you starve him long enough!"

"Why, you ungrateful little—"

"*What?*" Ji Fung screamed into Perique's face. "*What were you going to call me?*"

Perique had no answer. Ji Fung turned to Lin Bai, who was watching them in horror. "Will you stay and be his pet Chink, or are you coming with me?"

"Where?" Lin Bai's hands worked in unconscious operatic gestures of distress, shaping the stale smoky air of the train station.

"Where would we go? We need a friend." He turned to Perique. "You are Chinese. You are as entitled as anyone to criticize your own countrymen. Only try to be more compassionate. The lives of most Chinese people are not as good as yours."

"I'm not Chinese," said Perique in a strangled voice. "I'm not anything. My name isn't even LeBon, it's Lee."

"What?" said the boys in unison.

The crowd kept pushing and flowing around them. Their own silence spooled out. At last Perique said, "It doesn't matter. I suppose you'll want to leave, seeing as I'm not only a foreign devil but a liar too."

Lin Bai tilted his head. "What do you mean?"

"I told you I was born in Shanghai. That much is true. Everything else was a lie. I have no brothers or sisters. My father was Chinese, a trader of things legal and not. Mostly not, and he was extremely wealthy.

"My mother was a dance hall hostess from Paris, working in Shanghai. Not a whore, just a free spirit…but in my father's eyes it amounted to the same thing. He spent money on her, dazzled her, made her think he loved her. Soon enough he got what he wanted from her, and soon enough he tired of it and dropped her. She had other admirers, and wasn't one to chase a man. My father didn't hear from her until three months later, when she contacted him and told him she was going to have his child.

"At first he didn't believe that she knew he was the father, but she convinced him somehow. After that he took her in and treated her as his wife. She received the richest food, the softest bed, and the best herbal medicine. My father treated her exquisitely until the day I was born."

"Then what?" Lin Bai urged when Perique stopped. "Did he throw her out?"

"No. He had her killed."

The boys' eyes grew large.

"He sent two underlings into her room that very night. One held a hand over my mouth so I wouldn't cry and wake her. The other pushed a long hatpin through her nostril and into her brain.

My father had her body dumped off an opium junk in the middle of
the South China Sea."

"But why?"

Perique shrugged. "He wanted a son. He didn't want to be bur-
dened with a wife, much less a Paris whore, as he called her. I was
suckled and raised by an *amah*. I don't think he was really very interested in women. If I'd been born a girl, he would have killed me
too."

"How do you know all this?" Ji Fung asked.

"My father told me the story himself when I was ten years old.
He wanted me to know what sort of man he was, and what sort of
woman my mother had been. Like your uncle, Ji—he was worried
that I would turn out to be my mother's son. I suppose I did. Five
years later he called me a soft French faggot and ordered me out of
his house."

"Then how…"

"How do I live so comfortably? It's easy. Chinese family ties
can never really be broken. Until he died, my father paid me thousands of pounds a year to use a name other than his own. He promised that if I would live this way until his death, I would inherit his
fortune, and I did. Publicly he wanted nothing to do with me. But
whenever I was in Shanghai to collect a payment, he always seemed
to know what I'd been up to."

Perique stood silent, his arms hanging limp at his sides. He
looked tired and defeated. Ji Fung's heart went out to him in spite
of the snobbery and petty racism. These things seemed pathetic
now, like a man lashing out uselessly at a system that has ultimate
power over him.

Ji Fung felt a new kinship with Perique: they both knew the
pain of losing a beloved parent to a mad one. For Perique obviously
loved his mother's ghost, though he had spent only a single day
with her while she lived. Ji Fung imagined Perique as a child, a
sheltered prisoner in his father's world just as he and Lin Bai had
been prisoners of the opera school. But while they had had each
other, Perique had had no one.

He reached out and gave Perique's hand a quick squeeze. Perique looked surprised, then relieved. "So you don't want to go?" he asked.

Ji Fung allowed himself a slight smile. "Not unless you want us to."

"Don't tease me," said Perique as he stooped to pick up his share of the luggage. "You two are the first real friends I've ever had."

"Then let's find somewhere to store these damned bags, and you can start showing us the Whore of the Orient."

■ ■ ■

The Shanghai Club was as fabulous as Perique had described it. High ornate ceilings, cool shady rooms, long windows overlooking the rococo skyline. The world's longest bar was staffed by over a hundred expert bartenders and stocked with every potable poison in the world. Perique bought them Brandy Alexanders, frothy, creamy drinks whose sweetness cloaked a sharp alcoholic bite. They wandered tipsily through the library, trying to read the Roman characters stamped in gilt on the leather spines of the books, driving themselves into fits of laughter with their slurred pronunciations. They almost missed their six o'clock appointment with the Westerner. When Perique saw the clock and reminded them, they lost another five minutes saying "Herbert Hinchcliffe" to each other and laughing at the sound of it.

Taking a moment to sober up in the washroom, Ji Fung stood before the mirror breathing deeply, as he had often done just before going onstage. He tapped a fingernail against the brass lock on the red lacquer box, searching for a confidence he didn't feel. When he could delay no longer, he squared his shoulders and went out to speak to the maitre d'hotel.

The maitre d' was an officious little Fukienese fellow with threads of gray in his neatly trimmed moustache. He eyed Ji Fung and his associates with polite suspicion.

"I am looking for the American, Herbert Hinch—kwiff." Ji Fung struggled to keep his voice low and authoritative, though he knew he had botched the man's name.

"Who is it who is looking?" the man asked. His tone was supercilious, not quite rude.

"I am the nephew of Gong Sut Fo. I bring a package from my uncle to give to our client, Mr. Herbert."

"Hinchcliffe," Perique hissed. "The surname is Hinchcliffe."

But the little man did not seem to notice Ji Fung's mistake. As soon as he heard the name Gong Sut Fo, the man had gone from haughty and dismissive to desperately servile.

"Mr. Gong, I am happy to receive you and your friends in our humble establishment. Please allow me to offer you our finest meal free of charge."

"You are very kind," Ji Fung said. "But first, can you tell me where to find our American friend?"

The man's face fell as if he were suddenly the bearer of terrible news. "So sorry, Mr. Gong, but Mr. Hinchcliffe has not come in for three days." He scribbled quickly on a scrap of paper. "Here is his address where you might find him. If there is anything else I can do to assist you…"

Ji Fung pocketed the scrap. "Thank you," he said, his chin high. "That will be all."

"Well done," Perique murmured as the maitre d' led them to a table by the window. "I believe there's hope for you yet."

■ ■ ■

Herbert Hinchcliffe's house was in the French Concession, on Route Lafayette across from the Parc Francais. The little park was overrun with squatters, and the moist evening air was full of cooking smoke and the sibilant sound of Shanghaiese.

Ji Fung pushed open the heavy iron gates of the pristine white house. A brick path, green with moss, wound through a lush garden to the veranda. Shanghai had been built atop a river swamp, and the city was slowly sinking into its soft underpinnings. But the vegetation that sprang from this mud was riotous and verdant. The scent of night jasmine filled the garden and followed them up onto the porch.

The tall double doors were adorned with brass knockers shaped like lions' heads. Ji Fung was used to the Chinese lion, a smiling creature usually seen playing with a colorful ball. Herbert Hinchcliffe's lions were cold-eyed, their mouths frozen in eternal snarls. He forced himself to grasp one of the heavy brass rings and knock three times. Then he stepped back, listening for sounds of life inside.

It was a full five minutes before the door was hauled open by an old woman in a black cloth jacket. Her hair was thinning, her back twisted in a dowager's hump that reduced her height to less than four feet.

"We're here to see Mr. Hinchcliffe," said Ji Fung. At last he had gotten the name right. He held the red lacquer box before him like a peace offering.

The old woman shook her head. "Too late." Her Mandarin was clipped with a strong Shanghai accent.

"What do you mean, too late?" Perique asked.

"Gone." She made flapping wings out of her wrinkled hands. "Back to America. Afraid of war, he says. Chinese-Japanese fighting all the time now. I am afraid too, but I am old grandmother." She laughed. Almost any sentiment could be expressed by Chinese laughter; this was the laugh that meant *I am empty of hope.* "All my life I work for Hinchcliffe family. Tell me, where would I go?"

The old woman, whose name was Mrs. Yuan, gave them tea while they decided what to do about the box. It sat on the table between them, still locked, while the man with the key was thousands of miles away. Ji Fung found his fingers tracing the edges of the box while they debated their options. Should they leave it with Mrs. Yuan? Bring it back to Gong Sut Fo? Ji Fung's heart felt heavy in his chest. He was sure that, whatever action they chose, he had failed his uncle.

At last they decided to send a telegram to Gong Sut Fo asking for further instructions. They thanked Mrs. Yuan for the tea and left her alone in the empty house.

The car Perique had hired was still waiting outside. As they piled in, Perique took a long pull from his silver pocket flask and ordered the driver to turn on Route Pierre Robert.

Lin Bai accepted a dainty sip from the flask. "Where are we going?"

"I want to show you something." There was an odd light in Perique's strange eyes. He leaned forward and told the driver to go very slowly along Route de Zikawei. When they drew up alongside a set of tall iron gates much like Herbert Hinchcliffe's, Perique drained the flask and dragged the boys out of the car.

"This is the house where I was born and raised. It is where my mother was murdered, and where my father died in his sleep of old age."

Ji Fung and Lin Bai exchanged a wary glance, unsure what Perique wanted of them.

"I don't know who lives here now, but I'm sure they won't mind us having a wander through the garden. There used to be roses, every color you can imagine…"

"Perique, no." Lin Bai dug his nails into Perique's shoulder. "It's dark. These people won't want us sneaking through their garden. What if they think we're Japanese soldiers?"

But Perique was already pushing open the gates and striding in. The boys followed, intending to seize him. Instead they nearly ran into him, for he had stopped at the head of the overgrown path and was staring at the moonlit remains of the house.

The paint was gray and leprous, falling away in scabby clumps. The graceful windows were smashed, only a few jagged points of glass embedded in the rotten frames. The roses were still there, leggy and wild, their pale whorls edged with brown. The front door hung open, revealing an unhealthy darkness inside.

Perique stood as motionless as the moss-covered statues that inhabited the garden. His back was to Ji Fung, but the sag of his shoulders bespoke bitter disappointment. Ji Fung wondered what Perique had hoped to find here. "Let's go," he said, laying a hand on his friend's shoulder.

There was a low rustle from inside the house. Perique's chin snapped up. His whole body seemed to focus with a predatory intensity on the darkness inside the open door. Ji Fung looked too, just in time to see a young girl step out onto the veranda.

Painfully thin beneath her gray scrap of a dress, she was hauling the frame of a wooden chair with no seat. She saw them and froze.

Ji Fung could hardly believe what happened next, even though he saw it with his own eyes. Perique reached into his jacket and whipped out his tiny gun as easily as a cowboy in an American movie. Before Ji Fung could react, a firecracker pop sounded in the still evening air and the girl's dirty cheek exploded in a hot red spray. She crumpled like paper. The chair lost a leg as it hit the moldering tiles of the veranda.

The boys stood stunned as Perique ran up the steps and kicked the fallen girl. "Thief!" he shouted. "I'll teach you to steal from my father's house!"

He kicked the body again and again until it tumbled off the veranda and into the weeds. Falling to his knees, he carefully set the chair up on its three remaining legs.

"My father had eight of these chairs, and a table to match." Tears sparkled on his pale face in the moonlight. "At the banquets he gave for his business associates, I was always seated on his right side. It was the only time I ever thought he was proud of me."

Perique's sobs grew heavier, shaking his body.

"Everything is gone," he whispered. His voice was nearly lost beneath the song of crickets in the dying garden.

■ ■ ■

That night, Ji Fung could have sworn Perique dragged them to every bar and nightclub in Shanghai. Each place was packed with people who seemed desperate for a good time. Jazz lubricated the sultry night air. Glasses were filled and emptied and filled again. The impromptu carnival swelled and spilled out onto the streets, and the boys let it carry them like a warm alcoholic tide.

Ji Fung tried to hold himself aloof from the revelry. Under every gay drunken smile seemed to lurk a rictus of terror. There were soldiers here and there in the crowd, many of them pitifully young, all drinking as if it were their last day on earth. Prostitutes swarmed like rats. Even the oldest and the most diseased were doing a brisk business. The night soured early for Ji Fung, but it took hours to drag Perique back to the Cathay Hotel.

Standing alone by the window not long before dawn, Ji Fung stared out over the harbor. He could make out several Japanese boats, including a huge flagship flying the Rising Sun. Unease gnawed at his belly, and when Lin Bai slid warm arms around his waist, Ji Fung flinched.

"Things are going bad here," Lin Bai whispered, pressing his lips to the back of Ji Fung's neck. "Can you feel it?"

Ji Fung nodded. "I think there will be war soon in Shanghai."

"No, not just Shanghai." Lin Bai rested his chin on Ji Fung's shoulder and stared out over the harbor. "I mean all of China. You weren't paying attention tonight, but everyone is talking about war. About revolution. Crazy talk. There is fighting all over."

Lin Bai gripped Ji Fung's waist just above the swell of his buttocks. "I think we should leave."

Ji Fung turned his head to look into Lin Bai's face. "Go back to Hong Kong?"

"No." Lin Bai kept staring out the window. "To America."

"Don't be silly. Where would we get the money?"

"Perique has money."

Ji Fung turned to look at Perique, who slept restlessly in tangled covers.

"Leave the old world behind," said Lin Bai. His naked skin was warm and silken against Ji Fung's back. "Leave bad luck behind. Start a new life in Hollywood, like our dreams."

Ji Fung turned and took Lin Bai in his arms. The angles of his lover's body felt so precious, so fragile. "I can't leave my family," he said.

Lin Bai pushed away, his eyes dark and narrow. "I am your family. Perique would be too, if you let him."

Ji Fung was silent. His uncle had given him back his lost identity. He gave Ji Fung a lineage, a history, made him feel connected not only to his lost blood family, but to the greater brotherhood of the Triads. And, after finding his long-lost nephew, Ji Fung didn't think Gong Sut Fo would be happy to lose him again. In fact, if he did anything to make his uncle believe he was his mother's son, he suspected he would not be allowed to live.

"Bai," he said. His voice felt ragged, torn. "Please don't make me choose."

■ ■ ■

All next day they shopped. Perique was more manic than ever, throwing away money on whatever trinket caught his fancy, accepting first price on everything. He loaded Lin Bai's arms with jade bracelets and bought Ji Fung a shamefully expensive diamond tiepin. For himself, a new gold watch with his initials inside in fine, spidery script.

As the day wore on, Ji Fung found himself walking a few steps behind Lin Bai and Perique. Their petty squabbling intensified as the wet afternoon heat beat down on their skulls and glued their clothes to their bodies. Ji Fung usually found the little quarrels amusing, but now their sharp voices scraped his nerves raw. His head throbbed in time with his uneasy heart. Something was going to happen.

In a candy shop, Perique and Lin Bai argued over whether to buy chocolates or salted plums. Ji Fung leaned against the doorway, nauseated by the smell of burnt sugar. He had gone earlier to the telegraph office to wire his uncle, but the tiny storefront was packed beyond capacity, the anxious crowd spilling out onto the streets. He tried the telephone, but all lines had been co-opted for military use. Now he felt lost and adrift, disconnected from both his families.

The only useful article Perique had bought him today was a roomy black valise, perfect for holding the red lacquer box. Stepping out of the path of a fat European lady with a snarling dog under each huge white arm, Ji Fung squatted and unbuckled the valise, just to check. Just to run his fingers over the cool surface of the precious box, reassuring himself that it was still there. He had been afraid to leave it behind in the hotel room. He was almost certain that he had failed his uncle and the Triad brotherhood…almost. The box was his one link to that life. As long as he had it, there was a chance he still belonged.

At last Perique and Lin Bai came out of the candy shop with a box of chocolates, a bag of salted plums, and a handful of the fragrant, near-bitter black ropes Ji Fung had developed a taste for back in Hong Kong. Ji Fung chewed slowly as they walked, still uneasy, but beginning to be lulled by the drowsy heat. A light rain began to fall, slicking the sidewalks, turning the sky a watery gray, blunting the harsh edges of the afternoon. Perique's fragmented memories took them on a nonsensical route through the city, and Ji Fung let himself be led.

"Sincere's," Perique sighed as they reached the intersection of Nanking Road. "I must take you to Sincere's and buy you anything your hearts desire. I promised I would." His jade eyes were overbright in his flushed face.

Ji Fung tried to protest. "You've bought us enough. Why not go back to the hotel?"

"Let him keep buying," said Lin Bai. "It makes him happy; he loves to show off for us. And how do you know we won't need these things?"

"Jade and diamonds—"

"Can be traded for other things," Lin Bai said with an air of finality.

Sincere's turned out to be a vast department store with palm trees flanking its doors like sentinels at the entrance to some sacred temple. Inside it was dark and cool, redolent of fine cloth and subtle oils. Everywhere he looked, Ji Fung saw something he had never seen before. Candied ducks' tongues and torturous devices for curling ladies' hair. Jade carvings the size of small children. Shiny modern appliances and conveniences side by side with celadon goddesses and lucky red banners for long life and good fortune. Standing in the midst of all this wealth, Ji Fung could almost believe the promises made by the flowing golden characters.

There was a small commotion outside. At first Ji Fung ignored it, but it grew louder and louder. He drifted toward the doors, leaving Perique and Lin Bai with their heads bent over the glass jewelry cases.

"What's happening?" he asked a running boy in an American baseball hat.

The boy looked at him quizzically, poised to flee. Ji Fung clasped his shoulder and repeated the question in English.

"Chinese planes are bombing the Idzumo!" the boy said, squirming out of Ji Fung's grasp.

"The what?"

"The Japanese warship," the boy called over his shoulder. "Get down to the harbor or you'll miss it!"

Ji Fung stepped into the street and looked up into the pale gray sky. The rain had tapered off, but he couldn't see any planes. He heard distant thunder and the growling of engines in the east. All around him people were huddled together, staring into the empty sky.

A wry-faced old man with a cage of geese on the end of a pole was reporting to everyone around him. He had been on the riverbank when the attack began. "Pah!" he spat. "Not one bomb hit that ship. Just falling into the water, impotent. I am ashamed for the sons of China. How can we hope to save our country from the Japanese devils when our planes are worst quality and our pilots are untrained?"

"Look!" A pregnant woman with a baby on her back stabbed a finger at the sky. The whine of engines grew louder, and a brace of four Chinese planes cast their crucifix shadows on the cobblestones of Nanking Road.

"See how they retreat in shame," said the old man, shaking his white head and making his wispy beard fly about. "No hope for China."

"Grandfather." A young girl with ribboned braids tugged at the old man's sleeve. "What are those black spots in the sky?"

The old man's rheumy eyes grew huge, and nearly as round as a foreigner's. "It cannot be," he whispered. But the wobbling black specks grew and grew, their cylindrical shape and finned back ends becoming clearer as they fell.

A dreadful lazy paralysis gripped Ji Fung's bones as he watched the bombs falling toward him. Their descent seemed almost leisurely, like the gait of a man strolling to meet a lover he had known for years. He might have stood there staring until his eyes were boiled in their sockets by the blast, had an image of Lin Bai's face not risen before him like a foreshadowing of explosion. His sick complacency broke. He turned and ran back into Sincere's.

And then the bombs fell to earth.

There was only a split-second of terror, a split-second of Lin Bai's name hot in his throat. Then the muscular push of the shock wave filled his head with thunder, picked him up and threw him like the hand of an angry god. There was pain and vertigo and a huge soft impact that blotted out the world.

■ ■ ■

Ji Fung resurfaced with a feeling of great weight, of suffocation. He thrashed against the yielding mass that surrounded him until he reached light and air. He was battered but not seriously hurt, and he saw that he had been buried under bolts of fine silk. Their vibrant colors were dimmed with soot and plaster dust, stained with dark blood. He dug frantically in the pile, his heart screaming in his chest. Where was the box? Ji Fung knew he had lost it, had failed his uncle, his father, their brotherhood.

When his fingers touched the buttery leather of the valise, tears of relief filled his stinging eyes. He sank down into the pile of silk, clutching the valise to his chest for what seemed an eternity, his mind washed clean of thought.

Again the thought of Lin Bai penetrated his haze, a blinding aftershock that pulled him back from near-catatonia. Ji Fung heaved himself up, still clutching the valise, and began to look for his friends. The few landmarks he had noticed in the store were jumbled and broken, leaving Ji Fung disoriented, unable to locate the jewelry case where he had left them admiring a large ruby set into a heavy gold ring.

The store was in a shambles, all the beautiful things smashed and ruined. The cable that lifted the glass elevator to the upper floor had snapped. The elevator's twisted carcass lay at the bottom of the shaft, seeping oil and blood. The remains of its passengers were a mangled stew. The whole thing looked somehow organic, a monster of flesh and metal, freshly dead.

Toward the back of the store, the ornate ceiling had collapsed, crushing shoppers beneath tons of stone and plaster. The dead and dying were everywhere. They clutched at Ji Fung, pleading for help or a quick blow to the head, but he refused to see them. He picked his way through the wreckage like a blind man, the image of Lin Bai's face his only guide.

He found Perique first.

Perique's body lay twisted, head skewed at an angle that defied anatomy. When Ji Fung got closer, he could see the metal skeleton of the display case. A million shards of glass had exploded out of that frame, and Perique had been standing right in front of it. His handsome face was almost unrecognizable. Precious stones glittered in the flayed meat of his cheeks, diamonds and emeralds embedded there by the force of the blast. His eyes were filled with slivers of fine crystal. His white linen suit was scarlet with blood.

In the soft flesh under Perique's chin, Ji Fung saw the ruby ring Lin Bai had admired. It was reluctant to part with the open muscle into which it had sunk, but Ji Fung was determined. Eventually it came free with an unwholesome sound, and he tucked it into his vest pocket. A single thought filled his mind, blotting out the shrieks and sobs around him. Lin Bai had liked this ring. Ji Fung would give it to him. He had found the ring; therefore he would find Lin Bai.

But in the end, Lin Bai found him.

"Is he dead?" asked the familiar resonant voice. Ji Fung turned to see Lin Bai standing almost gracefully in the death and rubble. His silk stockings were laddered, his fancy red shoes spattered with darker blood. His face and arms were laced with cuts.

Ji Fung stood, longing to sweep Lin Bai into his arms, but unable. He wanted to laugh, scream, anything that would break the grip of this strange coldness.

Lin Bai dropped to his knees beside Perique and touched the shattered, jewel-encrusted curve of his jaw. Then he opened the white linen jacket and removed Perique's money clip. He hesitated for a moment, then took the new gold watch and the gun in Perique's waistband as well.

Ji Fung frowned. "Stealing from the dead?"

Lin Bai's chin was set, determined. "He will not need these things in heaven."

A woman began screaming just a few yards away. They could not see her, but her shrill sounds of agony pierced their brains.

"Come." Lin Bai took Ji Fung's hand. "It will be better outside."

It was worse. Shanghai was no longer an oasis of elegance and decadence, untouched by the inconvenient machinations of revolution. The gilded carapace that protected the soft-bodied foreigners from the reality of China was shattered forever. War had arrived at their doorstep, and when they failed to hear it knocking, had come smashing in.

Chinese and Europeans lay side by side, washed in each other's blood, some bodies driven into each other by the force of the blast. Limbs and unidentifiable bits of flesh lay bleeding on the rain-damp cobblestones. Drivers slumped over the wheels of expensive cars, their rich passengers cooked in the backseats like smoked ducks in a restaurant window. The old man who had feared for the future of China sat naked in the street, clothes ripped from his body by the concussion. His wispy white beard was reduced to char on his scorched cheeks. The old man held a mass of carbonized flesh to his scrawny chest. Ji Fung could barely make out the clutching shape of a tiny hand, the bright scrap of a colored ribbon in a smoking tangle of hair.

"No hope!" the old man cried. "No hope for China!"

Lin Bai pulled Ji Fung to a clear area in the middle of the street, away from walls that might crumble at any second. "Listen to me. We have to get out of China. You would not believe me before—believe me now. The old man is right. There is no hope in China, only death. We have no choice. We must open your uncle's box."

Ji Fung clutched the valise. "You are talking crazy. I cannot open it. And what would we do with the contents if I could?"

"The opium in that box is worth a fortune. We could sell it cheaply and still have more than enough for two tickets to America."

Ji Fung turned his face away. "I told you. I cannot betray my family."

"Tell me one thing," said Lin Bai. His fine black brows drew down over his eyes, which were spitting dark fire. "Where is *my* place in your new family? Will you leave me behind to marry some suitable girl of your uncle's choosing?"

"Of course not. I planned to introduce you as Perique's cousin—"

"Perique is dead. And your uncle lives today because he was not allowed to marry the woman of his choosing, your mother. What makes you think he would allow you to choose your wife?"

"I would not abandon you," Ji Fung murmured. But Lin Bai raged on.

"Even if he did, I am not a woman! Even if you have forgotten this, I have not. Do you expect me to play this role until the day I die? You have found your own identity, but you care nothing for mine. Who killed Master Lau so that you could live? Who has been like a brother and a lover to you? Was it your precious family?"

Lin Bai's well-trained voice sliced through the shrieks, moans, and crashes that made up aftermath of the explosion. Ji Fung's cheeks burned with shame, and he looked around to see if anyone could hear. The few people still able to stand and walk paid them no mind, but he cringed at the thought of this conversation falling on the ears of a dying person. "We mustn't talk here."

"Will you not listen?" Lin Bai lowered his voice. "We can sell or trade the opium and be on our way to America by tomorrow. Your uncle will assume you were killed in the bombing. He is rich. You know that he would not trust you with more than he could afford to lose."

"I cannot steal from my own family."

Lin Bai's face was dark with fury. "You dare to speak to me about stealing. You are stealing my future to please a man you barely knew."

"My father..." Ji Fung felt as if he were being pulled inside out, as if his heart were being fought over by dogs.

"I had no father. I have no uncle, no rich influential family. If I cannot escape from China, I will die. I do not want to be a ghost in your family's house."

He reached out to Ji Fung, still achingly beautiful under the plaster dust and sticky blood that streaked his face.

"Give me the box."

Ji Fung gripped the valise tighter. "I cannot."

Tears clung to Lin Bai's dark lashes, then spilled over, tracing crystal lines on his lacerated cheeks. "Then you leave me no choice," he said. He reached into his handbag and took out Perique's gun. As if in a dream, he pointed it at Ji Fung's face. "Give me the box."

For a long moment, Ji Fung was too shocked to speak. His mind raced with irrelevant memories. He recalled a time when Lin Bai had played the female warrior Mu Lan, and Ji Fung had been one of the evil henchmen. It was the only time they had had to fight each other, and throughout the scene they had to struggle to keep from laughing. But now there was no humor in Lin Bai's eyes, only a shiny glaze of desperation.

"You would shoot me?"

"I have no choice," Bai said. His agony was evident in his trembling voice, but the gun's barrel did not waver.

Ji Fung's chest was tight and icy. "Don't do this. Come home with me."

"Put the box on the ground." Now Lin Bai's voice was barely audible above the sounds of the wounded and dying.

Moving as if trapped in the thick syrup of nightmare, Ji Fung laid the valise on the pavement between them. He watched from what felt like a great distance as Lin Bai snatched it and pulled out the red box. Searching in the rubble, Lin Bai found a fist-sized stone and began smashing the brass lock. The gun was no longer aimed at Ji Fung, but he did not think of rushing Lin Bai. He knew the quickness of his lover's reflexes.

It took five strikes. The final blow smashed the red lacquer lid and sent lock and contents spilling across the bloody cobblestone.

It was sand. Fine white sand.

Lin Bai dropped the gun. He grabbed a double handful of the stuff, sifting it through his fingers, whipping his head back and forth in wordless denial. Ji Fung saw a scrap of paper in the splintered remains of the box and bent to retrieve it.

Triads

"Mr. Hinchcliffe," it read in English. *"If my nephew delivers this box to you unopened, please give him five hundred American dollars, which you will be soon repaid. I am very grateful for your assistance."*

Below this was the print of his uncle's name chop. Ji Fung let the note fall from his numb fingers.

Lin Bai's hands were still buried in sand, but now he turned his face to the sky. "Ji Fung. Listen..."

Again the drone of engines from above, coming fast and low. A young girl fell to her knees and began screaming. "No! No! We're already dead!"

Her screams were swallowed in a second volley of explosions. Ji Fung sprawled flat on the ground, his face pressed into the bloody sand.

When he was able to open his eyes, he saw Lin Bai's face washed with fresh blood from a deep gouge on his temple. He could not tell whether his lover still lived. As he gathered Lin Bai into his arms, Ji Fung began sobbing at last. It felt as if the sobs were being wrenched up from the depths of his trained lungs, from the pit of his belly, from the root of his genitals. He wanted to close his eyes and never open them again. But even as he realized this, he felt the faintest thread of a pulse in Lin Bai's throat, and he knew he could not die while Lin Bai lived.

■ ■ ■

The hospital was a fresh kind of hell. Doctors and nurses moved like sleepwalkers through an ocean of trauma, treating only those who seemed to stand a chance of survival, injecting the rest with morphine and leaving them in the hallways to die. It was full dark before Ji Fung could get someone to examine Lin Bai. The doctor was English, scarcely older than Perique. His blue eyes were ringed with purple fatigue, his arms gloved in blood past the elbows.

"Your wife has a concussion and I suspect a hairline fracture of the skull. You must try to keep the wound clean, since infection of the brain could result in death."

The doctor took out a handkerchief and wiped his sweating brow.

"I would give you medicine, but there is none left. I would give you extra gauze to dress the wound, but we have none to spare. There is nothing more I can do for her."

Outside, the night was hot and foul. The living had done their best to clear the dead from the streets, but the task was overwhelming and the heat unforgiving. The stench of burnt, rotting flesh had already begun to pervade the humid summer breeze. They walked along the Bund, where the river freshened the air a little, looking for their hotel. They could not find it. The Japanese ships were still anchored in the dark water, impassive, perhaps gloating over the city's self-destruction.

Ji Fung held Lin Bai while he vomited blood and chocolate against the Hong Kong and Shanghai Bank building. The smell of bile was almost welcome, for at least it smelled of life.

"Ji Fung," Lin Bai gasped as if reading his lover's thoughts. "I'm dying."

"Hush," Ji Fung whispered. "Stop that bad-luck talk."

"Bad luck is all we have," Lin Bai wailed. "The world is dying. No escape."

"Don't worry." Ji Fung smoothed back the sweaty, bloody hair straggling into Lin Bai's face. "We're going home to Hong Kong. We'll be safe there."

"No escape," Lin Bai repeated. "Oh, I'm so *dizzy*..." He crawled away from Ji Fung and began to vomit again.

A crowd had formed across the street, shouting and jostling. Taking a few steps closer, Ji Fung saw that the commotion was centered around a military jeep. The crowd seized its occupants and dragged them into the street, attacking them with stones, long jagged splinters of wood, whatever deadly thing came to hand.

As Ji Fung watched, a young Japanese soldier tore free from the mob and stumbled across the street toward him. The man's face was a bloody sponge, nose smashed, lips and ears split open. His uniform was in tatters. Beneath his close-cropped hair, Ji Fung could see deep gashes in his scalp. The skull gleamed dully through in several spots, and one hellish porridge of a wound exposed the man's brain.

Triads

The soldier grabbed Ji Fung's lapels and shouted something in rhyming staccato syllables. Then he was falling. Before he fully knew what he was doing, Ji Fung caught him and lowered him gently to the ground. The soldier's hands found his own, and Ji Fung gripped them tightly. The Japanese might be invading, torturing devils, but the Japanese were an abstract. This young man was like him, a pawn in an implacable system, set upon by forces beyond his understanding.

Ji Fung cradled the dying soldier, staring into his eyes. One of his pupils was blown, filling the iris with bottomless blackness. As Ji Fung gazed into that eye, it seemed that images from the man's damaged brain imprinted themselves on his own. People he had never seen, landscapes he had never known. A silent room where a master meditated, his still body a vessel brimming with the fluid motions of combat. A girl in a hand-painted kimono, cherry blossoms woven through her long black hair.

A bubble of thick blood swelled and burst at the man's lips. His body stiffened in Ji Fung's arms, and a long wet rattle came from deep in his chest. As life left the soldier, the images in Ji Fung's head seemed to foretell the future. He saw the man's body decomposing where it lay, bursting open in the wet heat, flyblown and ripe with the juices of decay. He saw an old man and woman reading a letter, their faces sagging with grief. He saw what looked like a line of ghost-children in a shadowed hallway, translucent and insubstantial, stretching into infinity. The children this man would have had, perhaps, and their children, and their children's children. Their little hands were curled against their chests as if they knew they would never be born.

The soldier's fingers closed on his sleeve, a reflex of death. And suddenly Ji Fung thought he was in a strange city, the city where this man and all his family had lived. Something had fallen from the sky—a bomb, but more terrible than any bomb Shanghai had seen. He was running from a fearsome heat that baked his skin and made his eyes feel as if they were frying in their sockets. His organs were cooking inside him. He could go no farther.

He fell, rolled over on his blistering back, and stared at a sight utterly beyond his comprehension. A swelling crown of fire rose into a striated sky. Beneath it was a great column of smoke in which he could make out blackened shapes twisting, swirling. It must be a million *li* high. How could anyone live in a world where such a thing was possible? He was not sure whether he had closed his eyes or been blinded, but either one was preferable to the sight of that devil's cloud.

Ji Fung blinked. He was crouching on the steps of the Hong Kong and Shanghai Bank Building cradling a dead man in his arms. Behind him, he could hear Lin Bai still gagging and spitting; it seemed only a few seconds had passed. He stared into the soldier's ruined face. "What have you shown me?" he whispered. "Would you have lived to see that? If so, then be thankful you are dead tonight."

He laid the soldier's body aside and went to help his dying lover.

■ ■ ■

On the crowded deck of an old junk called the *Devil Fox*, Ji Fung sat with his back against a pile of rotting hemp rope, cradling Lin Bai's head in his lap. It was a good spot, occasionally shaded by the ragged brown sails that made him think of huge curved insect wings. Ji Fung had traded his diamond tiepin, Perique's gold watch, and all but one of Lin Bai's jade bracelets for passage to Hong Kong, silently thanking Perique for that last frantic shopping spree.

Now their faces were burned by wind and sun, their lips dry with salt spray. He had eaten nothing since sharing the last of the candy with Lin Bai two days ago. Letting the thick chocolate melt over his tongue, it had been difficult to believe he had ever stood in the doorway of the candy shop on Nanking Road listening to Lin Bai and Perique squabbling. There was still fresh water on the junk, but with so many people on board, it wouldn't last more than another day or two.

Lin Bai stirred in his lap and whimpered softly, a hopeless painful sound. Ji Fung tried to soothe him, checking the crusted bandage that covered the wound in his temple. It was foul and stinking, but Ji Fung had used the last strip of cloth from his shirt and he was reluctant to start tearing up his jacket, the only sunshade they had.

"I'm thirsty," whispered Lin Bai.

"You'll have some water soon. They'll come round with the bucket." Ji Fung stroked Lin Bai's cheek. Neither of them needed to shave yet, but there was the faintest shadow of fine hair on the line of Lin Bai's jaw. Ji Fung wondered how much longer his lover would be able to pass for a woman, and what would happen if they were found out. Would the crowd of refugees gang up on them, throw them overboard to save a few dippers of water? Did the hatred run that deep? Or did the less important taboos fall by the wayside in desperate times such as these?

Luckily, the people closest to them were unlikely to notice anything amiss: an ancient half-blind man with three exquisitely carved cricket cages on a string; a pair of exhausted women with a brood of hollow-eyed children who demanded all their attention.

That night, the weather turned bad. They had come into the wake of a typhoon, and could not tell whether they were sailing around its edges or straight into its heart. Ji Fung covered Lin Bai with his jacket and huddled in the rain with nothing but his thin silk vest and bloodstained pants. The sea flexed angrily beneath them. Lin Bai's face was icy pale, his lips bruise-blue. He lapsed into occasional delirium, babbling to Ji Fung or Perique or Master Lau, then sobbing as if his heart would break. Ji Fung sang every song he knew trying to soothe him, but Lin Bai would not join in, not even when Ji Fung forgot the words.

The old man with the cricket cages gave them sips of plum wine from a small bottle he had hidden inside a cloth shoe, saying he would do anything to help young lovers. He told them a story about two lovers who had turned themselves into crickets to escape disapproving parents. Ji Fung was glad for the endless rain because it masked his fears.

In the morning the old man was dead, his toothless mouth filled with rain. The crew dumped him overboard and took the cricket cages. Ji Fung managed to salvage the bottle of plum wine, nearly empty now. He watched the swirling water toss the old man's thin frame until cruising sharks pulled it under. He shuddered and held Lin Bai closer. They were still three days from Hong Kong.

The rain did not let up. Instead the sea became more violent. Looking into the sky was like watching a gray veil slowly descending in a huge spiral pattern. Ji Fung's bones ached from cold and wet and from fighting the wind. Waves towered higher than the boat, walls of slate-green death that could swallow them in an easy second if the gale turned. Sometimes water would sheet across the deck, washing away seasick-vomit and untethered bundles. People lost the few precious items they had been able to salvage from the wreck of Shanghai. The waves around them were peppered with silk wedding dresses and gilded teapots, portraits of stern ancestors and lacquer chests much like the one Lin Bai had smashed open in Nanking Road. So many treasures, now all as worthless as a few handfuls of sand.

The water began to claim children and old people who could not hang on. Passengers were tying themselves to the masts and rigging, grimly aware that they were almost sure to drown if the junk capsized, but willing to risk it rather than be swept overboard. Ji Fung used a piece of wet hemp rope to lash himself and Lin Bai to a heavy iron hook embedded in the deck. His mind was empty of any thought but survival.

By the time they made it into Hong Kong harbor, more than half the passengers were gone.

The typhoon pulling the junk in its wake had already reached the island city. It was as if the destruction of Shanghai had followed them home. The junks and sampans in the harbor were battened down tight, but the swells still tossed them cruelly. At the top of a long pole on the pier, a warning flag fluttered. Two triangles, one stacked on top of the other, apex to apex. Ji Fung thought the symbol looked like an hourglass with its time running out.

It took almost all night to find a hotel. Thousands of travelers, refugees, and Kowloonese who had missed the last ferry were holed up waiting for the storm to pass. Finally he was able to trade Lin Bai's last jade bracelet for a tiny room in one of the rough hotels that catered mostly to foreign sailors.

He laid Lin Bai on the stained mattress, peeled off the torn stockings and wet rag of a dress, covered him with a thin blanket. It was not necessary; Lin Bai's naked flesh radiated the heat of sickness like a well-stoked furnace.

"Ji...tell the Master I am too sick to go to his room. I cannot bear it tonight."

He groped the air, and Ji Fung seized his hand. It felt like a fleshless claw, almost too hot to hold. "Master Lau is dead," Ji Fung said. "He will never touch you again."

"Chen Bau will have to play White Snake." Lin Bai's yellowed eyes roamed from side to side, unseeing. "Tell him to use the quail-feather headdress."

Ji Fung saw a crystal drop splash into the hollow of Lin Bai's collarbone. Was the wretched roof leaking? He touched a fingertip to it, then tasted it. Warm and salty. A tear, his own.

"Ji Fung?" Lin Bai's voice was thick and low, clotted with infection. "One day we'll leave this place, won't we? We'll go to Hollywood. No more boring Chinese operas for us. We'll be cowboys and gangsters."

"That's right," Ji Fung said. He undressed and slid under the blanket, enfolding Lin Bai's hot, skeletal body in his arms. "When you get better, I promise you we'll leave this place. But first you must promise me you will get better. Do you promise?"

Lin Bai was silent, his breathing ragged and tortured. Ji Fung spent the rest of the night holding him, trying to think of everything he had ever wanted to say, murmuring it all into the sweat-damp hair at the back of Lin Bai's neck. Sometimes he sang snatches of opera, pretending to grope for the words, trying to make Lin Bai join in.

"But those who were true have come together at last." He remembered Lin Bai lying limp in his arms after the near-fatal overdose. *"Even though thousands of miles apart..."*

But he could not bring himself to sing the next line, though his mind spoke it soft and clear.

Even though torn from each other by death...

Ji Fung looked down into Lin Bai's white face and knew that he was dying. As bloody light seeped into the sky, he lay listening to his lover's final breath, long and slow, the sound of his soul slipping out from between his parched lips. Ji Fung kissed those lips. They were dry, faintly sweet, as slack as death itself.

He lay holding Lin Bai's body for a long time, listening to the storm screaming outside. He was not afraid; he knew Lin Bai would never hurt him, had known it even when the gun was pointed at his face. But when he felt a chill stealing over the corpse in his arms, he shuddered and sat up to put on his vest, the only garment he had left.

As he did up the little carved buttons, he felt a lump in the left pocket. Unbuttoning it, he discovered the forgotten ruby ring from Sincere's and the jade chop that had once been the receptacle of all his hopes and dreams. The blood-dark jewel was as dazzling as it had been when Lin Bai pointed it out to Perique in the glass display case, a thousand years ago.

He imagined how Lin Bai's face would have looked when Ji Fung slid the ring onto his finger. But it was too late for that. The world was dead. Lin Bai was dead. There was nothing left. The family that had meant so much to him seemed worthless without Lin Bai there to share it. As worthless as two handfuls of sand. He curled up on the bed and sobbed into his lover's cooling shoulder, wishing he were dead too.

But as the day wore on, he found his wish unfulfilled. His body was stiff, filled with aches and covered with bruises, a far cry from the numb comfort of death. He turned the ring and the chop over and over in his hands. As the daylight died away, so did the typhoon. A limpid, eerie hush fell over the city. The eye of the storm had arrived, and Ji Fung felt the stirrings of a plan.

Selling this ring would give him enough money for the two things he needed.

First, a ticket to America. Second, a bottle of kerosene.

He thought Lin Bai would approve of both purchases.

■ ■ ■

Gong Sut Fo was taking his pleasure with an American singer, a red-haired, long-legged beauty with wide amber eyes and coral-pink nipples. Her temperament was as fiery as her coloring, and this tryst had cost him a great deal in both money and peace of mind. When a pallid, trembling servant interrupted with four taps on the door, he was furious.

"You dare to disturb me?" Gong Sut Fo yanked on a silk robe. "What is it that cannot wait until a man is finished with—is—is finished?"

"A ghost, Gwan." Ghost, indeed. Gwan was a fawning term of respect, ghost meant a matter that couldn't be discussed in front of the singer, and the servant looked as though someone had just murdered his only son.

The singer understood some Cantonese. She pulled the blanket up over her pendulous breasts and frowned. "A ghost! What's he talking about?"

Annoyed by this turn of events, his cock wilting like an old turnip, Gong Sut Fo found that her flat American voice grated on his nerves. He kissed her manicured fingers. "Mimi, my sweet..." He took a deep breath, remembered the cushiony feel of her body. "I swear I will return to you without delay."

As he rushed down the stairs, he could hear shouting in the alley behind the kitchen. He pushed the cowering servant out of the way and strode past the crowd of cooks and scrubbers, out through the servants' entrance, into the alley. The smell hit him at once, the unforgettable smell that had branded itself on his memory eight years ago in an upstairs hallway of his brother's house. It was an odor of burning tallow, of dripping fat, of frying hair and meat, foul yet somehow savory.

There was a burning corpse in his alley.

"Fools!" he spat, shoving servants toward the kitchen door. "Do you want the whole neighborhood to go up in flames? Go! Bring water!" The gawking servants quickly formed a brigade of water pots and buckets. Even so, it was several minutes before they extinguished the flames.

Gong Sut Fo knelt to examine the body. Its limbs were shrunken, drawn up into a fetal position. Its face was a nightmare rictus of charred flesh and scorched bone. But the feet were hardly burned at all, and he easily recognized the shiny black-and-white shoes he had ordered Chi Gwai to give his nephew. Gong Sut Fo felt a sinking sensation in his chest as he saw that the corpse was clutching something in its hand.

It was difficult to pry open the tight black fists, and he was able to do so only by snapping some of the fingers. They crumbled like burnt noodles. In the end, he found what he was looking for. The jade was cracked from the heat, but the carved characters still spelled out his nephew's name.

The servant who had disturbed Gong Sut Fo's pleasure now knelt before him, trembling even more violently than before. There was a folded piece of paper in his hand.

"This was found in the kitchen door," he said, and scuttled away as soon as Gong Sut Fo took the paper.

The English words were written in a scrawling, childish hand. The note read simply, *"I am my mother's son."*

When their master went back inside, the servants threw an old blanket over the smoking remains of the corpse and shooed a small crowd of onlookers out of the alley. In the shuffle to retreat, no one noticed the tall homely girl with a gray kerchief pulled down over her large ears. No one asked why she was smiling even though there were tears on her face.

PART TWO

Los Angeles, 1945

N an Blake piloted the cranky '39 Merc 8 up the coast high-
way with a kind of barely contained desperation, taking the turns
too fast, clenching her jaw against the questions that circled like
anxious zoo animals inside her.

Blake was twenty-six and looked sixteen, with red hair cut man-
nishly short and a tough freckled face like that of a hard-luck urchin
who'd been scooped up and scrubbed clean. Men who knew her
called her a straight shooter, the kind of no-frills gal a fellow could
count on to get things done. Women who knew her knew what she
really was. She got called "sir" on a regular basis and did nothing to
correct either the misapprehension or the appearance that caused
it. Today she was dressed as always, in sharp-pressed trousers and a
custom-tailored shirt with its collar open and its sleeves rolled up in
the dull August heat. Her shoes were slick brown-and-white
wingtips, far too expensive for her writer's salary. Her hands were
large, scarred from a rural childhood fraught with fistfights and hard
labor. She gripped the Merc's big steering wheel as if she wanted it
dead, wrenching it to the left and cursing softly into the creeping
Malibu fog.

Beside her, slumped in the passenger seat with his hat pulled
down low over his eyes, the Chinaman sat unmoving. His face was
as grim and taut as that of a man stoically ignoring a bullet wound.

She'd met Jimmy Lee just before the start of filming on *Terror Over Tokyo,* yet another Z-grade war picture Blake had cranked out during her indentured servitude at Topline Studios. Jimmy scored the role of a Jap soldier trying to torture information out of Richard Noble, the All-American hero. Blake had seen Jimmy around the lot before, playing evil henchmen, waiters, and the other miniscule no-tickee-no-washee roles, but not until *Terror Over Tokyo* had she actually gotten to know him…though she didn't think anyone really knew Jimmy Lee. He could play any character from a devious Jap villain to a kindly number-one son, but he gave away nothing about who he really was. She'd thought "inscrutable Oriental" was just a cliche until she met him.

But when he showed up banging on the door of Blake's office in the writers' warren over at Topline, he looked as if some kind of Chinese demon were snapping at his heels. He told her there was trouble out at Richard Noble's Malibu cabin, killing trouble. When he said Jean Jordan was involved, that was all Blake needed to hear. So now she was driving through a sudden, unseasonably chilling ocean mist that curled its way into the car and up under her collar, matching her outer temperature to the coldness that had settled into her bones at the thought of what they might be driving into. They passed deserted crab shacks and oyster bars that loomed out of the fog like pastel ghosts, disappearing as quickly as they appeared. Blake never would have caught the turnoff if Jimmy hadn't spoken up in a dead whisper.

"Here."

Blake swerved, the Merc groaning against this new torment, and pulled into the driveway of a little blue beach house that seemed to float eerily in the mist. The house was decorated with a jaunty nautical theme: an anchor surrounded by perfect seashells in the sandy yard, a net spangled with pale green glass floats above the bright blue door. All the curtains were pulled tight against the misty daylight. There were two cars in the drive already, a zippy little roadster that must be Noble's and a humpy black sedan Blake thought she recognized but couldn't be sure.

"I sure hope you know what you're doing," she said. Jimmy didn't answer. Before she could kill the engine, he was out of the car, running up the walk, calling out.

"Victor?"

The only answer was the sibilant shush of the waves.

Blake felt a childish wish that Jean would reply, her warm breathy voice laughing and asking what on earth they were doing all the way out here. Instead there was just that *shush, shush, shush* of the uncaring ocean. She knew something was wrong; her senses were telling her so as surely as they had the night her first love's brothers ambushed her and broke her nose and three ribs, back in the orange groves, in another lifetime. There was something terribly wrong inside that cheerful little house.

"Come on," she told herself. "Be a man." It didn't work—it never had—but after another minute she was able to get herself out of the car and follow Jimmy.

When Jimmy knocked on the door, it swung open. Dull orange light from the fireplace spilled out onto his face.

"Victor," he said again, softer this time because he saw Victor now and so did Blake and she probably would have screamed except there seemed to be no air inside her, no air at all. She took a step back and stumbled against the door frame. She recognized Jimmy's "Victor," that Chinese female impersonator from the Black Dragon, but there could be no doubt about his sex now since he was naked. It was not just the orange light from the fire that painted him with a ruddy glow. He was splattered from head to toe with fresh, running blood, but even that was not the worst thing about him. The worst thing about him was that he was *not there.*

His face was slack as a corpse's. His eyes looked painted on, the unseeing wooden orbs of a dimestore mannequin. It was as if whatever made Victor the person that he was had dried up and left this living shell behind. And the shell moved. It took a step closer to Jimmy and the blank dead eyes blinked slowly like the glass eyes of a tipped-back doll. Its arm came from behind its back, revealing some kind of short stubby sword, a Jap sword from the look of it, just like in the movie although this was no prop. It was as red as Victor himself, but still glinted wickedly in the firelight.

"What happened, Victor?" Jimmy asked. Blake was amazed at the steady calm in his voice.

The shell did not speak. It simply rotated its wooden face towards a doorway behind it, a doorway that appeared to lead to a bedroom.

Blake squinted into the darkness and thought she saw a tangle of blonde hair in the shadows. Her paralysis broken, she bolted in a crooked, sideways half-run, keeping her body facing that bloody maniac until she was through the door and into the dim bedroom. The expensive curtains blocked out all but the thinnest sliver of mist-pale daylight. Her feet slipped out from under her and she fell gracelessly onto the wet bed. Flailing and cursing, she finally found a bedside table with what felt like a small lamp. When she was able to locate the switch, she immediately wished she hadn't.

The bed was drenched in slowly cooling blood. Wrinkles in the linens held gelid, coagulating lakes. Blake found herself already covered with the stuff, her clothes sticky and ruined. The meaty stench of it was like a copper sledgehammer inside her head and Blake gagged and closed her eyes, biting deeply into her lower lip. She thought she had the nausea beat until she scrambled up off the bed and turned back to see what remained of Richard Noble.

His head was nearly severed, tilting his handsome face up and back at an impossible angle. The rest of his naked body was a raw mess of gaping slashes and stab wounds that seemed to radiate outward from the red and awful void between his legs. Sure, Blake had wanted Noble dead, had fantasized about killing him every day for weeks, but that didn't make looking at his guts any easier. She turned away, braced herself against the wall, and added the remains of her studio hamburger sandwich to the mess. She must have written a hundred scenes where the hero finds a stiff, and never once had she made the guy lose his lunch. She wiped her knuckles across her mouth. *Some hero.*

But where was Jean? The Chinaman had sworn she was here. That subtle gleam of blonde hair that had led her into this slaughterhouse in the first place teased at her reeling mind, but Blake didn't want to look back there, back against the far wall where she knew it was. She didn't want to look, but she did, and of course there was Jean, crumpled in the corner. Blake couldn't bear to look for more than a fraction of a second, but in that time she saw too much, far too much. She saw crooked slashes across Jean's smooth white arms like the clawmarks of an angry tiger. She saw blood clotting in blonde curls and on Jean's diaphanous dressing gown. She saw open empty eyes and a smeary slack mouth. Somehow Blake just couldn't equate that bloody ragdoll with the fresh, gutsy young actress whose bottomless ambition had broken Blake's heart.

Cops, she thought, visualizing the sane black shape of a telephone, fixing her mind on that basic logical thought. *Better call the cops.*

"Victor, come here," Jimmy was saying in the other room. "Come here and let me see what's happened." A pause, and Blake remembered that this was not a crime scene; it was a living, evolving *crime.* The man who'd done it was still here, still holding the murder weapon in his bloody hand.

"You've cut your cheek." Jimmy said. "It's very deep. Here, let me have a look."

"I'm sorry," Victor said. His voice was soft, toneless. Blake thought then of an Edgar Allan Poe story she'd read as a child, the one where a man was hypnotized at the moment of death. Poe had described the horrible faint voice that had issued from the dead man's throat, from beyond death, and Blake thought it must have sounded just exactly like Victor's. She knew then that all this was real, that Jean and Richard Noble really were dead, that she and Jimmy both were inches away from joining them.

"It's all right now, Victor," said Jimmy, keeping his voice miraculously neutral as Blake sidled over to the doorway and peered back into the firelit living room. It seemed impossible to imagine that it was just after four in the afternoon, that back in Hollywood it was still as bright and sunny as a picture postcard, just like every other cheerful August day. Here in this house, it had somehow been transformed into four A.M..

"I'm sorry, Daddy," Victor said, and Blake watched as he turned the sword and plunged it into his own naked belly. The wooden mask seemed to crack as he wrenched the blade through the tough muscle of his gut. He paused, and his brow creased as he seemed to really see them for the first time. His face showed only a sort of mild consternation, like a man who has just remembered that he left the kettle on. His hands dropped to his sides. The sword began to slide free, pushed loose by a bulge of purplish intestine, then clattered to the floor. Victor fell too, but Jimmy caught him.

Jimmy's face was still expressionless, but his eyes were bright with tears as he lowered the dying man to the floor and held him, unmindful of the blood ruining his cheap suit. They remained like that, frozen for a long minute. Blake didn't understand what happened next—not that she'd understood much of anything today, but she couldn't imagine why Jimmy's head suddenly rocked back as if someone had given him a stiff uppercut to the jaw. His hat flew off and his hands rose to his shoulders, fluttering helplessly. Victor's now-lifeless body slid to the floor.

Blake managed to squeeze Jimmy's name from her airless throat as she took a step into the living room. Jimmy raised his arms in a warding-off gesture, eyes as unseeing as Victor's, and Blake almost broke and ran. She would have done so if Jimmy hadn't shaken his head savagely and looked up, eyes full of fear but normal and alive. He began to whisper under his breath in what Blake thought was Chinese. His nose was bleeding, clean red mingling with the clotted smears across his worn gray lapels.

"What the hell happened, Jimmy?" Blake asked, finally finding some small ghost of a voice.

"Something unspeakable," Jimmy told her, his voice hoarse but steady as he stood and pushed aside the curtain covering the large picture window. He pressed his hand to the glass, staring out through the mist to the shushing sea. Somehow she knew he was not talking about the murders that had happened here in this little house, but about something else entirely, and that made her more afraid than she had ever been.

■ ■ ■

The blonde grabbed my wrist and dipped her cigarette into the flame of my lighter, her smoldering green eyes never leaving mine. She inhaled deeply, threatening the integrity of the soft white sweater that fought valiantly to contain her lush feminine curves.

"I can't think why you'd be accusing me of associating with a two-bit grifter like Harry Landry," she said.

I snapped my Zippo shut.

"Don't play kitten with me, sister," I told her. "The Van Hueron kid saw you leave Landry's place at 11:45 last night. She said you seemed upset."

Her green eyes flashed poison and her crimson lips arranged themselves into an elaborate pout. "She's lying."

"Look, I've read this one a hundred times already," I said. "Can't we just skip ahead to the tearful confession?"

She raised her hand to let me have it and I grabbed her wrist and pulled her to me, holding her firmly as she squirmed against me like a trapped alley cat.

"Let me go, you bastard!"

"Keep up the sweet talk and I never will."

I kissed her.

Blake yanked the paper from her aging Smith-Corona, wadded it into a ball, and tossed it towards the overflowing wastebasket. She missed and the ball rolled under her desk to join the legion of other crumpled pages gathering dust. Her latest novel was going nowhere fast, endlessly roadblocked by whatever pointless assignment Mansley saddled her with this week. When she did have time to work on it, she found herself hating every stale, thudding word. She rolled a fresh sheet into the typewriter and stared at it for several minutes before giving up in disgust and heading out onto the narrow walkway outside her office door. The day was hot and hatefully bright after the never-changing dimness of her cramped little hideyhole. Two floors down, the artificial life of the studio lot ebbed and flowed. Lighting the last cigarette in the crumpled pack, Blake leaned against the railing and watched a passing herd of hopeful starlets in their best stockings and cowtown dresses, all drugstore perfume and hunger. From her vantage point, she could see the black roots of one girl's peroxided hair. Blake chuckled softly to herself. All those gals were barking up the wrong tree. They were ready to offer themselves to Sherman Mansley in exchange for a plum role, but the producer had no use for their type, not unless they were packing a little something extra in their panties.

As she watched the actresses disappear around the corner, a single straggler appeared from behind the prop department. The girl was blonde and awkward, girlishly clad in a green skirt and plain cotton blouse with a Peter Pan collar. Her felt hat was cheap, as were her simple brown shoes. She carried a stack of photographs, and as she tipped her face up and met Blake's gaze, they fluttered out of her hands. Ditching her cigarette in an ashtray by the stairs, Blake headed down to help.

"Gosh, I'm so clumsy," said the girl as Blake approached.

"No harm done." Blake stooped and gathered up the photos, which included several of the girl in a white bathing suit. Her body was far more womanly than her childish getup let on. She was actually very beautiful close up, fresh and sweet with clear blue eyes and skin like winter butter. She smelled like tiny secret flowers hidden under mossy stones and there was something about her long, awkward legs and guileless smile that made Blake's heart kick under her ribs.

"I'm looking for Sherman Mansley's office," the girl said.

"You and every other skirt on the lot." The girl looked so crushed at this, and Blake silently rebuked herself. "Hey, don't worry. Those other dames got nothing on you."

The girl's face lit up.

"You mean that? My name's Betty Jean Hepple. I've come all the way from Sandpoint, Idaho to try and make it in pictures. I was Junior Miss Idaho last year and the rector at my church said I had the best voice in the whole choir. He said I had a real shot at being a star."

I'll bet he did, Blake thought, but only said, "Is that right?"

"That's right, so I saved my sewing money for seven months and bought a bus ticket to Hollywood. And here I am!"

"Here you are," Blake said, wondering exactly what she thought she was doing with this backwoods babydoll.

"Thank you so much for coming to my rescue, Mister..."

Triads

Blake's heart skipped a beat. She knew she ought to make an excuse and get back into her hole where she belonged, but the girl was batting her lashes and twisting her foot on the cement, and Blake was hooked.

"Uh...Blackline," Blake said, pitching her voice low. "Blake Blackline."

The girl said something unbelievable then. If Blake hadn't been hooked before, she was now, as surely as an Idaho trout.

"Blake Blackline? The writer?" The girl's wide eyes sparkled. "Oh my gosh, I've read all your stories in Black Mask and Dime Detective. And the novels too. Cherry Rocher, girl detective!" Betty Jean grinned. "She's only my favorite character of all time! I love murder mysteries. I can't wait to get to the end and see how they turn out. Boy, my first day in Hollywood and I've already met someone famous."

Now it was Blake's turn to blush.

"Well, I'm no James Joyce."

"Who wants to read that mixed-up gobbledegook anyway, outside the stuck up college set?" Betty Jean made a cute sour face. "You write real stories about real people just about anybody can relate to. Like Cherry Rocher. She's beautiful and tough, but on the inside she's got real feelings just like you and me. They ought to make a Cherry Rocher movie. A whole series of them where she could have all kinds of adventures. Wouldn't that be swell?"

"Sure," Blake said, trying to stay cool and not doing a very good job of it. "And I bet you'd make a dynamite Cherry."

"Oh go on! I'm way too plain."

"Don't sell yourself short." Blake looked back over her shoulder at the open door to her office and took a sudden, impulsive chance. "I tell you what though, I'm working on a war picture, and you'd be perfect for the hero's sweetheart."

That was how Blake met Jean Jordan.

■ ■ ■

Victor knelt under the huge mahogany desk dutifully sucking Sherman Mansley's thick, stubby prick. The intercom squawked and Mansley pushed him away roughly, a long string of spit still connecting them. "I thought I said to hold my calls," Mansley barked.

"Blake's here," said the tinny voice of the intercom. "With some girl."

"The writer?" Mansley stuffed his wet red erection back into his trousers and motioned for Victor to get up. Mansley was a fussy little man with an Errol Flynn mustache and chubby hands. He smoothed his tie. "Fine, fine. Send them in."

Victor stood and straightened his red crepe dress, hand touching the heavy black spill of his wig. He fished a compact from his tiny purse and began touching up his lipstick. His mouth burned, the tissue inside hot with loathing. He clenched his teeth.

"Don't fret, my pet," said Mansley. "We'll finish this later." He pulled a billfold from an inner pocket and handed Victor a thick wad of cash. "Go buy yourself something pretty and wait for me up at the house."

Victor took the money and tucked it inside the little purse. On his way out he passed the young redheaded writer with some blonde number. He did not meet their eyes for fear that they would be able to see the droplets of flame starting to leak from the corners of his eyes. Instead of buying something pretty, he bought a fifth of gin and drove the roadster Manley had given him back up to the little house off Mulholland Drive.

The house where Mansley had set him up was a study in Oriental fetishism. All red and gold, dripping with dragons and embroidered silk like a Hollywood fantasy of an opium den flash-frozen in 1928. Scattered copies of *Life* and *Photoplay* spoiled the effect a little. Victor was not the first boy to live here and probably wouldn't be the last, but he didn't care. It was a place to drink himself to sleep each night. He kicked off his slingback heels, peeled off the sweaty dress and smoky wig, and collapsed on a crimson fainting couch clad only in a black and red slip, mended stockings, and a tan wig cap. The wig cap pulled his smooth young features into something severe and emotionless. He poured a generous knock of gin into the golden glass that still sat where he had left it the night before, added a splash of tonic water, and drank it down, hoping to quench the increasingly unbearable heat inside him.

He clicked on the radio. "Ac-cent-tchu-ate the positive," Johnny Mercer sang. "Ee-lim-inate the negative...Hang on to the affirmative...*And don't mess with Mister In-Between!*" Victor hated this song. He was Mister In-Between himself, something that deserved a place in no sane world. He couldn't stand the sound of the radio, but couldn't find the energy to get up and turn it off either.

It seemed as if he'd just finished that first drink, but here the bottle was nearly empty already and the fire still smoldered sullenly in his mouth and belly. Johnny Mercer wasn't on any more; now it was Stan Kenton with "Sentimental Journey." Victor hated that song too. Actually, he hated almost all songs; music reminded him of his father. He stood and carefully made his way out of the suffocating red velvet parlor and into the cool green safety of the bathroom. The seafoam tiles soothed his burning eyes; the tiny blue waves that encircled the tub seemed to undulate with a calming grace. He turned on the tap and closed his eyes, luxuriating in the sound of water splashing against porcelain.

The silk of his slip clung to his skin as the water soaked it through and he felt the safe liquid embrace surround him, rendering the hateful fire as pale and distant as the sun viewed from beneath the surface of the ocean. When he turned off the tap, the faraway sound of the radio began to filter down through his safe green calm. He wondered where his father was at that moment. Was he playing in the band at Heart Mountain Internment camp with all the other persons of Japanese descent? Had he been drafted; was he flying over the Pacific fighting his parents' homeland alongside white soldiers who hated him? Did he think of his only son at night, his dead son Arthur, and blame himself for the boy's suicide?

The memories were strong tonight, in spite of the childish bathtub spell and the gin. He just didn't have the strength to fight them.

His childhood had been utterly American: steak and potatoes, baseball and Santa Claus, everything an American boy could want. Except little Arthur Omura was only half American, a fact that none of the other kids would ever let him forget. His father was Nisei, second-generation Japanese in love with everything American, particularly jazz music. He was the best Japanese saxophone player in Los Angeles, playing first with all-Japanese bands and eventually with a mixed, mostly Negro band called Duke Dalton and his Sixth Street Stompers. That was how he met Mavis Tate. Mavis was a bad girl with bobbed auburn hair and a cigarette permanently fixed in the corner of her cupid-bow lips. She fell head over heels for the dashing and exotic Billy Omura. Despite both families' explicit disapproval, they ran off together and got married in Tijuana. Little Artie was born six months later.

Billy used his savings to open a music store down on Central Avenue in the heart of Darktown, a colored neighborhood famous for its hot, authentic jazz and swinging nightlife at juke joints like Cafe Zombie and Dynamite Jackson's. Billy and his pretty wife lived above the store with their young son and everything was as good as it could be. Of this time, Artie had memories of musicians with kind brown hands and strangely fragrant cigarettes. Of parties that went all night, Artie curled up in his bed dozing off to the lullaby of clinking glasses and grown-up laughter and music, always music.

When Artie was nine, the family moved into a new house in a mostly white neighborhood. Billy spent long hours in the store to meet the mortgage note, and lonely Mavis' drinking got more and more out of control. She took out her frustration on her son, constantly berating him for ruining her fun and carefree life. Men started to visit Mavis and Artie would be sent to play outside until long after the sun went down. He had lost all his Negro friends after the move and made no new ones in this clean barren place where all the beautiful blonde children stretched up their eyes, stuck out their front teeth, and gobbled like turkeys whenever they saw him. He retreated into the movies, spending every free minute at the Rialto, entranced by the looming silver gods and goddesses who reigned over the dark theater.

Then Mavis' brother Larry showed up on their doorstep, unshaven and grinning and needing a place to stay until he got back on his feet. Even at that age, Artie could tell something was wrong with Larry. Something was wrong with the way his mother's smile froze into this roadkill rictus at the sight of her long-lost brother, with the way Larry looked at Artie and winked as if they were sharing some grown-up joke.

The years that followed, the death of little Arthur Omura and the birth of Victor See...those memories burned endlessly at the heart of his internal fire. The fire had been damped down for a little while, though, rendered dim and distant beneath the gin's juniper balm and the cooling water around him. Victor slid down in the tub until his face was completely submerged. He wondered if he might never need to breathe again.

■ ■ ■

When Blake arrived home that night, Zola fell upon her like a voracious lioness. "I'm simply starving," breathed the older woman, her long scarlet nails impatient with the buttons on Blake's shirt. Blake supposed Zola could rip the buttons right off if she wanted to; she'd paid for the shirt and its dozens of brethren in the rococo mahogany wardrobe. "It's my nerves. The party tonight. The strain is just excruciating. I must have my release this minute or I tell you I will die in your arms, darling."

The party. Blake had forgotten about the party. Dutifully peeling layers of perfumed silk away from Zola's full, hungry body, Blake silently cursed her and her damned parties. Once a month, regular as blood, Zola's sprawling estate was hung with colorful paper lanterns and drenched with champagne and laughter and women. Twenty years ago, back when silent screen siren Zola Marova was one of the hottest women in Hollywood, these parties had been like been something out of an erotic fever dream. The fiercely independent, Russian-born actress and director was known for her unabashedly sexual onscreen persona and scandalous behind-the-scenes hijinks. Her notorious women-only parties had been the source of much outrage and envy.

But now, with the sobering Depression already in the rearview mirror and all eyes on the war in Europe and the Pacific, Zola's brand of decadence had fallen out of fashion. The parties got smaller and the guests got older with the exception of the few kept butches, handsome young tomboys like Blake who let their aging lovers dress them in tails, who helped the older women pretend it was still 1928, that they were still young and beautiful.

Lately, for Blake, the pretense was getting more and more difficult. She felt genuine love for Zola, who was a truly amazing woman, mercurial, passionate, and utterly unapologetic. She had taught Blake everything: how to light a woman's cigarette, how to help her into her fur, how to make love to her the way a woman really wants. She had bought Blake handsome, expensive clothes and given her rooms here in the Marova mansion.

But she was living in a fantasy world. At first it had been fun playing dress-up and getting all the attention, but now Zola and her shrinking coven of worshipers seemed to have cut themselves adrift from the unglamorous tedium of reality. Their arrogance and narcissism annoyed Blake where it had once impressed her. Were they growing old, or was she growing up? Maybe both, but what was she supposed to do about it?

Worse, as Blake worked her tongue between Zola's generous thighs, she could not get Betty Jean Hepple out of her mind. The girl's smile, the way she twisted her foot on the concrete. That photo of her in the bathing suit, her firm young body and long legs and her smell, her sweet, secret smell. When Zola's much-needed release shuddered through her, Blake wondered how that same release would travel through Betty Jean, whether she would cry out or stifle any sound with her slender fingers. Blake knew it was a terrible idea, possible the worst she'd ever had, but she also knew she would do anything to find out.

■ ■ ■

Jimmy Lee wiped the bar with a damp rag and watched the faces of the customers watching the line of scantily clad Oriental girls who twirled paper umbrellas on the long, narrow stage of the Black Dragon nightclub. The crowd was mostly white, but included a few prosperous local Chinese businessmen and their assorted minions. There was also a fair amount of mid-range Hollywood royalty seeking refuge from the voracious press that swarmed the tonier nightspots like blowflies, endlessly hunting for even the tiniest open wound. The Black Dragon was a sanctuary for those who chose to indulge in shadowy liaisons best kept out of the spotlight.

On the far side of the club stood a well-known Chinese cinematographer and his white girlfriend. Closer to the stage was an older character actor drinking alone, watching the girls with a kind of wistful sadness. Freshly tattooed sailors on shore leave came to indulge the exotic new tastes they had acquired in the Pacific Theater. Crooked politicians took bribes, made gray-market deals and wooed young Chinese mistresses in the dim candlelit booths. By the bar, a cluster of pushed-together tables overflowed with rowdy young comedians and brash Burlesque dancers. The Black Dragon was always hopping on Saturday night.

Jimmy mixed a sloe gin fizz for a stunning Chinese actress with a silky Pekingese dog under her arm. He was about to take her money when his fellow barkeep, a roguish young third-generation American named Winston Chu, swooped down on her proffered bill and made change like a card sharp dealing out poker chips. Jimmy backed away graciously, smiling just a little when the actress sniffed and turned a spangled shoulder on Winston's wolfish grin.

"Get her," Winston said. "You'd think she was too good for her fellow countrymen."

Jimmy said nothing, just dipped his head slightly and pulled a draught for a young white man Jimmy thought he recognized from a recent yellow-peril serial he'd worked on.

"Did you see that latest picture of hers? The one where she's a whore who falls for a GI and kills herself rather than live without him?" Winston leered at the actress's slender backside. "She's wearing this little see-through number and she throws herself into the river."

"I must have missed that one," said Jimmy, though he had auditioned for a small role in the picture.

"I don't get it." Winston dropped a cherry into a whiskey sour and deftly swapped it for coins. "She acts all high and mighty, but all she ever does is play tramps on the screen."

"Maybe those are the only roles she can get. You know studios never hire Chinese actors to play the best roles. They hire white actors and glue rubber on their eyes."

"Yeah, yeah, what do you know about it?" Winston smirked. "They don't hire you for the best roles because you aren't as good-looking as me. Ought to get those big ears pinned back. Just wait till Hollywood takes a gander at my handsome mug. Move over, Gable!"

"Clark Gable has big ears," Jimmy pointed out. Winston was still trying to come up with a retort when the umbrella girls twirled off the stage and the lights went dim. When they came back up, the host was telling everyone to welcome the Black Dragon's own little mermaid, the exotic Tansy Chan. Jimmy's breath stuck fast in his throat. From the darkened wings came the petite singer whose eloquent hands and cherry lips tormented Jimmy, peeling back all the years of callus over his heart and filling him with a thick, desperate ache. He turned away, but the singer's image was caught in the golden depths of the bar mirror, red mouth wide open and that rich, heartbreaking voice coiling around him like spicy incense smoke.

Jimmy fixed drinks and washed glasses and wrestled with the memories the singer dredged up inside him, keeping his benign, friendly, at-your-service-sir face smooth and unchanging. He did not watch Tansy Chan; he saw only the amber splash of scotch on ice. He did not listen to Tansy's song; he heard only the slushy sound of the cocktail shaker in his trembling hands.

The singer played with the song's final note, stretching and teasing before letting it drift away as one hand drifted towards an elaborate pearl-studded coiffeur. Glossy coral nails disappeared into oil-black curls and pulled them away, revealing a man's short, slicked-back hair. Tansy Chan bowed as the audience burst into whistles and hoots.

"I have to take a break," said Jimmy. He whisked his apron off and headed out through the hinged section of bar before Winston could even answer.

He stood just outside the kitchen door with his eyes closed and his back against the brick wall. The smell of the Chinatown alley, rich garbage and roast duck, cooking oil and car exhaust and spent firecrackers, made him feel as though time had folded in on itself. Surely he was back in Hong Kong, and if he opened his eyes, Lin Bai would be there beside him.

Of course he wasn't. There was only a single sleek rat cleaning its whiskers between two trash barrels, ignoring him completely. Jimmy felt a crushing loneliness so powerful it left him nearly breathless. He felt ancient, as if each of his eight long years alone in this land of plenty had become a decade. It was the singer, whose bruised beauty and delicate, almost tragic grace slipped so easily through Jimmy's defenses. It was as if Lin Bai's ghost had come back to haunt him, robed in someone else's flesh.

The Black Dragon's burly cook chose that moment to poke his head into the alley. *"Hey, Big Ears,"* he called in gruff Chinese. *"Dreaming of your dinner?"* The cook tossed his cigarette butt into a pool of oily water and wiped his hands on his stained white jacket. *"Boss catches you goofing off, there will be trouble. I made spicy pork buns for the staff. Hurry up or they'll all be gone."*

"Thank you," Jimmy said softly. *"I'll be there in a minute."*

When he looked back over toward the trash barrels, the rat was gone.

■ ■ ■

Blake sneaked in through the side door, creeping silently through the stacks of scenery to where Betty Jean was shooting her screen test. The actress wore a navy rayon dress splashed with pale daisies. Her hair hung loose and shining. She was reading the obligatory scene in which the girl tells the hero she will always love him and will wait faithfully for him to return.

She was good. Blake got more and more biased with each passing minute, but she was really amazingly good. Her lower lip trembled just a bit when the guy reading the hero's lines told her he might not make it back. Her big blue eyes sparkled with brave tears as she told him not to say that, to say he'd see her again soon, just as if she might have a date with him the very next day. Blake had written those lines on two hours' sleep and countless pots of bad coffee the night before the deadline, but Betty Jean made them sound as if they were coming straight from her big, honest farm girl's heart.

Mansley and the director, a well-meaning hack by the name of Sid Steckler, had obviously been sold on her before she even opened her mouth. The smile on her face when they told her she had the part was brighter than any spotlight. Blake had planned to sneak back to her office, but Betty Jean spotted her and called out. "Blake! Blake, I got the part!"

She ran over, and before Blake could stop her, she flung herself into Blake's arms.

"Congratulations, Betty." Blake looked over the girl's shoulder at Mansley, who was scowling at her.

"I thought they would have to talk it over or show the test around to different people, but what do you know, they gave it me right on the spot! They've given me a new name too. Jean Jordan. Do you like it?"

"Very classy," Blake said. "I can picture it up on the marquee already."

"You can still call me Betty. You know it never would have happened without you, Blake." The girl was looking up into Blake's eyes in a way that made Blake feel hot and dizzy. Then the smile again, and an effervescent giggle bubbled up out of her. "I think this calls for a celebration!" She took both of Blake's big hands in hers. "Where are you taking me?"

"Well, I..." Blake looked back up at Mansley, who arched his thick eyebrows and gave a tiny shake of his head. "Tell you what. Why don't you go change into something devastating and I'll pick you up at eight? I've, uh, got some work to finish up here first."

"I don't think I own anything devastating, but Myra, that's my roommate, I bet she'd have something I could borrow. Eight o'clock, then. Gosh, I just can't believe it!"

She scribbled her address on the inside of a cigarette pack and hurried away. Blake raised a hand to wave, but Mansley grabbed her arm.

"Sid, will you excuse us," Mansley said.

"Sure thing," said Steckler, eyes already preoccupied behind his tiny round glasses as he scuttled away. "See you later."

When they were alone, Mansley spoke low and close to Blake's ear. "Listen, Blake, we love this girl. We think she's really got something, and believe me, this studio could use a little something. But you gotta tell me, is she…is she part of Zola's crowd?"

"No way, boss." Blake shook her head. "Nothing like that."

"Because if she is, I need to know. We nearly lost Noble to a sissy scandal when some Mexican kid he'd jilted tried to sell photos to the tabloids. Cost me a fortune to bury that one, not to mention the years off my life. The studio can't afford any more of that trouble." He paused significantly. "*I* can't afford any more of that trouble. Do you follow me?"

"I swear, Mansley, she's a decent kid." Blake's eyes went to the door Betty Jean had passed through. "She's only sweet on me because she thinks…"

"Thinks what?"

"Well, that I'm a man."

There was a pause between them, and Mansley's dark eyes began to sparkle.

"What are you saying?" Mansley pressed a hand to his cheek and stared open-mouthed at Blake's crotch. "My God, you're not…you mean to tell me all this time…That's it, you're fired!"

He burst into wheezing gales of thick, nasal laughter.

"Cut it out, Mansley." Blake smoothed her trousers. "Believe me, there's nothing under there you want to know about."

"Look." Mansley wiped his mouth on the back of his hand. "I know how it is. Frankly, I don't care what you do with Betty Hepple or Betty Grable or Bette God Damn Davis just so long as you play it smart and keep it under the covers. Tell her whatever you gotta tell her, but I can't have my new star hanging all over Zola Marova's pet writer on the set."

Stung, Blake nodded.

"So go get ready for your date." Mansley took a pack of Egyptian cigarettes from an inner pocket and offered one to Blake, who shook her head. "Take her to the Black Dragon. No one will even notice you there, and you can check out Tansy Chan, the female impersonator I want you to write into *Terror Over Tokyo*."

"What?" Blake frowned. "There's no female impersonator in *Terror Over Tokyo*."

"There is now." Mansley sucked in a deep drag and gestured with his cigarette. "Put her in the scene where the Jap officers have that big party with all the liquor and dancing girls."

Blake grimaced. She hated that scene and resented having to add it in the first place. Though she was no expert on Japanese culture, she was pretty sure they didn't have rowdy parties with strippers in skimpy belly-dancing costumes left over from a low-rent Ali Baba movie. But Mansley had insisted.

"Look, you get your little piece in the picture and I get mine," said Mansley. "It'll just make those dirty Japs look even dirtier. Remember, Blake, villains can get away with anything in pictures, just as long as they get what's coming to them. I ought to know. I made my fortune on Bible pictures. You can have all the Sodom and Gomorrah you like as long as you bring down the wrath of God in the final reel." Mansley smiled thinly under his patchy pencil mustache, and Blake realized how much she disliked the oily little fairy. "Besides, I happen to know the Japs have men dressed up like women in that Kabuki theater of theirs. I'll bet you never knew that, did you?"

"It's your movie, boss."

"So go chase your little farm girl and have the new pages on my desk by Monday."

Blake nodded, wondering for the hundredth time exactly what she thought she was doing.

■ ■ ■

In his dressing room at the Black Dragon, Victor sat before his vanity preparing for the show. The mermaid dress, nearly twenty pounds of crystal and sequins in every shade of green known to man, lay over the arm of the divan. Victor felt desperate for its heavy, snug embrace. More and more he relied on the costume, the makeup, the lights and the crowd to coat his burning pain like pearl over a grain of irritating sand. He had a crystal decanter of gin on his vanity and kept his glass full as he applied thick black liner around his not-quite-Asian, not-quite-American eyes. He placed the jeweled wig on his head and stood, a little wobbly on silver heels. When he was sure he had his balance, he hefted the dress and slithered into it, tipsy fingers struggling with the regiment of tiny hooks running up the side from hip to armpit. The dress had a panel of flesh-colored netting across the belly, and Victor adjusted it so that the green glass jewel he had glued into his navel winked through the sheer fabric.

A stagehand knocked on the door and then kneed it open, arms full of yellow roses. Mansley. Victor motioned for the smirking boy to place the flowers on the vanity beside the decanter.

My beautiful yellow rose, read the card. *Your dream has come true. Yours, M.*

So Mansley had arranged a part for Victor in the new movie, just as he'd promised—a legitimate movie, not like the one reel stag films Mansley often shot with Victor and other pretty Oriental pansies up at the Mulholland house. As vile and awful as the producer could be, he did have his moments. Surrounded by the sweet stench of roses, Victor found himself remembering the first time he had ever seen Mansley, beckoning from the back of a long black car.

"Are you Chinese?" Mansley had asked the newborn Victor, pressing a glass of champagne into the boy's dirty hand.

"Yes," Victor told him. Why not? The half-Japanese boy he had been was dead now, drowned in the cold ocean less than three months ago. He could be anything.

"What's your name?"

"Victor," he said, using the name he had been telling the men who gave him money to use his body. Victor like the actor Victor Mature, whose dark, handsome face he often pictured as he closed his eyes and earned his liquor money.

"Victor what?"

Victor blinked, turning his face away towards a billboard advertising chocolate. "See. Victor See," he said, hoping that sounded Chinese enough to fool this rich white man with his oily face and tobacco breath.

The man nodded and refilled Victor's glass.

"You are very beautiful, Victor See. As beautiful as a girl, one might say. Did anyone ever tell you that?"

Then he took Victor's hand and pressed it against the hot swelling beneath his expensive trousers. The rest was easy.

A few weeks later, Mansley had Victor installed in the Mulholland house and fitted for a wardrobe that would have made Anna May Wong jealous. Victor found the feminine clothing safe somehow, as if the satin and fur was yet another layer between the burning memories of the boy he had been and the person he was now. The house was a ridiculous fantasy, an Oriental brothel dreamed up by someone who'd never been to the Orient, but the only thing that really bothered him about it was a collection of Japanese swords on the wall. The blades seemed to speak to him, whispering in a hot smoky voice that sounded just like Uncle Larry, until he moved a painted screen in front of them.

From there he fell into a dim unchanging dream punctuated only by sweaty visits from Mansley. He might have just drunk himself into oblivion without another glimpse of the outside world if not for that *DOWN WITH JAPS!* button.

One day Mansley brought Victor a little button and fastened it, smiling, onto his blouse. *DOWN WITH JAPS!* it said in red block letters. And under that, in smaller blue ones: *I'm Chinese.*

Victor looked down at it with a strange dead feeling in his heart while Mansley explained that things were getting dangerous for Japanese-Americans on the West Coast. There was even talk, Mansley said, of moving them all inland whether they wanted to go or not.

"For their own safety, of course," Mansley said. "Plus we can't take any chances with sabotage or spying. Just be glad you're Chinese. I couldn't stand anything to happen to you."

Then he started unbuttoning the blouse, but Victor could not take his eyes off that button. He stared at it while Mansley whispered meaningless sound against his neck and slid his cock up into Victor's churning guts. He thought of his father's broad, smiling face, the smell of his aftershave and the brassy glare of light off the skin of his saxophone. He could almost hear Billy Omura's gentle voice telling little Artie to finish up his chores if he wanted to go to the ball game on Sunday. He thought of the single visit from his father's sister, how she had tried to speak Japanese and Billy told her this was America, that his family spoke only English.

Victor wore the button several weeks later when he got up the courage to drive down Central Avenue, past Omura's Music Shop. It was dark, one window smashed and boarded up. A sign on the door said CLOSED UNTIL FURTHER NOTICE, and under that, a handwritten note thanking everyone for their business and declaring with painful optimism that the Omuras would be back to serve them as soon as the war was won. And last of all, in his father's brave, bold hand, GOD BLESS AMERICA!

Speeding away from that cold, empty store and hopeful hand-written note, Victor had had the first of his total blackouts.

It seemed impossible to believe all that had happened nearly four years ago. Time did not seem to exist inside the plush trap of the Mulholland house. Now Victor stood before the dressing room mirror, a vision of shimmering underwater light and coiled black hair. It was almost time to sing, to lose himself again in the smoky blue glamour. The decanter beside the yellow roses was already empty.

■ ■ ■

Blake stood before the full-length mirror in her room, body singing with nervous energy as she studied every inch of her reflection with a critical eye. She had changed several times before deciding on an olive-green, single-breasted suit with a heavy cream shirt and her two-tone wingtips. Inside her underwear, she wore an appliance Zola had taught her to make by filling a rubber prophylactic with soft cotton batting. It was subtle and realistic, adding just the right amount of extra weight inside the left leg of her trousers so that if Betty wanted to slow dance she would feel exactly what she was expecting.

Blake had dressed like this for Zola and her cronies a hundred times, but she had never ventured into the real world in full male attire. It was one thing to wear slacks and loose shirts that hid your figure, to have people mistake you for a man. Going out in a man's suit, with the deliberate intention of fooling people, was something else entirely. Zola's crowd knew who she really was and loved her for it. If she failed in her masquerade now, people would have an entirely different reaction.

But it felt so good. A mad delicious rush, like being just drunk enough to believe the whole world was yours for the asking. Looking at the man she had become, she felt like a spy, like a dashing secret agent on a mission to seduce Hitler's mistress. She felt daring and handsome and cocky. But as she selected a green and orange abstract tie from the rack and fumbled through a clumsy Windsor, she wished for Zola's clever fingers to smooth the knot and was immediately stung with a sharp pang of guilt. Zola, who had bought the tie and the shirt and the suit and everything Blake was. Zola, who took a rough-knuckled street kid with a penchant for storytelling and made her into a civilized gentleman. Zola, who saw enough promise in a handful of callow mystery stories to get her a job in pictures. Zola, who loved her.

Blake eyed her reflection. A secret agent couldn't afford to blow the mission by getting mushy over some girl back home. Betty Jean was waiting.

When Blake arrived outside Betty Jean's apartment on Ivar Avenue, she sat out front in Zola's Merc 8, telling herself she ought to stand the girl up. It really would be the best thing for her. Best thing for both of them. But she got out and went up to the door anyway.

"Betty Jean Hepple," Blake told the woman at the desk, pitching her voice low and looking furtively around the shabby lobby.

"Yeah," the woman said over the top of a gossip magazine. "Who may I say is callin'?"

"Blake Blackline," Blake said, beginning to sweat under her good jacket.

"Yeah, right, she mentioned you'd be here." The woman glanced at the clock above her head. "You're late."

She spoke into a phone. A few minutes later the elevator slid open to reveal Betty Jean Hepple in a jaw-dropping burgundy cocktail dress that hugged her curves like a roadster and left very little to the imagination. Her hair was swept into an elaborate updo, her mile-high legs clad in perfect smoky-dark stockings that must have cost her a favor or three in these days of wartime rationing. Her feet glittered in golden heels. She was barely recognizable as the girl who had dropped her photos the day before in front of Blake's office. Only that dazzling smile was the same, and it lit up her face when she saw Blake.

"Is this devastating enough for you?" she asked. "I borrowed it from Myra. She did my hair for me too. She's way more sophisticated than I am."

"Consider me officially devastated." Blake offered her arm and her heart raced as Betty Jean took it, enveloping her in that intoxicating secret scent. "Shall we?" she managed to say.

"We shall," Betty said.

At the Black Dragon, Betty blushed over the scantily clad revue, giggled at Tansy Chan's gender-bending performance, cooed and fussed when Blake ordered her a second champagne cocktail.

"You're not trying to ply me with champagne so you can have your way with me, are you?"

"Actually, I was hoping to ply you with my clever wit," Blake said, although she did figure a little champagne might help to drive away any pesky questions. Such as, how did Blake manage to get such a close shave?

"I'm not that kind of girl, not for drink or wit." Betty put her hand on Blake's arm, looking up into her eyes with a frank invitation that seemed to pay no attention to the sounds her mouth made. Blake excused herself to collect what wits she still had. The evening was going unbelievably well so far, so well it was scary. Betty's gaze made her feel as if they were alone in the universe. There was not even the slightest hint that Betty suspected anything unusual under Blake's expensive suit. The doorman, the waiter, everyone was treating Blake just like the other men in the place. It was working, and it was fantastic. Blake was a little drunk and extremely high on Betty's smile when she unthinkingly pushed open the door to the ladies' room.

A piercing shriek hit her like a bucket of ice water. She backed out, heart pounding, apologies clogging up her throat. As she turned to get away, she felt rough hands on her shoulders, spinning her around to face an oversized goon in a too-tight suit.

"What's the big idea?" The guy's breath fairly dripped with the stench of stale beer. "You some kind of sex-fiend weirdo trying to peep on the dames in the powder room?"

"No, nothing like that, I just had a few too many and couldn't make out the sign." Blake tried on a laugh that didn't quite fit. "You know how it is."

"I don't know nothing about peeping." The guy's face screwed up like an ape trying to figure out how to drive a car. "Say, wait a minute, you some kinda sissy? You look awful soft to me with that soft voice. What would a fairy like you want with peeping on girls in the john?"

This was going to hell faster than a stone-cold killer strapped into the electric chair. Blake wanted nothing more than to get away from this drunken gorilla as quickly as possible. She couldn't see Betty from where the guy had her cornered, but she was terrified that the girl would decide to wander over and find out what had happened to her.

"I told you I didn't see the sign." Blake pulled away from the goon. "It was an honest mistake."

"Honest mistake my eye!" The goon reached out and grabbed a handful of Blake's shirtfront and the worst possible thing happened. Buttons flew, her undershirt tore, and the goon stared at the tight binder that encircled Blake's chest.

"What the hell kinda shit is this?" His big hairy fingers wrenched the binder down and Blake's right breast sprang free over the top. Pure terror exploded in Blake's heart, not fear of the beating she was surely about to get—that was nothing new—but of Betty, beautiful innocent Betty coming around the corner and seeing her like this. She squeezed her eyes shut in preparation for the blow she knew was coming but instead she heard a calm voice with a Chinese accent.

"No fighting here," it said and when she opened her eyes she saw the bartender, a Chinese fellow with big ears and slicked-back hair. She knew she had seen him somewhere before, but she couldn't place him just now. The way her mind was whirling, she probably couldn't have placed Humphrey Bogart just now.

"The hell you say!" The goon pulled back to take his swing at Blake, but before he could let fly, the Chinaman had his arm wrenched up behind him and was hustling the big man out through the kitchen door. "You came to the wrong bar," Blake heard him telling the goon. "Everywhere else, men are only men and women are only women. Things aren't like that at the Black Dragon."

Blake had barely collected her senses when the Chinaman re-appeared with a folded shirt. "Here, put this on." He held the shirt out to her. "Your girl is looking for you."

Blake looked up at this oddly familiar man and saw that he understood exactly what was happening. He'd spoken only two sentences to her, and she hadn't said a word to him, but somehow she felt as if she could trust him with her life. She felt suddenly, absurdly like crying, something she hadn't done in ten years. Instead she nodded, adjusted her binder, and slipped into the new shirt. It was far too big, but it would have to do. She was fastening the last button when Betty came around the corner, pretty face creased with worry.

"Oh my gosh, Blake, what on earth happened?"

"There was a fight," the Chinaman said. "Your friend caught a man trying to peep on the ladies here." He pointed towards the rest-room door. "He was drunk. I had to remove him from the club."

"Oh my gosh," Betty said. "Blake, are you all right?"

There was something in Betty's face, not just genuine worry but some other kind of raw emotion as she looked into Blake's eyes. It was so intense that Blake had to look away.

"Oh, sure." Blake fixed her tie and glanced over at the Chinaman. "Never better. Guess I told that big lout a thing or two."

"You sure know how to show a girl a good time!" Betty said.

"Casanova ain't got nothing on me," Blake replied, smoothing her shirtfront. "You wanna dance?"

Betty's blue eyes shone. "Actually, I think you better take me home."

Blake felt so weak in the knees that she could barely stand. She was simultaneously aroused and terrified by Betty's unmistakable invitation.

"Thanks for saving my skin there," Blake told the quiet Chinaman, meaning so much more.

The Chinaman nodded, meaning so much more.

■ ■ ■

In the car in front of Betty's apartment, Blake sat nearly delirious from the smell of Betty's perfume and her closeness. Every detail seemed too real, too sharp. The quiet street, every window blacked out, sealed against a warm night sky that could erupt with Japanese bombers at any moment. The feel of the leather seat, and the way the space between her knee and Betty's seemed alive with potential. She was sweating profusely under her binder. Blake gripped the wheel with both hands, scared to even turn her head.

"I had a really great time," Betty said softly, touching Blake's arm.

"Yeah, me too." Blake still couldn't let go of the wheel. Betty's touch felt electric through the fabric of her sleeve. Blake felt her hungry female anatomy pulsing beneath the masculine attire, seeming to strain against this phony cover-up, demanding recognition. She felt as if she might rip the wheel loose from its moorings, but her grip on it was the only thing stopping her from clutching Betty and never letting her go.

"Y'know, most of the dates I've been on have been just like octopus wrestling. Fellas trying to grab a cheap feel every chance they got. But you haven't tried anything funny all night. You're a real gentleman."

Blake didn't say anything, but she could feel hot blood coursing under her skin.

"I guess what I'm trying to say is…" Betty paused and took one of Blake's hands off the wheel, holding it in both of her own. Blake finally turned and looked into her face. The girl's blue eyes were wide and dilated in the dim interior of the car. "I *want* you to try something."

Blake knew there were a million reasons why she should not be doing this, but she couldn't think of a single one. She put her hand on Betty's cheek, caressing the girl's jawline with her thumb. The skin there was so soft, Blake felt almost ashamed to be defiling it with her scarred, ugly hands. Betty closed her eyes and sighed. Blake leaned in and paused for a moment with her lips less than an inch from Betty's, breathing her breath and relishing the intensity of her desire.

She kissed Betty first lightly, then opening the girl's lips gently with her tongue. Betty was trembling as Blake pulled her close, dizzy from the smell of her skin and hair. The lush satin of the evening dress slithered under Blake's touch. Blake tentatively brushed her palm against the inside of Betty's nylon-clad thigh, and the girl made a soft, tiny noise and let her knees drift apart. Emboldened by this reaction, Blake's fingers slid higher to the magic spot where nylon gave way to warm, luscious flesh. She ached to move even higher, to slip beneath the wispy lace that covered Betty's sweet young cunt and sample the wetness she knew she would find there. But that was going too far too fast. Instead, Blake broke the kiss, keeping her arms around Betty. The girl rested her cheek against Blake's lapel, and Blake stroked the back of her neck.

"I can't invite you in," Betty said. "I want to, but entertaining male visitors is grounds for eviction."

"Sure," Blake said, her mind racing. She couldn't risk bringing Betty up to Zola's, but she couldn't bear to let her go either.

"Isn't there anywhere we can go?"

Suddenly Blake had an idea, a terrible, wonderful idea. "Listen," she told Betty, "go check in at the desk and then sneak out the back. I'll meet you there in 10 minutes."

Betty smiled that killer smile and kissed Blake again with such fierce intensity that Blake knew she would do anything to be with this girl. Then she was gone, out the door and into her building, leaving Blake to rest her forehead against the wheel and wait for her heartbeat to slow to something like normal.

■ ■ ■

Waiting behind Betty's building, Blake went through a hundred kinds of hell, tormenting herself with doubt and guilt. As soon as Betty had gone, Blake grabbed her leather satchel full of rewrites from behind the seat. Under the crumpled, coffee-stained pages was another present from Zola, wrapped in a plaid scarf. It had seemed insanely ambitious to bring this thing, and now, even with Betty seemingly ready willing and able, Blake had absolutely no idea whether she would be able to pass it off as the real McCoy. It might work; the few young women she'd been with outside of Zola's circle were amazingly ignorant about such things. But this was different; Blake cared for this girl, and she could not even imagine what might happen if Betty discovered her ruse. Again and again she told herself to drive away and go home to Zola where she belonged. When Betty finally appeared in the alley, sneaking up to Blake's parked car with an expression of sweet mischief on her face, all the doubt dissolved.

It was only a short drive to the studio lot. "Get down," Blake told Betty as they turned into the driveway leading up to the gate. Betty scrunched down in the well under the dash, giggling.

"Evening, Blake," the ancient guard called around a mouthful of egg salad. "Mansley got ya working late again, huh?"

"Can you believe he wants me to write a female impersonator into *Terror Over Tokyo?* What'll they think of next?"

"A female impersonator?" The guard snickered. "Didn't know they was filming Mansley's life story."

"Yeah, what can you do?" Blake was filled with nervous hilarity. "We're all just slaves of the Topline empire. Ours is not to question why, ours is just to do or die."

"Guess we all gotta do our part for the war effort," the guard said as he waved Blake through.

When they were out of sight of the guard booth, Betty popped up. "What did he mean about Mansley's life story?" she asked as Blake pulled into one of the writers' slots behind the commissary.

"Nothing." Blake glanced around nervously. It was very dark, all lights blacked out. She slung her satchel over her shoulder and squeezed Betty's hand. "Come on."

She led Betty through the deserted streets of midtown Manhattan, past an Egyptian temple, through a dusty Western town complete with tumbleweeds. Finally they came to a studio marked B3 above the airplane-hangar-sized door. Sparking her lighter, Blake

illuminated a large interior mockup for a Japanese POW camp. The
Zippo filled the room with flickering shadows. Rows and rows of
narrow military cots stood side by side.

"I'm sorry we're doing a war picture right now and not some
Grecian epic set in a queen's boudoir." Blake took Betty in her arms
and let the flame of her lighter die. Total darkness enveloped them.

"It's perfect," Betty whispered, her breath warm on Blake's lips.
They began to kiss again.

Betty let Blake lay her down on a narrow cot and gasped softly
as Blake's fingers found the hooks on her dress and slowly undid
them, peeling the satin away. Beneath was a thin slip the girl removed herself, leaving behind only stockings and the garter belt
that held them up. Blake wanted more than anything to see this
lovely girl's exposed flesh laid out before her, but she was also grateful
for the darkness that allowed her to slip Zola's gift from the satchel
and position it nearby for easy access.

She spent several long minutes worshiping the length of the
girl's body, first with her hands and then with her mouth, lingering
on spots that seemed to evoke the most response: the back of the
knees, the taut, gracile muscles of her inner thighs, the soft perfection of her tender belly. She tried to picture each part as she touched
it, wondering if the small, tight nipples that capped Betty's generous breasts were pale pink or chocolate-brown like Zola's. She was
drunk on the scent of sweet girlsweat and that secret perfume, and
finally could wait no longer to spread the silky hair that hid Betty's
warm, full-lipped cunt and embrace it with her mouth.

"What are you...?" Betty breathed but her words dissolved into
a sound of pleasure that was nearly more than Blake could bear. She
threw herself into the delicious task with more relish and determi-
nation than she ever had, loving the complex and subtle battle to
interpret Betty's sounds and movements and adjust her own actions
accordingly. When the girl began to thrust her hips rhythmically
against Blake's questing tongue, making muffled animal grunts,
Blake slid a finger up into her slippery depths. Encountering no
virginal resistance, she added a second finger and was rewarded by
a shudder and a sweet gush of fluid. Giddy with desire, she worked
the fingers in circles on the inner wall while her tongue worked

counter-circles on the outside, feeling the tension building and building to swift, sharp contractions. Betty cried out, forgetting herself in the dark as her young body shook, fists gripping the rough wool blanket beneath them.

Blake's arousal was at its peak, the ache beneath her trousers like a pulsing fever, and she was hit with a perfect idea. While Betty lolled in the aftermath of her release, Blake slipped Zola's gift from its hiding place, undid her trousers, and removed the smaller, flaccid appliance from the harness that held it. Instead of setting the artificial phallus facing outward in its place, Blake pulled the harness aside and inserted Zola's gift into her own vagina, allowing her body heat to warm it. When the time came, she hoped Betty would not feel cold, lifeless rubber but something hotter and more realistic. She replaced her clothing and took the insensate girl in her arms, kissing the sweat from her upper lip.

"My God, Blake," Betty whispered. "I've never felt anything like that before."

Blake was filled with an absurd kind of pride, so strong she felt as if she could get away with anything. The length of the dildo inside her was warming fast. She kissed Betty again, lingering.

"Baby," Blake said softly as she broke the kiss. "We can stop right now if you like. We don't have to do anything you don't want."

"I do want it," Betty said. "I don't think I've ever wanted anything so bad in my whole entire life."

That was all Blake needed to hear. She had her fly open and the dildo reversed in seconds. It was slick and hot as flesh in her hand as she guided it between Betty's open legs. She slipped the head in, then paused. Betty held her breath. Her whole body sang with tension that Blake could nearly see swimming between them in the blackness. When she sank the full length of it, she caught Betty's gasp in her mouth, kissing her without moving the rest of her body. She cupped Betty's damp, naked ass in both hands and began to fuck her slowly, drinking in her breath, feeling the friction of the harness straps against her own cunt like an exquisite torture. Betty's long, nylon-clad legs wrapped around Blake as she sped up her thrusts. The girl began to sob Blake's name in the darkness, and the friction from the straps gave way to sharp, nearly painful orgasm.

Blake's whole body shuddered and Betty wrenched herself away with an alarmed cry.

"What is it?" Blake asked, still shaken from the sudden orgasm and terrified that she had given herself away somehow.

"It's just…" Betty gasped, fingers groping between her legs in the dark. "I can't have a baby right now."

Blake laughed, letting all her breath tumble out in a gush of relief.

"Don't worry," Blake said, swapping out the dildo for the other appliance with shaking hands. "I…uh…I didn't, you know, inside you."

"I don't smell any," Betty whispered. "Just girl stuff."

That nearly set Blake off laughing again. Instead she bit the inside of her cheek and lay down beside Betty, wrapping the girl up in her arms. They were silent for a long time in the dark, listening to each other breathe. Finally Betty spoke up in a quiet voice totally unlike her former breathy, girlish tone. "I have to tell you something."

Blake frowned in the dark. "What is it?"

"I…" Betty paused. "I haven't been quite honest with you."

You and me both, sister, Blake thought, but said nothing.

"You see," Betty whispered against Blake's neck, "I'm not really from Idaho."

"Oh?" Blake said cautiously.

"I was born in Lincoln Heights. I've lived in Los Angeles all my life."

"Yeah, well, I like the Sandpoint angle. It suits you." Blake said. "Besides, we've all rewritten our life stories now and again."

"There's more. I knew you were the writer on *Terror Over Tokyo,* so I went out and read up on you and then waited till I saw you outside your office and dropped those photos hoping you'd come to my rescue."

Blake had to laugh again. Clearly Betty hadn't done quite enough research to figure out that Blake Blackline was really Nan Blake. It was all so preposterous. Who was fooling whom here? "I shoulda known," she said. "No dame in her right mind ever read *Black Mask!*"

"But listen," Betty said, speaking too fast. "I had the most amazing time tonight. No lie. I mean, I guess you can tell this isn't my first time, but I swear Blake, I never ever felt like that before with any other fella. I mean it. I already got the part so it's not like I'm doing this to get ahead. Being with you tonight was for *me*, get it? For me. Since we met, I knew there was something special about you. You're so…so different somehow. Can you forgive me for trying to put one over on you?"

Blake put her finger to Betty's lips.

"Shhhhhh, baby," she said. "Don't give it another thought." She found herself remembering Mansley's warning. "But listen. On the lot we do need to play it cool. Maybe you batted your eyes at me to get the part, and maybe I let you, but you don't want anyone else thinking you screwed your way in." Blake swallowed, hoping the excuse sounded believable. "If you're all over me on the set, people are gonna get the wrong idea."

"Sure…"

"So I just want you to know in advance that if I give you the cold shoulder on the lot, its not because I don't want you. God knows I do. I just think it's best if we keep things low-key between us in public from here on out."

Betty snuggled against her. "Whatever you think is best, Blake."

■ ■ ■

Victor arrived late for the first day of shooting on *Terror Over Tokyo*. He was horribly nervous and needed a bottle and a half of gin and three baths in order to make it out the door. When he got to the set, they had already shot the majority of the party scene without him. All that was left was the Tansy Chan number and the cutaways of the hero watching the party through the grate.

The set was noisy and full of workers fixing costumes, setting lights, making notes, doing a thousand large and small jobs. Several women and a man descended on Victor the moment he arrived. Within minutes they had him done up in a sexy, sheer costume that left his legs exposed to mid-thigh and a preposterous wig like some reject from a high-school performance of the *Mikado*. He felt like a bad joke, and was wondering how hard it would be to sneak away without anyone noticing when Mansley poked his head into the dressing room.

"Fantastic!" he said. "We're ready for you, Victor."

Victor wobbled out onto the set in too-high heels, trying to pull the insubstantial pink fabric tighter around himself. The tables were filled with Chinese and Korean actors in Japanese military uniforms. Their faces were emotionless, but their eyes blazed at him. He could hear their disapproving whispers swelling and fading like the ocean, though no one's mouth moved. A burning nausea began to churn inside him. He closed his eyes and stepped forward. Some thick black cable tangled around his feet, and he would have gone down if strong hands hadn't caught him by the shoulders, steadying him. When he opened his eyes, he saw the quiet bartender from the Black Dragon. The bartender was wearing a Japanese uniform like the rest, but his eyes were not hateful and suspicious. There was some other emotion there, something Victor could not read as the man helped him up the stairs to the small stage, then ducked away. A blinding light hit his face, discordant music welled from unseen speakers, and it was time to sing.

They made him do the number several times, shooting from several angles. Then, abruptly, it was over. The light was still in his eyes as he staggered from the stage. Someone took him by the elbow—the bartender again? No, these fingers were hard and hurtful. "Very pretty," said a deep voice.

For a single hideous moment Victor knew it was his Uncle Larry. Uncle Larry had found him here and was about to announce to the whole studio that Victor was really a Jap, a dirty spying little Jap. Chinese men in Japanese uniforms would surround him and beat him to death with their bare fists. He twisted away and ran. A glance over his shoulder revealed the movie star Richard Noble, tall and perfect, blonde, rock-jawed with a quintessential all-American face and cold blue-gray eyes. Noble was laughing—Uncle Larry's laugh, coming out of that handsome mouth.

Even though Victor was out of the bright light, it still burned his skin. He had to escape this terrible set, to return to the safety of the bathroom in the little house. He'd gotten turned around somehow, and instead of winding up back at the dressing room, he found himself in some kind of storage area full of dusty old props. Of course he hadn't gotten away at all. Noble must have been able to follow the smell of the fire inside Victor, because all at once he was there, a cigarette smoldering between his fingers.

"You can't get away that easy," Noble said. He caressed his crotch with the hand that held the lit cigarette. The terror inside Victor was so intense that he was nearly paralyzed. He heard that laugh again, Uncle Larry's laugh, but now it seemed to be coming from the end of Noble's cigarette.

"You like me," Noble was saying. "I can tell." Now he caressed Victor's cheek, smearing Victor's thick lipstick with the ball of his thumb. "I know what pretty things like you need."

"Dirty little peeper," Uncle Larry said. "You like watching, don't you?"

Victor could feel the lit tip of the cigarette inches from the underside of his cockhead, even though Noble had parked it between his lips as he began to undo his trousers. He could not move until Noble forced him to his knees. The actor's cock was huge, looming monstrous in Victor's face. The fire tore through his insides, burning the slender tethers that bound him to his flesh until the last one snapped and Victor plummeted away, down a muddy well deep inside himself. Miles away, at the top of the well, he could see a circle of light like a distant movie screen. He could see himself on his knees before Noble, doing what Noble wanted like a good boy, but here in the well he felt nothing but dull numb coldness. He could see other things happening up there, other dirty things, and that boy up there liked it. He had always liked those bad, dirty things. The only time Victor felt anything was when Noble grabbed that boy by the hair and slapped his face. In the well, Victor thought he felt something like a faint warmth on his face as if he were leaning in close to a naked light bulb.

When Victor next came to awareness, he was lying on the concrete alone. Noble's smoldering cigarette had been crushed but not quite extinguished on the floor less than a foot from his face. It kept on whispering and whispering until Victor reached out and grabbed it, stuffing it into his mouth and swallowing, unmindful of the new burning on his tongue, of the taste of hot ash in the pit of his belly.

Triads

The cheap pink fabric of his costume was cold and slimy at the crotch. Slowly, rhythmically, he began to hit his forehead against the cement, sending bright yellow sparks flying across the floor, bouncing off the old rotting props. Childishly he hoped the sparks would catch, burning him up for good, and the whole rotten world with him. He hit his head harder and harder until blackness swallowed everything.

■ ■ ■

Blake adjusted her white bow tie and tried to remember what had become of her top hat. Last she'd seen, Zola had been wearing it and little else. The party was beginning to wind down, pairing off into twos and threes for more intimate party games. Zola had been directing some complex parody performance in which a woman dressed as Hitler was bound and flogged by a woman dressed as Uncle Sam, but now she came to Blake with her cheeks full of color and her hair tumbling over her eyes, tugging at Blake's sleeve like a child. She had exchanged Blake's top hat for the sequined Uncle Sam hat and clearly wanted Blake to take part in some liaison with another young butch. Blake just shook her head.

"Tell Zola what is wrong, darling." Zola looked up into Blake's face, her dark eyes full of real concern. Blake didn't know what to say. She couldn't tell Zola that Betty wanted Blake to call her Jean now, that the girl was growing more and more distant. That tonight, even as they spoke, the hot young ingenue Jean Jordan was on yet another studio-orchestrated dream date with that no-good Richard Noble. Blake knew what that was all about, had seen the way Noble looked at Mansley's dress-up dolly. Noble needed a clean, pretty, 36-24-36 cover story. Betty was naive, but she wasn't stupid. Why couldn't she see how she was being used?

"He took me to the Trocadero!" Betty had gushed. "Isn't that grand? I thought I'd go blind from the cameras flashing all around us! And you'll never guess—Hedda Hopper wants to interview me tomorrow afternoon!"

"Guess you've really got it made, huh?"

"Aw, don't be that way, Blake. Mansley says it's good publicity for the movie..."

"I want to be alone tonight, Zola," Blake managed to say now. She just couldn't stand another performance.

"I will allow it this one time, my handsome darling. But don't you make a habit of it, or I shall be forced to send you back to the orange groves whence you came."

Blake barely registered the catty barb. She wondered if Noble were fucking Betty right now, if Betty was telling him he was the best ever. She wanted to die.

■ ■ ■

Jimmy was whipping Richard Noble, trying not to hurt the man as much as he wanted to. The white actor who played the Japanese general was interrogating Noble in a high-pitched fake-Oriental accent that made Jimmy want to turn the whip on him. Instead he focused on making his front teeth stick out as the director had demonstrated and transforming his hatred for the handsome Noble into an approximation of a loyal Japanese soldier's hatred for his enemy. He had seen Noble hanging around Tansy Chan, had seen the beaten compliance in Tansy's face, knew what was really happening. The singer was always there, always lingering in the corner of Jimmy's eye. When Noble called 15, the two of them always disappeared together. Noble would return from the break cocky and smiling, slapping the director on the back. The singer would not return until several minutes later. Sometimes there would be blood on his dress; sometimes his haunted eyes nearly cut Jimmy's heart out. The singer's pain made Jimmy want to smash Noble's handsome, smirking face. He was doing such a good job of hating Noble that the director decided to add a closeup of his face.

The other Chinese extras were annoyed by Jimmy's perfect English, and mystified by his refusal to discuss his family or his past in a world where family ties were everything. The fact that he had one of the better roles only made him more unpopular, but Jimmy didn't care. He cared about nothing but acting. He was not alive unless he was being someone else; that was the only time he still allowed himself to feel, like a reformed alcoholic stealing tiny sips from a bottle that does not belong to him. Nothing else mattered. Nothing but…

Tansy Chan was there again, silent as a mouse on the outer fringe of the set, and the bound Noble seemed to smell him. The moment the director called it a wrap, Noble slipped his bonds and left the set.

Jimmy knew he should go home, knew he should mind his business. Instead he followed Noble to his dressing room, catching a brief flash of an anxious Tansy Chan inside before the door slammed. Jimmy was about to slink away, huge dark ache growing inside him, when he spotted Sherman Mansley storming towards him. He flattened himself into the shadows as the angry producer kicked open the dressing room door. Jimmy heard shouts and the sounds of a scuffle. The door burst open and out came Tansy Chan with a split lip and a rapidly purpling eye. The singer ran, and Jimmy could do nothing but run after.

He followed Tansy out into the lot. The storm that had been brewing all morning had burst loose while they were filming. Cool rain sluiced over Jimmy's hot skin. Tansy stopped in the middle of the street, head tipped up to the rain as tears and makeup washed down his cheeks. Inexplicably, this posture helped Jimmy find his voice.

"Tansy?" The name was nearly lost beneath the hammering of rain on car hoods and concrete. "Are you all right?"

The singer looked at Jimmy, seeming to see him for the first time. Then he touched his own throat with a slender hand in a gesture so evocative it hurt to see. "My name is Victor," said the singer, and took a step closer.

"Victor," Jimmy repeated, heart racing.

Victor closed the distance between them and kissed Jimmy. His lips tasted like rain and blood. Jimmy could not put his arms around Victor. He could not kiss him back. He was shaking so badly he felt as if the force of the rain would smash him to pieces. He was so afraid. Afraid that after so many years of not feeling, of not being touched, his hard-won armor would crumble under this beautiful boy's delicate hands, under his mouth that was so like Lin Bai's mouth.

Victor broke the kiss. "Don't be afraid," he said. "The rain will protect us." He peeled the soaked Japanese officer's jacket off

Jimmy's compliant body and dropped it to the ground. "Come with me."

■ ■ ■

Victor drove through the silvery sheets of rain with the tall bartender beside him. Mansley had given him this car, just as Mansley had given him everything else, but Jimmy didn't need to know that. Soon they were driving through the tawdry streets of New Chinatown. Victor hated the place, hated the cold stares from the women and singsong taunts of the children, hated the constant fear that someone might discover he was not who he claimed to be. When he performed at the Black Dragon, he parked out back so he could enter through the stage door instead of having to walk these glittering, jeering streets. Now, with Jimmy leading him silently down a fish-stinking alley behind an illegal gambling parlor, Victor kept his eyes down and his arms wrapped tight around himself, waiting for someone to point at him and cry "A Jap! A dirty Jap!"

The stairway up to Jimmy's tiny room was occupied by a scrawny underage prostitute with her cheap China-doll dress hiked up around her waist. Her client was a balding fat man with a loud jacket and a bulge in his armpit that screamed *vice cop*. The pair hardly seemed to notice as Jimmy and Victor sidled by.

Jimmy's room was the last one down a long, littered hallway. Inside, the walls were painted a safe gentle green. The clicking of ivory mah-jongg tiles from a game room below played counterpoint to the percussive song of the rain.

There were almost no personal touches here. A narrow bed, a tiny stove, a shallow sink. It was like a hundred other rooms. Jimmy did not speak to Victor or meet his gaze. His loneliness was as deep and inviting as the cold depths of the ocean. Victor knew there was something under there, some profound sadness that was like the opposite of fire. He wanted to drown himself in Jimmy.

Jimmy was stiff and resistant at first, but Victor persisted. When Jimmy finally gave in, his passion was like the passion of the ocean, pulling Victor under. Jimmy cried when he came, speaking someone else's name in a voice softer than the slackening rain. In the aftermath, Victor held him and dried his tears, feeling for the first time in his life that the fire inside him had not only died, but had never really been there in the first place. As if Jimmy's tears had quenched it for good.

"The other Chinese actors don't like you either, do they?" he asked, cradling Jimmy's head in his lap.

Jimmy shook his head in the dark. "It's true."

"They hate me." Victor sucked in a long breath. "I'm Japanese."

Jimmy sat up. Victor could not see his expression in the dark.

"Half Japanese," Victor said, waiting with his eyes closed to see if Jimmy would hit him, almost wanting him to. Jimmy said nothing.

"No one knows," Victor said. "But I am. My mother was white, but my father was Japanese."

Another long pause between them and Victor spoke up again.

"The only other Japanese person I ever met was my father's sister. She came to our house one day to tell my father that my grand-father was dead. I never met my grandfather, but my Uncle Larry…"

Victor paused, fearful that speaking Uncle Larry's name might set up some destructive echo that would destroy the green safety of Jimmy's room. When nothing happened, he continued, words stumbling over each other like children running. "My Uncle Larry said my grandfather did Hairy Carrie because of me. Do you know about Hairy Carrie?"

Jimmy shook his head.

"It's when you cut your own stomach open with a sword and all your guts come out. My aunt said he did it because of honor and gambling debts and other things I didn't understand, but Uncle Larry said that was a lie, that the only time you did Hairy Carrie was when something made you so ashamed that there was no way to get better." Victor paused, wishing Jimmy would say something, do something. "Uncle Larry said that finding out about his dirty little half-breed grandson was the real reason he did it. That he was so ashamed of me he couldn't stand to live. I used to have a picture of my grandfather, but it…got burned."

Victor could still see that photo of the stern-faced man in what looked like a dark bathrobe. His eyebrows were thick, his stony features nothing like the gentle face of Victor's father. Sometimes Victor thought he felt those stern eyes on him when he was getting fucked by Mansley. He used to have nightmares of his grandfather standing in his bedroom with his bloody intestines trailing behind him, telling little Artie that it was all his fault.

"I didn't want to be Japanese any more. So now I pretend I'm Chinese. White people can't tell the difference, and Chinese people don't look too close at me because I'm...a pansy."

Victor's tears were hot and acidic, burning his cheeks. Jimmy held him. "Sometimes people have to change," Jimmy said. "Become someone different, for all kinds of reasons. I understand that. Your secret is safe with me."

"Do you have anything to drink?" Victor asked. He couldn't even stand to look at Jimmy anymore. All this talk of the past had brought the fire back. If Jimmy noticed, he would surely be horrified, disgusted.

Jimmy shook his head. "Just tea."

"I'll get us a bottle," Victor said. "I'll be right back."

Jimmy reached for him. "No." His voice was choked with emotion. "Please don't go."

Victor paused, heart twisting in his chest, shriveling in the heat. "I'll only be a minute."

Jimmy dropped his reaching hand, head bowed. He nodded. Victor struggled into his clothes in the dark and left Jimmy alone on the bed. Uncle Larry's voice whispered to him beneath the click and shuffle of the mah-jongg tiles, chasing him down the stairs. He knew he would not come back to this safe green room.

It was only a short drive to Richard Noble's apartment.

■ ■ ■

Jimmy walked along the back lot's phony New York streets, barely seeing the workers ripping down the hollow brownstone facades and uprooting the streetlights. He could not stop thinking about Victor. Spots on his skin that Victor's mouth had touched seemed to ache like deep-tissue bruises even though it had been nearly a month since the singer had come home with him.

His tiny room had never seemed so empty before Victor was there. Now every corner seemed to resonate with an aching loneliness, as empty and hopeless as the endless gray stretch of Jimmy's life. It was as if he had been moving through his days without really being alive, seeing only the next ordered drink, the next role. Now the memory of Victor's body next to his own made his loneliness seem almost unendurable.

When Jimmy first arrived in the States, he'd had to endure sexual encounters in exchange for a place in a certain man's stable of Oriental extras. Hollywood wasn't the luxurious fantasyland Lin Bai had dreamed of. You could see that land from a distance, but when you got close, you realized the silver glitter was rubbing off on your hands and the sharp edges could cut you. But Master Lau's training had paid off; it wasn't long before directors began selecting him for speaking parts. Soon he was getting roles on his own, and he told the "casting agent" to go to hell. The "agent's" threat of exposure kept Jimmy up nights until the man turned up in a Chinatown trash bin with his throat cut. Jimmy and nearly three dozen other Chinese actors let out a great sign of relief when that item hit the morning papers. That man's soft, meaty hands had been the last to touch Jimmy, and as the years went by, he began to feel as if his body no longer existed below the neck. He might as well have been a disembodied mind controlling a life-sized, flexible puppet.

Then Tansy Chan was hired at the Black Dragon where Jimmy picked up extra income tending bar on weekends. Jimmy was smitten. Something about the singer awakened all his emotional and carnal memories of Lin Bai. He was tormented by fierce, insistent erections like a teenager's. He was still struggling to get a handle on this uncontrollable desire the day Victor kissed him in the rain.

Victor's pain had been so much like the pain suffered by Lin Bai years ago, and Victor's hunger made Jimmy lose all sense of time. Holding the slender boy in his arms, Jimmy ached to help him somehow, to ease the torment that was burning him up inside. When he left, Jimmy stayed raw and open like the wound beneath a fresh-torn scab.

As the days passed with no sign of Victor, the ache in Jimmy's heart stubbornly refused to fade. It grew stronger and stronger until

Jimmy thought he might go mad. He dreamed of holding Victor's dying body in the heart of a howling storm. He dreamed of explosions and blood, of watching Victor pause with his hand on the doorknob, saying *I'll only be a minute...*

Now he could not stand to stay trapped inside his room. It was as if he could still feel the heat of Victor's body in his single lumpy pillow, in his threadbare blanket. So he walked. He walked the gaudy streets of New Chinatown and the fantastical maze of the Topline back lot, trying not to think, not to feel. He was barely aware of where he was or where he had been. He didn't even notice the young redhead until she called out to him from the second-floor walkway of the writers' building.

"Hey there," she said. "Jimmy, isn't it?"

He looked up at her and nodded. "Hello," he said, keeping his face and voice pleasant and neutral.

She motioned for him to come up. He stood there for a moment, wondering, then headed for the stairs.

"Name's Blake," she said. Jimmy refused the cigarette she offered him. She shrugged and stuck it between her own lips instead. "You're making me dizzy down there. I feel like I'm in a shooting gallery."

"I don't understand," Jimmy said. He still felt nervous, unsure of the writer's motives.

"You must've passed by my office a dozen times in the last hour." She blew smoke from the corner of her mouth. "What gives?"

"I'm sorry," Jimmy said. "I was just thinking."

"About Tansy Chan?"

Jimmy looked away.

"Look, I don't mean to pry or nothing." Blake smoked in silence for a minute, looking out over the lot. "You remember Betty, that girl I took to the Black Dragon?"

"I remember."

"Mansley has her doing publicity dates with Noble." Blake did not look at Jimmy, but she scowled at the prop department roof.

"Because of Tansy Chan?"

Blake nodded, crushing her cigarette out against the railing.

"They're together all the time now. The papers are screaming wedding bells and I think they might be right. Mansley needs something to quench any potential questions about Noble's character. I'm sure he thinks marrying him off to a hotsy-totsy like Jean Jordan is just the ticket."

More silence. Finally Blake spoke up again.

"I know it's hopeless between me and Betty." She shook her head. "But I just can't let it go somehow. I keep thinking if Noble were out of the way maybe I'd have a shot. Maybe we both would."

Jimmy frowned.

"What are you saying?"

"I'm saying he's a piece of shit that doesn't deserve to live." Her face was fierce, jaw set. "You've seen how he treats Tansy. How long before he starts on Betty?"

"You want to murder him?" Jimmy asked, incredulous.

"Do I want to murder him?" Blake spat, pulled out another cigarette but did not light it. "You better believe I do. Not that I'm gonna. I'm a mystery writer. I know there's no such thing as a perfect murder. The killer always gets caught."

Jimmy nodded, thinking of Lin Bai. He had never been punished for the murder of Master Lau, but he had been caught nonetheless. Just as surely as a carp with a hook buried in its flashing throat, he had been caught.

"I understand," was all Jimmy said. "I too have thought of killing Noble." He paused and looked away. "Not how to avoid being caught, just…just how good it would feel."

"I know, I know." Blake held the matches in her hand, thumbing the book open and shut, open and shut. Finally she lit one and touched it to the cigarette. "Well, I guess I better get back to work. It's the only thing that makes sense anymore." She pocketed the matches. "Maybe we can't kill Noble, but I can make sure some fictional piece of shit gets what's coming to him."

Jimmy nodded. "You are lucky to have that."

The writer looked as if she might say more, but Jimmy turned to go. "Good-bye, Blake."

"Yeah, right, see ya."

He felt the writer watching him as he walked slowly away.

■ ■ ■

Victor lay on the floor of Noble's beach house staring into the cold black fireplace. Soot and ash formed a desolate gray landscape in which Victor imagined himself, one inch high, walking amidst the char like a character in a German expressionist film. Somewhere behind him, at the top of the well, Noble strained and sweated until his cock refused to cooperate. Then he beat Victor with wild, drunken fists that missed as often as they hit. None of it seemed as important as the texture of the ash.

"See, this is what I'm talking about." Noble's voice echoed down to Victor. Up on the little round movie screen, Noble staggered back, collapsing into a chair. He wore only a pair of socks and a misbuttoned shirt. Victor watched him pour an inch of whiskey into a glass. "Goddamn worthless piece of Chink trash. What goddamn good are you?"

Victor returned to the fireplace. It was safe now, chill and lifeless, but Victor knew the fire was never really gone. The sooty bricks remembered the heat; the ash still held on to dreams of fiery glory. The potential for burning never really went away. The little one-inch boy could be burned to cinders at any moment.

At the top of the well, Noble drank down the whiskey and continued to rail. Victor barely heard him until he stood suddenly and kicked Victor in the ribs. "I've had it with you, you worthless cocksucker. You see this?"

He waved a blue velvet box in Victor's face, then dropped it. Victor seemed to fly up the well to meet it until it struck him on the chest. As he sat up, the box bounced away and popped open, revealing an obscenely large diamond ring. Noble stepped on Victor's wrist before Victor's reaching hand could touch the box.

"You think that's for you?" Noble laughed. "You're dreaming, pansy. Faggot whores like you don't get diamonds. I wouldn't waste one red cent on a faggot whore like you. See, I'm getting married. To a legit lady. Not some..." His words were slurred and juicy. "Useless...fuckhole." Noble scooped up the ring and set it on the table beside the whiskey bottle. "Get out."

Triads

Victor clutched the torn front of his slip and looked up at Noble, whose face was red and mean, his eyes like nailheads.

"Are you deaf or something?" Noble hurled the empty glass at Victor. It exploded inches from Victor's knees. "I said..." He grabbed the crumpled pile of Victor's clothes and threw them. They bounced off Victor's chest and landed in the broken glass. "Get out!"

"I'm sorry," said Victor, gathering up his clothes and feeling the bites of a hundred tiny shards of glass against his chest. "Please. I'm sorry."

Noble looked down at the ring, weaving slightly.

"If you tell anyone about this," he said without looking up, "I'll kill you."

"If you tell anyone about this," Uncle Larry whispered, "I'll kill you."

Paralytic terror washed over Victor. He couldn't remember what he wasn't supposed to tell. His blood felt like lava in his veins as his heart burned broiler-hot beneath his ribs. He thought he had gotten away, but the gravity of Noble's cruelty kept pulling him back. Now even Noble didn't want Victor any more.

He bowed his head. All at once a strange cold calm was congealing inside him. It felt wonderful, and now he knew what he must do.

"I understand," he said.

From the ashes, his grandfather nodded approval.

■ ■ ■

When Jimmy heard a hesitant knock on his door, he knew instantly that it must be Victor. He was appalled by the way his heart leapt and mad hope surged through him as he stood with his hand on the knob.

When he opened the door, he was overwhelmed with raw, painful emotion. Victor's pretty face was a map of bruises, his eyes bright with unshed tears. His dress was disheveled and unwashed, his stockings laddered. Jimmy took the boy in his arms, feeling how thin he was, how fragile, like a wounded bird or a child's bamboo toy.

"Victor," Jimmy said into Victor's hair. "You came back."

"I need…" Victor broke the embrace and looked up into Jimmy's face. "Will you take a ride with me?"

Jimmy nodded, though he had no idea where Victor wanted him to go. He sat silently in the passenger seat of Victor's car, wishing for a way to see through Victor's battered face to what really lived inside the boy's heart. He wanted to tell Victor how he felt, but he couldn't. He could only stare down at his hands in his lap.

When he looked up again, they were on the ocean, speeding up the coast and then down a sudden, sharp turnoff to a sandy dead-end road. Victor pulled over and shut off the engine, sitting motionless for a few moments and then wrenching the door open. "Come on."

What else could Jimmy do? He followed Victor over a tall grassy bluff and down onto the beach. The tide was high, leaving only a thin scrap of sand. The ocean was rough, dark swells smashing into the scattered rocks. The smell was deep green, salt and seaweed and smashed mollusks dying slowly in the sun. In the time Jimmy had lived in California, he had visited the beach only once, in Santa Monica. That beach had been much more civilized, full of fat ladies and shrieking children and colorful umbrellas. Up here in Malibu, the beach was wilder, the Pacific Ocean far more savage.

"That's Richard's house up there," Victor said, pointing to a charming little blue cottage on the top of a distant bluff.

Jimmy wished he could move, put his arms around Victor, something, but he just looked up at the little house. His belly churned with thin, greasy hate. He found himself remembering his conversation with the writer.

Victor picked up a rock and hurled it into the water. "When I was fifteen I tried to drown myself in the ocean."

Jimmy frowned and waited for him to continue.

Victor turned back, looking up at Jimmy as if he were gauging Jimmy's reaction. Then he looked back out over the ocean and began to talk.

■ ■ ■

Triads

Victor let the story spill out after years and years of being buried deep inside him. He could feel the salty breeze on his naked skin, the nighttime ocean cold as death on his scrawny legs. The fire was loose and raging in him, pulsing in the shiny spot of burnflesh on the underside of his penis. That burn had been fresh then and the salt water had stung like acid as he waded in deeper.

I'm sorry, Daddy, he'd written on a sheet of notebook paper he slipped inside a purple velvet pocket of his father's saxophone case. He had wanted to write more, but could not find the words.

"You get back in here this minute, you filthy little Jap whore!" Uncle Larry called, his voice not really mad at all. More...teasing. Almost affectionate.

Artie didn't even know what made that day worse than any other. Ever since Uncle Larry arrived things had been hellish, each day a fresh horror. But something about that Sunday night—the way the clouds streaked the sky like claw marks, the way you could smell the ocean from miles away—had told Artie it was time to go. When Uncle Larry finished fucking Mavis over the arm of the sofa, he had wiped her shit from his dick with a fistful of curtain and swaggered over to untie Artie from the radiator. "Get my cigarettes," he said, chucking the boy under the chin and winking.

The walk down the hall to where Uncle Larry hung his jacket over the back of a kitchen chair was always excruciating, but that night it was like a dream, still frightening but unreal somehow. The spot where Larry always burned Artie's penis was still raw and blistered from earlier that day. Artie stood in the dim kitchen holding the package of cigarettes and the flashy lighter with the naked girl on it and realized that the only way to get away was to die. It was so obvious. From the shadows by the pantry, his grandfather watched in stony silence as Artie wrote the note to his father. The old man's trailing guts gleamed in the pale light from the street. Artie knew he was not brave enough for Hairy Carrie, and he could feel his grandfather's eyes condemning him for a coward as he stole two bottles of gin from the liquor cabinet and slipped out the side door. Uncle Larry's voice trailed after him as he ran into the night, running and running towards the subtle briny scent of the ocean.

He had never had a drink before that night, and his young body took the force of the guzzled alcohol like a hit from a speeding train. He kept graying out as he waded in deeper, sometimes turning back to see the sad little pile of his clothes on the empty beach, sometimes closing his eyes and picturing his burning guts trailing away into the cold healing water. The world spun and the waves tossed him and he went under, icy brine filling his mouth and sudden sobering terror racing through his veins. He struggled, flailing and dogpaddling and then nothing but black unconsciousness swallowing him like the black water.

When he came to, he was coiled around a slimy wooden piling beneath a long pier. He had no idea how he had ended up there. He could hear music and see flashes of colored light through the boards above him. He vomited repeatedly into the damp sand, body wracked with shivers. It took him several minutes to realize he was not alone.

"A little late for skinny dipping, don't you think?"

A high, horrible laugh and Artie looked up to see a very tall man zipping up his trousers. Behind the man, a thin, fey Chinese boy with bad skin was giggling into his hand.

"Had too much to drink, didja?"

Artie nodded, wiping his mouth on his forearm. The tall man came forward and took off his jacket, setting it around Arite's shivering shoulders. It smelled like sweet aftershave and felt so warm and good that Artie started to cry. The Chinese boy hung back, pouting.

"I can help you," the tall man said, lifting Artie to his feet. "We can help each other. What's your name?"

"Victor," Artie said, beginning to understand that he really was dead.

That man was named Sonny and he taught Victor that he did not have to give himself away for free. Victor was pretty, he explained, and pretty things cost money. At first Sonny kept all the money men gave Victor, but Victor did such a good job that Sonny let him keep more and more. Victor spent every dime on his newfound passion, liquor. Soon he was drinking so much that Sonny had to come looking for him every morning, usually finding him passed out in some alley, or in the backseat of an abandoned car, or sprawled on the beach where the papers said the police had found his clothes that first night, confirming the verdict of death by suicide and closing the case of the missing Arthur Omura.

Sonny began to use his fists more and more on the uncaring Victor. When Victor disappeared into Mansley's dim velvet cage, he didn't think Sonny lost any sleep looking for him. No one in the world really cared for him now, no one but Jimmy. Jimmy who listened, who didn't use ugly words to judge him. Jimmy who smelled liked tea and rice paper, whose gentle hands and melancholy eyes tortured Victor with childish hope for something like a future.

"That was more than three years ago," Victor told Jimmy. "Actually, it will be four years tomorrow." He looked away. "Exactly four years to the day. Of course, it wasn't this beach."

Suddenly disoriented, Victor looked down at the sand. He wasn't sure where this was, *when* this was. He thought he saw the pile of Artie's clothes, but it was only a knot of rotting seaweed. But then he looked up at Noble's blue house and he knew exactly where he was.

Jimmy took a step closer to him. Victor could see the conflict in his face. He reached out to Victor, and Victor curled against his chest, terrified by how good it felt.

"I sometimes wish I had died back then," Victor said, looking over Jimmy's shoulder at the restless ocean. "I should have just dissolved into the water. Then I wouldn't have to do it."

"Do what?" Jimmy cupped the back of Victor's neck and looked down into his face. "What do you have to do?"

Victor looked away. "I don't remember," he admitted. "I was so sure, but now I just don't know."

"I'm afraid I don't understand."

Why did Jimmy have to be so kind? Why did he have ruin everything by filling Victor with jagged doubt and fear?

Victor's grandfather stood shin-deep in the dark waves, scowling. His bloody insides floated around his pale, bare legs, turning the seafoam sickly pink. Victor gasped and turned Jimmy's body so the old man was behind him, terrified that Jimmy might see.

"I *am* Japanese," Victor said, his voice tight and desperate in his constricted throat. "Don't you see? There's only one way to make it right."

He pulled away from Jimmy, no longer able to endure his touch. His head was filled with a cacophony of jagged memories. The old man was scowling at him, drilling into him with cold black eyes, and Uncle Larry (or was it Noble?) kept on whispering terrible dirty things that made it hard to hear anything else. Didn't Jimmy understand that he only loved Victor because he didn't really know him? That anyone who really knew him, who looked inside him and saw how bad, how filthy and horrible he really was, would run screaming? Victor knew he had been wrong to bring Jimmy here, wrong to try and reach out to someone so clean and good.

"I'm sorry," Victor said. "I have to go now."

"Victor..." Jimmy was hurting, his voice full of pain. Victor knew it was all his fault again, just like always.

"Don't worry," Victor said as he turned and began to walk away. "I'm going to fix everything." He looked back up at the little blue house. "I'm going to end it."

Then he ran, unable to look back. Deep inside, he found himself wishing Jimmy would chase after him, pull him close and tell him it would all be OK. Take him back to the safe green room and love him forever...but that was a child's wish. Not even Jimmy's love could stop him now.

■ ■ ■

Blake sat in the car in front of Betty's apartment on Ivar again. She clenched the wheel and refused to look over at Betty sitting in the passenger seat smelling so good it hurt. It was a warm blacked-out night just like their first one together, but that was where the similarity ended.

Betty had wanted to meet for the first time in nearly a week. Blake had been avoiding the *Terror Over Tokyo* set, throwing herself into the next script with mindless intensity. It was a dull comedy about a girl from the wrong side of the tracks who gets mistaken for a society dame and hijinks ensue. Blake couldn't help seeing Jean

Jordan as the plucky lead. She had worked late every night in a kind of trance until Betty phoned and asked to meet her here.

"Blake," said Betty.

"Yeah."

"Richard and I, well…" She toyed with the hem of her dress. A classy, expensive dress, something chic and Parisian with cut-glass beads around the neckline. She always wore such things now. Blake wondered what had become of that navy rayon dress, the one with the daisies Betty had worn for her screen test. It hurt to think that it had really been just another costume.

Another long, uncomfortable silence and Blake kept on gripping the wheel, this time to keep from slapping Betty's pretty face.

"He's asked me to marry him," Betty said at last. Even though Blake had known it was coming, the words still felt like a slug in the guts.

"Congratulations," Blake said, managing to make it sound like the vilest insult.

"Blake, please." Betty tried to take Blake's hand. There was a huge diamond ring on her perfectly manicured finger. How had Blake missed it before? She hadn't wanted to see it, that was how. "Blake, listen to me. I'm sorry about this, but I can't spend the rest of my life sneaking around to be with you. I need a man who's proud to be seen with me, a man who's not afraid to kiss my hand in front of reporters."

That stung, but in her heart Blake knew it was all bullshit and had been since day one. How much did Betty know? How much had she *ever* known? Blake suddenly felt sure Betty had known everything all along, had known Blake Blackline was really Nan Blake, had played her like a hooked trout anyway. The thought sickened Blake to her core, but she couldn't shake it. "Get out of my car," she said.

"I'm sorry it had to end this way."

Could the girl never stop mouthing cliches? "Get out," Blake said again, and pounded her fist against her thigh. "Go home, Jean."

A pretty, hurt look flashed across Betty's face, complete with a faint sparkle of tears. Not a *spill* of tears—that might ruin her makeup—but a perfect little shimmer. Blake couldn't stand to look at her. All she saw was acting.

Betty pulled the Merc's door open and climbed out, slamming it behind her. "Best of luck with your career!" Blake shouted at the retreating girl as she punched the gas and sped away.

Blake hadn't cried since the night she had lost her first real love, but she was crying now, hot tears of anger and shame as she slunk through the back door of Zola's mansion, up the servant's stairs and into her own familiar room. She smelled the smoke of Zola's cigarette before she spoke.

"Blake," said Zola. "Have a drink."

The older woman offered a snifter of brandy. Blake took it, trying not to childishly snuffle up the tearsnot that was beginning to slide down her upper lip. She drank the whole glass down in one shot, throat burning.

"Zola, I..."

"Shhhhhhh." Zola sat on the edge of Blake's bed and opened her arms. The tears returned as Blake stumbled forward and knelt before Zola, burying her head in Zola's lap. Thick, smoky perfume enveloped Blake, comforting in its poignant familiarity.

"Do you know why you have a broken heart right now?" Zola asked, caressing Blake's disheveled hair.

Blake looked up at Zola. She was still so beautiful, her movie-star perfection softened but not destroyed by age. Her dark eyes wrinkled at the corners, but they were wise and bright with understanding. Blake felt a kind of desperate love for her, a love underscored by guilt for having betrayed the one woman who really loved her.

"Your heart is broken because you were trying to be something that you are not," Zola said. "You think I do not know the thrill of masquerade? You think I did not walk the streets of Paris with my first lover, both of us dressed in perfect masculine style, seducing all the plump country girls we could get our hands on? Oh yes, I know the power when someone says *Yes sir, right away, sir.*" Zola took a long drag on her cigarette. "But that is false power. And the love that sort of girl gives you? False love."

Blake rested her cheek against Zola's tear-damp thigh, nodding silently.

"Your Jean Jordan will always be looking to the next step up. Even if you were a man, she still would have left you. She was using you from the beginning. Perhaps she knew what you really were, perhaps not. It wouldn't have mattered to her. She only loved what you could do for her, for her career and for her body. She never loved Nan Blake, not like I do, my handsome girl."

"I'm so sorry, Zola. I'll go if you want."

"Where would you go, darling?" Zola took Blake's face in her hands and tipped it up to hers. "Let the outside world keep its Jean Jordans. You belong here, just as I do."

Zola stood and took Blake's hand, pulling her to her feet and standing her before the large mirror on the far wall. Smiling, she undid the buttons on Blake's jacket, loosened her tie and opened her shirt and trousers. Standing in a pile of discarded men's clothing, Blake allowed Zola to unwind her binder. Released, her breasts tingled in the night air, nipples hardening as the sweat cooled on her skin. Zola teased a nipple with her long sculpted nails as she pulled down the shorts and removed the harness beneath. Now Blake stood naked before the mirror.

"Look at yourself," Zola said, caressing Blake's ribs where the cloth of her binder had left deep pink wrinkles. "You are so handsome, so perfect. Your beautiful shoulders, your strong thighs, your luscious little breasts. You are not a man, you are not a woman. You are just perfect."

Zola put her mouth on Blake's nipple, fingers questing between Blake's legs. Blake knew Zola was right, had been right all along. "I love you so much," she said, voice rough with emotion. "I'll never leave you again, I swear. I'm yours forever if you'll have me."

Zola laughed and pulled Blake onto the bed. "Forget the promises," she said. "I am not so young any more, and forever is not that long. Better to stop talking and start loving."

Blake laughed too, shakily, and did as Zola asked.

■ ■ ■

Sitting in his empty room, the staticky old radio underlaid by the sound of mah-jongg tiles, Jimmy was racked with guilt and anxiety over Victor. He knew something terrible was going on inside the boy's head, but felt powerless to help him. His story of abuse and torture had been hard to listen to, filling Jimmy with impotent rage and a fierce empathetic pity. Why did some people have such an urge to hurt the beautiful? Were they simply envious, or were they somehow trying to capture that beauty for themselves, to subjugate it and cage it up like a trained cricket?

All through the story, Jimmy had been unable to shake the feeling that Victor was trying to tell him something more. Hitchhiking back the long miles from Malibu, Jimmy had gone over the disjointed conversation, searching for some hidden key or subtle meaning that would help him understand. He was afraid Victor planned to commit suicide, but had no idea where to find him or how to change his mind. Today was the day, four years to the day from the Victor's first attempt at oblivion. All night Jimmy had driven himself mad, worrying at the conversation like a Chinese puzzle box.

The walls of his room were suffocatingly close. He needed to walk. He pulled on his jacket, grabbed his hat, and went out into the hot afternoon streets of New Chinatown.

He saw nothing but Victor's battered face as he walked down Broadway, smelling the salt breath of the ocean instead of the sickly-sweet aroma of bland impotent food from the gaudy tourist restaurants. He replayed the conversation endlessly, searching for a way in. When the answer came, it was so simple that Jimmy could hardly believe he hadn't realized it sooner. As he passed a newsstand, a single *Photoplay* cover snapped into focus. Jean Jordan and Richard Noble, their beautiful blonde heads tipped back, laughing open-mouthed in a rain of rice. *Wedded Bliss for Topline Costars!* declared the headline.

Jimmy picked up the magazine and flipped it open to the article. There was a lot of ridiculous detail about Jean's dress and hair, about the flowers and the bridesmaids and every other meaningless excess, but only one sentence really leapt out at Jimmy.

The happy couple will be honeymooning by the sea at Noble's cozy Malibu hideaway…

Malibu hideaway?

"I'm going to fix everything," Victor had said, looking back up at the little blue house. "I'm going to end it." Jimmy had hailed a cab and told the driver to take him to Topline before he even knew what he was going to do.

■ ■ ■

Victor stood before the collection of Japanese swords that had always seemed to whisper to him. His little house on Mulholland was very quiet. There were no whispers now, no jeers, just a faint sound of a car passing by somewhere far away.

One pair of flashy swords sat together on a fancy gilded rack. They dripped with jewels and red silk tassels, much bigger than he remembered, impossibly long and wicked. As he reached up to touch the smaller of the two, he saw the old man standing by a lacquered screen in the corner. The old man shook his head a little, and Victor pulled his hand away, confused. Sneaky doubt began to sabotage him from deep within. What was he doing wrong? Wasn't this what his grandfather wanted?

The old man's eyes flicked away, and Victor followed his gaze to a different, plainer sword the size of a large kitchen knife. It was not very clean. The handle and scabbard were wrapped with black thread in a sort of diamond pattern, the thread very old and worn, dull with age and beginning to unravel. He looked back at his grandfather and saw the old man nod. When Victor took down the smaller blade, he knew it was the right one. When he turned back, the old man was gone.

■ ■ ■

He couldn't remember getting in his car and driving out to Malibu, but somehow here he was in front of Noble's house. He felt good. Focused. The fire in his belly had gone cold in expectation of the blade's cold penetration. It was the right thing to do. It was perfect. To kill himself in front of Noble would be his way of making all the wrong things in his worthless life finally and unquestionably right. His grandfather had killed himself to restore his lost honor. Victor didn't think he had any honor to restore, but he felt sure that by doing Hairy Carrie in front of the enemy who had defiled him, he might gain honor after death. He might make the Japanese ancestors he had denied for so long feel proud, rather than ashamed of him. All the hateful voices and the hot clutching hands of the past were gone, replaced with a pure, clear resolve. He knocked on the door.

When the blonde girl answered, Victor stood frozen, speechless. It had never occurred to him that she might be here. Her blue eyes were hazy; her breath burned with the scent of liquor. Her pretty face creased in annoyance. "What the hell are you doing here?"

Anger surged inside Victor. She was going to ruin everything. This pretty, perfect bitch with her soft body and white skin had been ruining things from the beginning, and now when Victor needed Noble more than ever, here she was sneering at Victor and standing in the way of his last chance to make things right. When she turned to call Noble, Victor leapt at her and knocked her to the floor, pulling the Japanese blade from its scabbard. The girl screamed like an air raid siren into Victor's face. The blade skidded across the bone in her arm and slipped out, its tip raking across Victor's cheek. He yelled and raised a hand to his face as she kicked out and staggered away, into the dim bedroom, screaming for Noble.

There was a fire, a cheerful romantic fire in the fireplace. Victor could feel its heat throbbing in his cut cheek. He shook his head and went after the girl. She was sobbing and shaking a naked and insensate Noble by the shoulders. Noble made cranky, sleep-laden sounds, then suddenly shoved her hard enough to make her stagger back, tripping and bouncing her head against the wall.

"I said shut up, you crazy bitch," he said as he rolled over and buried his head in the pillows. Victor quietly made the girl do as Noble said. When she was finally quiet, he crawled up onto the bed.

"Richard," he said softly, stroking Noble's chest with bloody fingers.

Noble made more incoherent sounds and brushed at Victor's fingers.

"Richard," Victor said again, more firmly. "Wake up, Richard, I have to show you something."

Noble rolled onto his side and made a wet sound with his mouth, but he did not wake up. A desperate frustration started to build inside Victor. This was not how it was supposed to be. Nothing ever worked as it should for Victor. What had made him think he could be strong enough to do Hairy Carrie? He couldn't even drown himself like a girl. He was a pathetic embarrassment to everyone. The fire started inside him again, filling him with an uncontrollable fury. *"Wake up!"* he shouted into Noble's face, pressing the blade to Noble's unshaven throat. "Wake up or I'll kill you!"

At last Noble's bloodshot eyes rolled open and slowly, blearily registered Victor's presence. He lurched up towards Victor and the blade bit deeply into his neck.

Victor pulled back and dropped the sword, horrified. He pressed desperate, ineffectual fingers to Noble's throat as thin hot blood sprayed from the wound, terrifying in its velocity and power. This was all wrong. Noble was dying and Victor was still alive, still uselessly alive. He had failed again. He heard a howling animal sound of sorrow and anguish and then he was tumbling down the well again, so deep he could no longer make out what was happening on the tiny thumbnail-sized screen above him. There was blood and cutting but it was all mixed up and out of context. Then the cold mud at the bottom of the well started to close over his face, sealing his eyes and ears, blotting out everything.

■ ■ ■

The writer looked shocked to see Jimmy, her eyes full of suspicious questions, but Jimmy told her there was no time for explanations. Jean Jordan was in trouble, he said. They needed to get out to Noble's place in Malibu as quickly as possible. He knew she would help even before she nodded and grabbed her satchel off the back of her chair.

The drive seemed to take eons, neither of them speaking. Jimmy kept his teeth clenched, trying to convince himself that he was crazy, that he was reading too much into all this, that he should mind his own business as he had done for years. He could not make himself believe any of it. When Blake pulled into Noble's driveway, Jimmy jumped out and ran to the door calling Victor's name. Blake was saying something, but he didn't listen. He couldn't. He knocked on the door and it swung open easily, revealing Victor standing naked and bloody in the firelight. They were too late.

"What happened, Victor?" Jimmy asked, although he didn't really need to. He had seen this look before, this same blankness on Lin Bai's face the night he had murdered Master Lau. He was not at all surprised when Victor took a step forward, revealing a short Japanese sword in his sticky fist.

Behind him, the writer ran into the darkened bedroom, but Jimmy kept his eyes on Victor. His heart was fluttering in his chest, the same sick hopeless sense of loss he had felt in Hong Kong when he realized Lin Bai was truly dying. The light went on in the bedroom and Jimmy heard soft retching. If Victor registered the sounds or the light, he did not react. He remained still as a mannequin, dead eyes focused somewhere a few inches to the left of Jimmy's shoulder.

"Victor, come here," Jimmy finally said. His blood sang with adrenaline. "Let me see what's happened."

Victor did not move his eyes, but took a single, shuffling half-step closer to Jimmy. Jimmy saw that a long gash parted the smooth skin of his face.

"I'm sorry," Victor said, his voice a hollow whisper. Now, for the first time, Jimmy felt real fear. Fear that the boy who had kissed Jimmy's tears away and held him in his slender arms was really gone, that he was talking to a murderous walking corpse.

"It's all right now, Victor," Jimmy said, struggling to keep his voice steady, knowing his life and Blake's depended on it.

"I'm sorry, Daddy." Victor's unseeing eyes rolled up to meet Jimmy's, but held no recognition. He began to shift his grip on the sword, reversing it until it pointed inward. Jimmy almost cried out, wanting to throw himself at Victor and wrestle the blade away from him, but he was paralyzed. He could not move or even breathe as the boy sank the sword into his own naked belly. Jimmy remembered kissing that belly, the musky taste of his skin so vivid it was appalling as he watched the boy slice himself open.

Then, for a scant fraction of a second, Victor was back, looking up at Jimmy and really seeing him. His brow creased and he looked into Jimmy's eyes as if it were all some mistake, and couldn't they just laugh it off and pretend it had never happened? Then the blade clattered to the floor and glossy dark innards started to push out through the fatty yellow slice Victor had made in his belly. Victor fell to his knees, then nearly collapsed, but Jimmy caught him and held him. He hated Victor now, hated him for making Jimmy feel again, only to make him feel this. He hated Lin Bai too, for leaving him to live his life alone in this bright, sunny land where everyone wore a mask. Most of all he hated himself for failing, for being unable to save anyone he loved. As the boy's life drained away, Jimmy choked back tears, smelling bile and shit and blood, so much blood and then it all vanished in a flash of blinding light and Jimmy was on the Bund in Shanghai, holding a dying Japanese soldier in his arms and that cloud was in the sky again, that horrible giant cloud like a demon's fist and it wasn't Shanghai, it was some other city, a quiet port city that had been charred down to the bone by some hellish new weapon. People burned beyond race or gender staggered through rubble burning skillet-hot under that terrifying, unnatural thing in the sky. Jimmy's skin crisped like a duck's, his eyes boiled, but somehow he could still see that devil cloud leering over them all. It hit him then that this was not the hazy, distant future. This was real. This was now. As he ran, hair frying and skin crackling, he felt sure that the fire of Victor's madness had somehow been unleashed on the world. And now that it was loose, nothing would ever be the same.

As quickly as the vision came it was gone again, leaving Jimmy holding yet another lifeless young lover in his arms.

"*Why must everyone I love die?*" Jimmy whispered, reverting in his anguish to his native tongue. "*Why must I be left alone to live on in this world of death and burning?*"

"What the hell happened here?" the writer said from somewhere nearby. Jimmy had forgotten that she was there. He let Victor's body drop and stepped to the picture window, pushing the heavy drape aside. Outside, the pale silver mist pressed in, nearly obscuring the deep green ocean. Somewhere beyond that ocean, the world burned. Jimmy closed his eyes.

"Something unspeakable," he said.

Blake wiped her mouth compulsively, seemingly unable to look away from Victor's corpse.

"We better call the cops," she said.

Jimmy looked back at her, at Victor, and shook his head. "No cops," he said. "Not yet."

"What do you mean, no cops? Are you nuts?"

"Please," Jimmy said. "Please, listen."

The writer narrowed her eyes and cocked her head, nodding for him to go on.

"You don't want this scandal to get out, do you? Jean Jordan may be dead, but let her die a pretty young star whose career was cut tragically short. Not a failed cover story for a queer actor murdered by his crazy lover."

"What are you suggesting?"

Jimmy told her.

■ ■ ■

As they drenched the cute little beachhouse in kerosene, Jimmy paused, wrinkling his nose at the biting stench. Blake figured the tears might just be from fumes, but there seemed to be something deeper in his face. She wanted to say something to him but couldn't think of what. Instead she took the match he offered and lit it, setting fire to the remains of the girl who had made her feel so hurt and angry and so wonderful. She searched inside herself for some way to say good-bye to Betty, but there was nothing except a dull needle of pain and a swiftly fading image of a beautiful girl in a white bathing suit.

They drove down to the end of the road and watched the fire in silence from a high bluff. At first the flames were tentative, pale and struggling against the stiff ocean breeze, looking as if they just weren't up to the task set before them.

"What if it doesn't burn hot enough?" Jimmy asked, watching the house framed in the movie screen of the Merc 8's windshield. "What if the police are still able to...somehow..."

"Look." Blake gestured with her chin to where the long tongues of flame were tasting the dry clumps of beachgrass around the feet of a long metal tank beside the back door. "That's propane. My uncle had a fire on his ranch when I was a kid. Propane tank went up. You couldn't tell the horses from the chickens."

Jimmy nodded, frowning slightly.

Blake turned the ignition and the roar of the engine was swallowed by the deep, throaty growl of an explosion. The windows rattled and the air inside the car seemed to press in on her eyes and ears as the whole back of the cottage blossomed with extravagant black-and-orange flame. Jimmy turned away from the sight as if it hurt to watch.

They drove Victor's quilt-wrapped body out to a deserted stretch of beach out near Point Dume. Jimmy didn't need to tell Blake to hang back; she knew he needed to say his own good-byes.

She watched him wade into the water with Victor's body in his arms. For the first time in more years than she could remember, she was wearing a dress, a summery thing printed with blue and yellow tulips. She had found it in a closet, and it still smelled painfully like Betty. None of Noble's clothes had come anywhere near fitting her. Even Jimmy, who was several inches taller and broader than Blake, looked like a little boy playing dressup in the shirt and trousers he had taken from Noble's suitcase. Their own clothes were in a bloodstained bag in the Merc's backseat, waiting to be burned later.

Jimmy was nearly lost in the mist as he let the undertow take his dead lover away. The waves whispered on the sand as if asking what had taken Victor so long to come home to them. Victor had once wanted to die in the cold embrace of the ocean. It seemed only fitting that he should go back there now.

"Just remember," Blake said as she drove back toward Hollywood. "You came to talk to me about some background info for a novel I'm writing, a book about a private dick who solves crimes in Chinatown. You offered to buy me a drink and I took you up to Zola's for a freebie instead. She'll back us up, no questions asked."

"Fine," said Jimmy. He seemed so tired, diminished somehow, and his eyes were lost in shadow. They drove for a few more miles in silence. Then Jimmy spoke up. "Blake?"

"What?"

"Thank you."

Blake nodded. She could say nothing that would express how she felt, but she knew Jimmy understood. He was probably the only person on earth who could understand.

Pulling up in front of Zola's house, Blake saw the older woman standing by the koi pond, beneath the fierce stone Amazon with her notched arrow eternally ready to strike down any foe. Zola had had the statue custom-made, and when it arrived with two breasts, she'd sent it back to have one chiseled off. "Wonderful news, darling!" she called. "You remember Lester, don't you? That silly little blonde thing who wants to be Veronica Lake when he grows up?"

Zola noticed Jimmy now, and blinked at him for a moment as if trying to place him. "Anyway, Lester has been seeing this military man—a very prominent one, I might add—and this fellow says we have a special new bomb that's going to win the war for sure. They dropped one on Japan today, and they plan to drop another one soon. Those terrible Japanese will have no choice but to surrender. Isn't it wonderful?"

Blake nodded. Jimmy did too, but he looked as if he were about to faint.

Zola turned back to Blake and seemed to see her for the first time since they had arrived. "My God, what are you wearing?"

"It's a long story."

"Well, never mind then. Come inside and have some champagne to celebrate our imminent victory. Nat and Marta and Patsy are coming over tonight with Davis and his boy, and Theo as well. He's single now, you know."

Zola nudged Jimmy, who tried on a smile that looked painfully thin and sad. They allowed themselves to be dragged inside.

Blake soon excused herself to change out of Betty's dress. She showered and put on her normal trousers and shirtsleeves, but couldn't bring herself to face the arriving guests. Instead she lay on the bed, and had slipped into a half-doze by the time Jimmy appeared in the doorway. She motioned him in gratefully. It seemed the quiet Chinaman was the only person she could stand to be around just now.

"Do you think they've found the bodies yet?" Blake asked, looking up at the ceiling.

"What bodies?"

Blake nodded and closed her eyes.

"Are you really going to write about a Chinese detective?" Jimmy asked.

Blake turned to look at him, but couldn't read the expression on his face.

"Well, he was gonna be a white guy who just investigates in Chinatown," said Blake, amazed that she was capable of thinking about the next book, or about anything beyond the events of this day. "But I guess he could be Chinese. Be tougher to sell, but could be interesting. Maybe someday you could play him."

She suddenly found herself thinking of the conversation she and Betty had had about Cherry Rocher on the day they met. She wondered how she was going to live the rest of her life with all these little connections like mousetraps, waiting to drag her thoughts back to Betty, back to this day.

"Funny," she said. "In books and scripts, crime doesn't pay and criminals always get caught. You never read about the guy twenty-five years after the crime, just living every day knowing what happened and going on anyway. We didn't commit a crime, but I still don't know how to move on because…well, because I've never written it like that. It's like I've lived beyond the end of the book and I don't know where to go from here."

"Listen to me, Blake." Jimmy came forward and sat on the edge of the bed. "You go on living because the sun keeps on coming up no matter how you feel. No other reason. The days keep passing and before you know it it's been a year or two or ten."

He sounded as if he spoke from experience, and Blake nodded again. A particularly raucous cheer floated up the stairs.

"Think you can stand to go back down?" Jimmy asked.

"Yeah, I think so," said Blake. If she was going to go on with her life, she supposed she might as well get started.

■ ■ ■

PART THREE

■ ■ ■

Los Angeles, Present Day

■ ■ ■

J

ake Ryan sat cross-legged in the center of his empty living room staring into the glass pitcher from his blender. Only a few gritty swigs of MuscleMax MegaProtein were left in the bottom. He made himself gulp the rest of the shake, shuddering at the weird cake-mix texture and strident artificial banana flavor. He had no furniture yet, so he set the pitcher on the floor beside him and wiped his mouth on the back of his hand.

This new place was so quiet it was creepy. In North Carolina he had lived in a big country house with his mother, grandmother, three little sisters, four dogs, six cats, and an African Gray parrot. He had never experienced long stretches of silence. Now the place he called home was as quiet as…he wouldn't think graveyard, that would be bad luck for sure, but as quiet as a hospital.

The place was in Hollywood (*right near that sign!* he had written home the day he signed the lease), a once-grand old 1920s estate that had been divvied up into flats. His apartment was on the top floor with big breezy rooms and windows that looked down into the city. There was no pool—he'd thought every place in Hollywood was required to have one by some movie-star zoning law—but there was a pretty courtyard with a koi pond and a fountain shaped like a naked woman with a bow and arrow. One of the statue's breasts had been chiseled away—by vandals, Jake thought at first, but upon

161

closer examination he saw that the scar had been professionally smoothed over. More important than goldfish or statuary was the big shady back yard with plenty of space for Jake to do his morning t'ai chi. There was even an orange tree so he could have fresh juice all the time. There was an avocado tree, too, but he had to go easy on those. With principal starting on *CyberCommandos* in three days, he couldn't afford the fat content.

Everything in Jake's young life seemed to be going unbelievably well just now. He had been "discovered" at a martial arts tournament in Pasadena last spring. Two weeks after that, he was on a plane to Hong Kong with a three-film contract in his pocket. Now he'd made it to Hollywood, and while he was not the lead in *Commandos*—just the best buddy whose noble sacrifice motivates the hero to go out and kick alien ass—he still had *Extreme Impact, Future Force,* and *American Dragon 3* under his belt. Even better, he was on the short list for a spot in an upcoming Brett Davis film that supposedly had Chase Black attached.

But sitting here in this echoey apartment by himself on a Friday night, he felt lonely and a little pathetic. Though he'd been here three weeks, he had yet to make a single real friend. He'd had plenty of offers from industry predators both male and female, all of whom swore they would make him the next big thing while he just put on his big sweet hick smile and acted like he didn't know what they meant. He'd been invited to parties, but the few he went to seemed either incomprehensibly shallow or like being trapped in the censored scenes from a bad where-are-they-now show.

The guys at the gym were the friendliest people he had met. Some even made it plain that they'd love to have him over for a private workout. In a couple of cases, Jake wouldn't have minded taking them up on it. He was too scared, though. Not of the sex itself, but that someone would find out and his one chance at stardom would go down in a volley of tabloid nightmare headlines. Even big mainstream stars like **** ***** and ** ***** couldn't afford to be openly gay; what hope was there for an action-flick nobody like Jake Ryan?

Jake had always been pathologically discreet about his sexual orientation. All the girls he'd dated back home marveled over what a gentleman he was. Of course, it was easy to be a gentleman when kissing these southern peaches and holding their soft bodies close to his was about as interesting as petting a friendly dog.

On the other hand, the locker room at school, the showers at the dojo, these were places where being a gentleman was pure torture. He would stand with cold water sluicing over him, willing himself not to look, to keep his eyes on the mildewed grout between the tiles, to ignore the wet muscular flesh all around him. He had known since childhood, but he hid it deep inside himself, focusing instead on mastering the martial arts, spending every waking hour in near-compulsive training, pushing his body to be stronger, faster, more graceful, honing his mind to focus above and beyond the animal needs of the flesh. Only once had he allowed himself to give in, and that had been years ago.

The boy's name was Ronald Gary. He was a skinny kid with pale blonde hair and girlish hands. Everyone in school knew he was a fag. He was into theater and sewing. Other boys talked about how Ronald would give any guy a blow job out behind the equipment shed. It wasn't really gay to let him do this, they said, because a mouth's a mouth and it wasn't as if they touched him back.

Fifteen-year-old Jake could not stop thinking about Ronald. It must have shown somehow, because late one Indian-summer afternoon, Ronald approached Jake on the track field. Jake meant to tell him to fuck off, but instead found himself behind the shed with his zipper open and Ronald kneeling in front of him in the dirt doing the most amazing thing Jake had ever experienced. He couldn't take his eyes off the sight of Ronald's mouth sliding up and down the length of his cock, and beyond that, the blurred movement of Ronald's hand inside the fly of his own expensive designer pants. The idea that Ronald was hard too, that he loved sucking Jake's dick so much that he had to jack off, put Jake over the edge. He came like a firehose, twisting his fingers in Ronald's thin blonde hair. It should have ended there. Jake should have zipped up and walked away like every other guy in the school, but looking down into Ronald's flushed face, into his green eyes, Jake lost all power of rational thought. Before he knew what he was doing, he hauled Ronald to his feet, pressed him up against the shed's splintery wall, and kissed him. Not the gentle kisses he dutifully showered on his various girlfriends; he crushed his lips against Ronald's, artlessly thrusting his tongue deep inside the semen-slick mouth that had brought him such unbelievable pleasure. The boy made a soft, delicious noise and kissed him back, matching Jake's hunger, grinding his hips against Jake's thigh. Jake tore at Ronald's clothes, desperate to get at the smooth flesh beneath. Ronald's cock was larger than Jake had expected, rock-hard in his hand. When he squeezed it tight, Ronald gasped and pumped his hips, shuddering as he came all over Jake's belly. The boy went limp in Jake's arms and Jake held him, smelling his shampoo and his sweat and the fabric softener in his clothes.

They couldn't seem to get enough of each other, kissing and touching and not even seeing the sun going down as Jake took Ronald's cock into his mouth, totally beyond caring about anything but the feel of warm silken muscle sliding in and out of his mouth, the sweet clean smell, the soft sounds of pleasure when Ronald came again, filling Jake's mouth with a sharp taste that was both like and utterly unlike his own.

They met nearly every day for two weeks. Jake could think of nothing else. He would sit on his bed at night with his arms wrapped around himself and feel a kind of madness chasing its tail inside him. He was terrified of getting caught, yet he seemed incapable of stopping. It was as if all the fantasies that haunted him had suddenly grown teeth. Before, they'd been abstract and easy to ignore—everyone had a poster of Bruce Lee on their wall, and so what if he jacked off to his? He went on dates with cheerleaders and talked trash with all the other guys about this one's tits and that one's ass. He could play the part so flawlessly that no one was the wiser. Now this pale geeky boy had unleashed a furious desire that Jake could no longer control. Ronald's touch, his mouth, his cock, they were real. Once the monster inside Jake had tasted living flesh, it grew more and more reluctant to get back into its cage.

But one afternoon in the back of the school stage, lying together on a dusty pile of old theater curtains, drenched in sweat, still kissing even though their faces were chapped raw from rubbing together, Ronald pulled back and looked up into Jake's eyes.

Triads

"I love you," Ronald told him, and cold terror gripped Jake's heart, cutting off his breath and making his sweat turn to ice. He suddenly saw himself crumpled and half-naked with his arms around this skinny boy everybody knew was a fag. He pushed Ronald away like a bloody murder weapon, pulled his clothes together, and ran, ignoring Ronald's pleas to tell him what he'd done wrong.

Ronald kept trying to talk to him the next day, but Jake froze him out. Out on the track field, Ronald appeared again saying he just wanted to talk. He put his hand on Jake's wrist.

"You don't have to love me back," he whispered. "Just let me…"

"Get off me, faggot!" Jake yelled, shoving Ronald much harder than he'd meant to. Other boys sniggered as Ronald staggered and tripped, sprawling on his ass in the dirt. Ronald started to cry then, but what really made Jake feel worthless was the bleak acceptance he saw in those big green eyes as he turned away.

Jake won his first tournament that fall, and his training schedule became so intense that he no longer needed excuses to avoid Ronald. A few months later Ronald's family moved away and Jake never saw him again. That was the last time he had allowed anything like that to happen. Sure, he'd had a boy or two in Hong Kong, but those were discreet one-night stands that never affected him above the belt: pretty Asian boys with slim hips and shiny black hair and no expectations.

And now he was in Hollywood, in his very own apartment, feeling blue and vaguely horny, not that there was any chance of doing anything about that. It just wasn't worth the risk. Better to head down to the gym and put in some extra back and chest work, drown his desire in physical exertion. His watch said ten-thirty, so he still had plenty of time to make it down there before they closed. This late at night, there would be a shorter wait on the most popular machines. Jake grabbed his *Impact* crew jacket from the hall closet and headed out.

As he passed the koi pond, he paused a moment to watch the glinting, spiraling fish beneath the water's murky surface. In a shadowed archway across the courtyard he thought saw someone, a man in a dark suit standing still and silent with his hands stuffed into his pockets. When he looked again, no one was there.

■ ■ ■

Jake had finished with his morning workout and was waiting anxiously by the koi when the *CyberCommandos* driver showed up forty-five minutes late. The man, who looked like a mummified surfer, only shrugged hazily in response to Jake's nervous questioning. Jake wasn't familiar enough with the endless sprawling geography of Los Angeles to estimate the length of the trip. His belly churned with anxiety about being late. The wide streets were choked with traffic, but the sidewalks were almost empty; no one walked here. Only the dark-skinned people waiting for buses gave any life to the scene. Jake found himself folding and refolding his call sheet into lopsided origami as the driver lurched through red lights and wandered in and out of lanes. Amazingly, they still made it out to the set by seven-fifteen.

A bored woman in a headset ignored Jake's apology, gave him a quick once-over like a chef examining a crate of tomatoes, checked his name off on some list, and pointed him towards a huge feature-less building the size of a zeppelin hangar. Inside, the building was church-quiet and full of echoes. Jake followed a skinny corridor formed by the back of some set and the exterior wall, stepping over nests of wires and crumpled bits of black foil until he found a human—a grip, he figured—wearing a tool belt, a backward baseball hat, and a Walkman. Jake had to poke him to get a response, but the guy eventually managed to communicate that he should go down to the end of the corridor and through a red door to makeup.

There was no red door at the end of the hallway, only a locked gray door and a white door that opened to reveal a bathroom reeking of pot smoke. Jake turned back and slipped through a gap in the set to find himself on the deserted bridge of a spaceship. Feeling increasingly stupid, he retraced his steps to the place where he had spoken to the grip, only to find him gone. He was already late, and he would be even later if he didn't find someone with a clue right away. In Hong Kong he'd had a translator who never left his side and a rotating entourage of facilitators making sure he got where he needed to be. Here in Hollywood, in his own country, he felt like a

Triads

geeky transfer student late for his first day of third grade. He was about to go back outside to look for the woman in the headset when he spotted a chipped, dented door at the other end of the corridor. He supposed some people might call it red, though it really looked more purplish to him.

The room on the other side of the sort-of-red door wasn't much more than a skinny closet with a row of chairs set before a long mirror. At the far end of the room, a pale dumpy girl sat with her head tipped back and her sock feet up on the counter, snoring softly. Jake cleared his throat, feeling embarrassed and unsure.

"Um…excuse me?"

The door banged open and in came a slender young Asian man with spiky maroon hair tipped in black. Something dark was smeared around his eyes, as if he'd worn makeup last night and hadn't bothered to wash it off. Perhaps that was the case, though Jake had never met a man who wore makeup before. The young man held two cups of coffee, and his mouth was twisted into a sardonic smirk that did not quite disguise the girlish beauty of his lips. "Marcy," he snapped, "get up off your lazy snatch and make with the Aquanet. Talent is in the house!"

As he stretched across to set the coffee before the blinking hairstylist, his purple Glamourpuss t-shirt slid up over his smooth belly. Jake looked down at his own feet in their black cloth shoes.

"What's your name, honey?" asked the young man, looking up into Jake's face. It felt so nice to have somebody actually notice him that he blushed.

"Jake," he said softly. "Jake Ryan."

"Well, ain't you sweet?" replied the young man in a dead-on imitation of Jake's soft drawl. His gaze was teasing, but there was no meanness in it. "Welcome to the Miki and Marcy Show. I'm Miki Lau and I'll be your waitress this morning. What'll it be?"

"What?" Jake was completely flustered now.

"I mean, what's your poison?" Miki took a sip of his coffee. "Java? Tea?"

Jake let his breath out. "Is there any fresh juice? Orange or maybe carrot?"

167

"Honey, on this set it's all about stale chips and supermarket cola." Miki rolled his eyes extravagantly. "You'd be lucky to get an Orange Crush."

"Well, water then, I guess."

"I'll get you some from my private stash."

Miki winked and slipped away. It took several minutes for Jake's heartbeat to return to normal. Marcy the zombie hairdresser had Jake's short cropped hair done in less than a minute and was already asleep again by the time Miki returned with two sweating bottles of Fuji water.

"Thanks," Jake said, cracking the top and taking a deep swig.

"OK, so, Jake Ryan..." Miki flipped though a battered notebook. "Jake Ryan, right. Sergeant Mark Hunter. The buddy. Looks like a lot of rhubarb this morning. Establishing shit, all beauty. Action in the afternoon."

"Where is everybody, Miki?" Jake asked, setting his water on the counter.

Miki pulled open a drawer in his enormous makeup case and rummaged around. "Still sleeping off last night, I'm sure," he said, dabbing at Jake's chin with a triangular sponge.

Having Miki leaning so close was intensely disconcerting. He smelled like chocolate and lipstick and his dark gaze kept snagging Jake's, playing with him, making some small joke and never looking away. Jake forced himself to look down at Miki's hands instead. There was picked-off glitter polish on his nails, and the crotch of his left thumb and forefinger was stained with different shades of red, purple, beige.

"Is it always like this?" Jake asked Miki's hands.

"On a Millbank shoot, you better believe it. Look up." Miki smoothed beige cream under Jake's eyes. "We're on Miller time."

A tiny woman pushed her way in through the not-exactly-red door. She was wan and colorless, nearly lost in a huge T-shirt and sweats.

"Morning, Tyler," said Miki. "You're looking radiant." The woman just gave Miki the finger and sat down beside the hibernating hairstylist.

"Chop chop, Marcy." Miki clapped his hands. "Miss Cane is in desperate need of your attention."

Marcy came to like a plugged-in machine and started picking out mathematically precise sections of the woman's blasted blonde hair and rolling them on curlers. "Is that Tyler Cane?" whispered Jake, disbelieving.

"Not yet," Miki said. "But give me an hour and she will be."

Jake turned away and laughed softly through his nose. Miki fished out a Polaroid camera and took a shot of Jake, leaving him blinking from the flash. "You're done, honey."

Jake looked at himself in the mirror. He didn't look made up, just...better. "Hey, thanks," he said, finishing off the rest of the water.

"Don't mention it," said Miki, flashing that wry smile that made Jake go all hot and shy again.

"Well," he said into his own lap. "Now what?"

"Wardrobe," Miki said. He glanced back at Marcy, hard at work over Tyler Cane's bowed blonde head. "C'mon, I'll show you."

Wardrobe was another reddish door farther down the maze of artificial hallways that wound between the sets. Inside the door was a tiny room packed with racks and racks of clothing inside labeled plastic bags. "Corrine is probably off shooting up or blowing some grips or bitching about how Millbank won't let her express her creativity by making everyone look like extras from a bad eighties *Road Warrior* knock-off, so wardrobe is gonna be pretty much self-serve on this set," Miki explained. He riffled through the hanging bags until he found one with Jake's name on it. It contained a black uniform like something a futuristic SWAT team member might wear. Also included were boots, a belt, and a weird gadget-heavy helmet.

"I just saw Mrs. Park over by craft services," Miki said. "If you need any alterations, she'll be the one to look for."

"Thanks a lot."

Miki smiled again, reminding Jake how close they were standing and how empty this part of the building was. He found himself looking down at that little slice of pale skin above the waistband of Miki's low-slung black jeans and forced himself to look away, feeling a thick flush of blood to his face and groin. He was very glad he was wearing the athletic supporter and rigid, heavy-duty cup he'd bought in Hong Kong the day after he took a knee to the tenders during a rooftop fight scene.

"Well," Jake said, just to say something.

"Well well," Miki said. "Guess I'd better start spackling Miss Cane back together. I'll leave you to meditate on the deep inner motivations of Sergeant Mark Hunter."

When Miki was gone, Jake dropped the bag of clothes and closed his eyes. He took three deep breaths, raising his palms to his sternum with each inhalation and pushing them down again on the exhalation. When he opened his eyes again, there was a dour-looking Korean lady in the doorway with a cloth tomato stuck full of pins tied around her wrist. She made a low wordless grunt and walked away.

■ ■ ■

Jake got home well after midnight. He was completely drained, emotionally and physically. Meeting Miki had been the high point of his day. After that it went downhill like a car with no brakes in a bad adventure serial. The director and the brainless hunk playing the lead disappeared every ten minutes and came back with runny noses. Tyler Cane spent the whole day complaining about the lighting and her hair and everyone else's performance. The has-been actor hired strictly for his name was so sauced by midafternoon that he threw up on one of the spaceship control panels, put his hand up the dumpy hairdresser's shirt while she was trying to nail down his toupee, knocked over two sets, and eventually had to be sent home to sleep it off. Worse still was the stunt coordinator, a beery old cowboy whose idea of a good fight scene was throwing wide comic-book punches and hitting people with chairs. Jake had known this was not a martial arts movie, but he'd expected fight scenes that might be believable to someone over the age of twelve. Grappling with out-of-shape rodeo clowns in bad rubber alien suits that gave off toxic chemical fumes so overwhelming Jake had a migraine after less than three minutes, the only thing that kept him from flying into a murderous rage was a glimpse of Miki standing just off-set. A black apron full of brushes and Polaroids was slung round his narrow hips, and his secret smile seemed meant just for Jake.

Between takes Miki would crouch over him, daubing fake blood on his temple and at the corner of his mouth, making some quiet, biting remark about one or another of his costars. These remarks never failed to make Jake laugh.

"You know you're too good for this direct-to-video write-off," Miki told him. "But you're a tough guy. You'll survive. Just do what I do. Close your eyes and visualize a check being deposited into your bank account." Miki patted his arm. "And be thankful they decided not to shoot in Hungary."

Then the cranky A.D. called for everyone to settle and Miki slipped away. Watching him go, Jake visualized a check, then visualized using some of the money to take Miki out to a really fancy restaurant. That made him visualize other stuff, so he sank his teeth into his lower lip and concentrated on not laughing out loud when he had to yell, "Die, alien slime!"

Shooting in Hong Kong had been physically grueling, so much so that there were mornings when he could barely get out of bed, but there was a sense of forward motion and teamwork. Jake had been exhausted when he got to the hotel at night, but it was a good physical exhaustion combined with the satisfaction of having canned some great fight scenes. Here it was like being trapped in one of those endless nightmares where you run and run and get nowhere. They were always waiting. Waiting for the director to come back from packing his nose or getting a blowjob from the star of his next film or talking on his cell phone. Waiting for FX guys to revive the third alien to pass out in less than an hour, peeling off his lumpy rubber head and splashing water on his red, rashy face. Waiting for Miki to trowel yet another layer of cover-up onto Tyler Cane's implant scars. The entire day was less physically strenuous than his normal workout, yet by the time he got home, Jake felt drained. He was barely able to walk straight as he headed past the koi pond and toward the stairway that led up to his apartment.

He was nearly there when he spotted the man in the suit, the one he thought he'd glimpsed the night before. The man was closer now, but still shadowed. Jake could see that he was Asian, roughly handsome with big hands and prominent ears that seemed larger because of his old-fashioned, slicked-back hairstyle. Maybe it was because Jake was so tired, maybe it was the shadows that dappled the man's pale face, but looking at him seemed inexplicably difficult, as if he were very far away or behind a pane of dirty glass.

"Hello?" Jake said, frowning a little.

The man looked at him with sharp black eyes that seemed full of secrets. There was something vaguely familiar about his face. He gestured with his chin for Jake to follow him, then turned and walked away.

Jake wanted nothing more than to go upstairs and curl up in his old Boy Scout sleeping bag. Instead he walked down the long hallway behind the stranger in the dark suit. Eventually they came to a rounded wooden door at the far end of the corridor. The man reached out a pale, soft-focus hand to push it open.

It did not seem strange to follow him in. They entered a modest studio apartment lit only by the pale yellow streetlight that filtered in through the sheer curtains over the single window. For a moment in the dimness, Jake lost sight of the other man. Long ticking seconds passed as he stood there feeling foolish, smelling tea and old books, someone else's private smell.

He was about to turn and go when suddenly the man was there, body and mouth pressed against his with a voracious hunger that caught Jake so off guard that he could do nothing but allow himself to be drawn down on a musty single bed, hands greedy under his clothing and a dreamy lust enveloping him, swallowing him.

It seemed impossible to sort out individual physical acts; there was just this sense of hot flesh against his and an aching sort of wet dream pleasure surging though him. Jake found himself thinking of Miki, of his wry mouth and pale belly and laughing eyes, of kissing him, fucking him. As he felt something warm and wet sliding over his engorged cock, he stopped trying to understand what was happening and instead closed his eyes and made love to Miki in the empty wardrobe room. When he came, it was Miki's name that lingered unspoken behind his lips.

Triads

He woke confused and stiff several hours later. The sun was just below the horizon, staining the eastern sky outside the window a deep, smoky violet. He was alone.

He fumbled around with the lamp on the bedside table, nearly knocking it over before figuring how to turn it on. He stumbled to the small bathroom, looking around while he pissed. Legions of orange pill bottles. Plastic boxes with compartments for each day of the week. Hemorrhoid cream. Chinese herbal preparations for arthritis and prostate health. Old guy stuff. He flushed the toilet and returned to the main room.

With the light on, he noticed the dark green walls were covered with framed photographs. Jake suddenly realized why his mysterious lover had looked familiar. He was clearly related to the man in the photos: Jimmy Lee, a Chinese character actor Jake had seen in a zillion bad action movies. He had played a hundred wise old senseis, a hundred saintly grandfathers whose senseless murders drove countless young heroes to dish out vigilante justice. Here on these walls was young black-and-white Jimmy looking uncannily like the man Jake had been with the night before. Jimmy in the forties and fifties posed with actors Jake recognized but couldn't name. Jimmy in color posed with actors from Jake's childhood Saturday matinees. Jimmy with Bruce Lee, Chuck Norris, Cynthia Rothrock. Jake couldn't help wondering where Jimmy was now.

He felt uncomfortable being alone in this stranger's apartment, but he was also terrified that one of the neighbors might have seen him come in with the man last night and would now see him leaving the next morning in the same clothes. He was working up the nerve to dash out and sneak back up to his own apartment when he noticed a small desk, empty except for a stack of silk-covered Chinese notebooks held together with a fat rubber band. Looking up at a faded snapshot of Jimmy with a very young redheaded boy, Jake ran a finger over the pale green silk cover of the top notebook. It was none of his business, but his lover from the night before had obviously deserted him and no one would ever know if he just took a quick peek.

Poppy Z. Brite & Christa Faust

Inside the book, the handwriting was thick and intense, gouging deeply into the soft rice paper. Jake opened to a random page and started reading.

It was less than a week before the sickness took over. There were 211 passengers when we left Hong Kong but by the time we arrived in Hawaii there were only 43 left. The stench was beyond description. I was terrified that my false papers and feminine masquerade would not hold up to scrutiny once I arrived in the U.S. but luck was with me as I made the acquaintance of a dying man named Fong Fu Sheng three days before our arrival. He was traveling to Hollywood, California to meet his mother's cousin, a man who could supposedly get handsome young men work in the cinema. Fong Fu Sheng was terrified of dying alone, and as the fever ravaged him, he was so grateful to have a sympathetic girl hold his hand that he did not look too closely. Watching the life ebb from his face, a face very much like my own, I found myself re-experiencing the agony of losing my beloved Lin Bai. But when his last breath passed through his lips, I did not hesitate to do what must be done. Although there was very little privacy, the sick and hopeless people around me did not notice when I became another dead man. Yet another identity shed like a snake's skin and a new one taken on like a freshly painted face. I stood on the deck with the salt wind on my new-shorn scalp and a dead man's clothes pulled tight around me against the chill, and I wondered if there was anything left of who I really was.

Jake looked up from the scrawl to notice with horror that it was already six-fifteen. Just enough time to run upstairs, down a protein shake, and change clothes before he had to race back down and meet the driver by the koi pond.

■ ■ ■

"Good morning, glory," Miki said as Jake slipped in, trying not to meet Miki's gaze.

After the bizarre experience last night, Jake was determined to be professional but cool towards Miki. He could not afford to let anyone get any ideas, least of all himself. "Morning," he said, gruffly, sitting down beside the slumbering Marcy.

As Marcy came to and ran a handful of gel through Jake's buzz cut, Miki leaned down under the counter and produced a

174

Triads

Tupperware bottle from a cooler. He poured a plastic cup full of thick orange juice and handed it to Jake. Jake felt like a heel as the luscious morning scent of fresh oranges hit him like a piece of home. "Gee, Miki," he stammered. "You didn't have to do that."

"It's no big thing, honey. My roommate makes a ton of the stuff every morning."

The orange juice turned to battery acid in Jake's mouth. *Roommate.* Jake knew what that meant. Boyfriend. Lover. Of course it made sense that someone as great as Miki would have a boyfriend. Jake had absolutely no right to be jealous, yet he was, so much so he could barely swallow.

While Miki did Jake's makeup, leaning in to lightly brush a cheekbone with the pad of his thumb, Jake silently drove himself crazy imagining the "roommate" waking up next to Miki every morning, squeezing oranges for him, fucking him any time he wanted. He also imagined himself in his own empty apartment, working out as much as he could stand, jacking off when he absolutely had to, and he felt more lonely than ever.

The day was very hard. They were filming Sergeant Mark Hunter's big death scene, and the idiot man-bimbo lead in whose arms Jake had to die was either too stupid or too stoned to remember his lines. He kept repeating famous lines from other movies, ad-libbing the strangest things, cracking himself up even though no one else thought it was funny. The FX guys couldn't get the disemboweling gag to work; they had to repack and reset the sticky rubber guts four or five times while the alien that was supposed to kill him kept walking into walls because his big lumpy head didn't fit right. The director seemed utterly uninterested in anything other than how many scenes were left before Tyler took her top off again. The food was atrocious, each gluey, fat-saturated basin of unidentifiable muck more horrifying than the last. Jake was getting way behind on his protein intake. By the end of the day he felt weak and shaky and on the verge of tears. Miki found him leaning against the wall of the alien warship with his palm pressed against his forehead.

"You OK, honey?" Miki asked, looking up at him with genuine concern.

"I guess," Jake said. "It's just…so different than Hong Kong. It's like no one cares if this movie is good or not."

"Oh, honey. Of course they don't." Miki took Jake's chin and lifted it until Jake met his gaze. "It's *CyberCommandos*, not *Citizen Kane*. Just do your best. That's all you can do. Remember that check?"

Jake nodded.

"Are you visualizing it right now?"

Jake smiled a little. "Yeah," he said.

"OK then." Miki took him by the arm. "On your feet, soldier!" His voice dropped an octave as he reeled off a chunk of Sergeant Hunter's dialogue. "We'll show these no-good alien scumbags how we do things on Planet Earth!"

Jake laughed and thought maybe he could get through this after all.

That was how it went all through the first week of shooting. Working from eight A.M. till midnight with nothing but Miki's fresh juice and scathing sense of humor to keep him going, then coming home and finding himself in front of that rounded wooden door, wondering about the man in the suit and the silk-bound notebooks. He became more and more curious about the old actor who apparently lived there. One morning he saw one of his landladies sitting out on the back porch of the guesthouse she lived in and decided to ask her. "Good morning, Mrs. Blake," he said as he approached.

The old woman on the porch smiled at him. She looked rather like a hip Mrs. Santa Claus, hair tucked into a soft bun, eyes magnified behind tiny glasses, ears and fingers sparkling with amber jewelry. "You know, you're the first person who ever called me that," she said. "I kind of like it."

"What do people normally call you?" Jake asked.

"Ms. Farburg," she said, sipping her coffee. "Ms. Blake's still asleep."

"I am not," said a voice behind her. The screen door creaked open, revealing another person who must be Ms. Blake, though Jake would have sworn the skinny old thing with short white hair and a man's blue bathrobe was a man.

"You're the new boy, huh? The actor."

"That's right, Ms. Blake. Sorry about the mix-up."

"No harm done, kid." The newcomer eased herself into a chair and patted Ms. Farburg's chubby thigh. "You want coffee? Get the kid a cup of coffee, Sarah."

"No thank you, Ms. Blake. I don't drink coffee."

"Health nut, huh?" She shook her head and gave Jake's bare chest a quick cynical once-over. "And lose the Ms., willya? At my age there's no point even bothering. Just Blake's fine."

"OK, Blake." Jake already felt more comfortable with these old women than he had with anyone he'd met in L.A., but he wasn't sure of the best way to ask about Jimmy Lee. "This is really a great house," he said.

"Thanks. An old friend left it to me. Don't have much else in the world, but it hardly matters. I've got a home. Got my health. And I've got Sarah, of course. Don't know how I'd keep all the paper straight without her."

Jake realized belatedly that the two old women were a couple. It seemed everyone was paired up but him. Well, it didn't matter. He had other things on his mind. "You know," he said, "I heard one of my favorite actors lives here. Did a lot of action films. His name is Jimmy Lee. Do you know him?"

"Sure," Blake said. "I've known Jimmy for years. He used to do odd jobs for me in exchange for an apartment. That was before the stroke."

"Stroke?" Jake frowned. "When did that happen?"

"Just a couple days before you moved in. He's been in the hospital ever since. I keep his apartment like he left it in case he gets better, but the doctors don't have much hope. Coma, they say."

Jake shook his head. "That's awful," he said. Then, before his brain knew what his mouth was doing: "Can he have visitors?"

"I don't see why not." Blake looked at Jake curiously, as if trying to see inside him and gather his intentions. "Sarah and I try to see him every week, but he can't talk or anything."

"I've just always been a big fan. I watched all his movies when I was a kid. I sure would like to meet him."

Blake frowned. "Well, I don't know. I'm not so sure he'd want you to see him like he is now."

Jake had no idea why it was suddenly so important to see Jimmy Lee, but he just couldn't let it go. "Please, Ms....I mean, Blake, don't you think if he can hear what's going on around him, he might be cheered up by a visit from a young actor who was influenced by his work?"

Sarah smiled and nudged Blake in the ribs. "What can it hurt, Blake? Jimmy might like a visit from a handsome young fellow."

"Yeah, I guess you're right. As always." Blake took a small notebook and pen from her robe pocket. "He's at Queen of Angels, room 307." She wrote down the address, then tore off the sheet and handed it to Jake. "Go see him if you want to. You seem like an OK kid."

Jake heard the set driver's horn. "That's my ride. Thank you so much for this."

Blake made a dismissive gesture and sipped her coffee.

On the set, in the makeup chair, Jake found himself telling Miki about Jimmy Lee. He didn't mention being inside Lee's apartment and certainly didn't mention the man in the dark suit, but he wanted Miki's approval of his plan to visit Jimmy in the hospital. He wasn't even sure why he was doing it.

"I swear, honey," said Miki, "you have got to be the sweetest boy who ever lived. I'm sure that old guy is all alone in the world and it's really wonderful of you to go and visit him."

Jake grinned sheepishly.

"Not that I will ever be old," Miki added, "but if I were, I know I'd want a cute boy like you to come visit me."

Jake had let down his guard for a moment and looked up at Miki's face. Now he blushed and looked back down into his lap.

Later, Miki took Jake aside and pressed a small, colorful flyer into his hand. "I'm doing a show tomorrow night at the Horn of Plenty," he said breathlessly. "I'd love it if you'd come."

Jake looked down at the flyer. A drag show at a gay club. His heart kicked in his chest. "I don't know," he said before he could stop himself.

"It's no big deal." Miki shrugged and began to turn away. "If you can make it, fine, if not then not."

Jake realized with sudden clarity that Miki was nervous. Miki who was always cool, who always had a naughty joke or some catty comment, was suddenly as nervous as Jake. He realized that he wanted more than anything to know Miki outside this crazy artificial movie world. More than that, he wanted be the one squeezing oranges for Miki in the morning. That thought led to another, and before he could stop himself he said, "Will your roommate be there?"

Miki frowned. "My roommate?" Then understanding flooded across his features and the wry smile was back, making his eyes sparkle. "Yes. All four of my roommates will be there. Two of them are in the show and have more boyfriends between them than you can shake a stick at. The other two are married. To each other."

Profound, almost physical relief flooded through Jake, and he burst out laughing. Miki laughed too and Jake wanted to kiss him so badly that he had to turn away. He was in so far over his head that he had no idea what to do. He knew that being seen at a drag show with Miki was probably akin to hanging a rainbow flag in his window, but just for the moment he didn't care. Miki wanted him too, he was sure of it. The Closeted-Movie-Star Manual would no doubt tell him to fuck Miki in secret and ignore him in public, but that didn't seem right. Miki deserved better.

"OK," Jake said.

"OK what?" Miki asked.

"OK, I'll be there."

When Jake got home that night he found himself back by the rounded wooden door. It wasn't locked.

As exhausted as he was, he devoured the silk-covered diaries one after another. The story was so engrossing that he did not notice when the sun came up. Jimmy Lee had lived a thousand lives, each more tragic and fascinating than the one before. Jake read until his eyes felt like hot sand in his head, until he could barely see. When he had turned the final page of the final book, he collapsed on Jimmy's narrow bed, dreaming before his head hit the pillow of Miki and the man in the suit, of the young Peking Opera fugitives Ji Fung and Lin Bai, of the heartbreaking Victor See. He slept for nearly ten hours.

■ ■ ■

Poppy Z. Brite & Christa Faust

The Horn of Plenty was in West Hollywood, and Jake got lost several times before finally turning a corner onto a wide, glitzy street that fluttered with rainbow flags and teemed with handsome young men. He gripped the steering wheel of his cranky '64 Mustang, sick with nervous jitters, sure he ought to just keep driving and pretend he was on his way to somewhere else. There were no parking places anywhere and he was about to give up and turn around when a pair of shirtless muscle boys climbed into a Jeep and pulled out of a spot just ahead.

He sat in his car for nearly ten minutes, stomach churning. When he finally worked up the courage to get out, he walked as quickly as he could towards the address on the flyer, keeping his head down and refusing to look either left or right. He gave the flyer to the boy at the door like a man buying a ticket for a porno movie. He was astonished when the boy pressed a stamp into an inkpad and stamped a large red penis on the back of his hand.

The club was hot and dim, crowded with mostly men and drag queens but a few real girls too. On the small stage, a black drag queen was doing Billie Holiday terrifyingly well. When she finished "Tain't Nobody's Business If I Do," the audience applauded and whistled. The queen smiled and touched the gardenia in her hair with one large white-gloved hand, then slithered offstage. A momentary lull of low bar noise was soon swallowed by stamping and hooting as an upbeat rockabilly number shook the speakers and a rich, fruity voice demanded that everyone give it up for Miss Cherry Blossom.

Miki came out dressed as a pinup artist's cowgirl fantasy, tiny shorts and silk-piped Western shirt knotted between petite artificial breasts. A gunbelt with two shiny toy pistols hung low on his slim hips. His long black wig was done up in pigtails, and a tiny red cowboy hat perched on the back of his head. He pretended to blow smoke off of his toy guns as he lip-synced to some bubbly girl singer from the '50s. While he was flawless in his representation of cutesy-girl femininity, Jake wasn't sure how to feel about the act. He loved seeing the full exposed length of Miki's muscular belly, but his familiar face seemed lost under all that makeup. Only his bright eyes were recognizable.

Triads

People think I'm crazy
Stone deaf and dumb
But I can cause destruction
Just like the Atom Bomb

Miki spoted Jake in the audience and gave him an extravagant wink.

'Cause I'm a Fujiyama mama
And I'm just about to blow my top

He aimed his pistols at a trio of leather-clad men to the left of the stage.

And when I start erupting ain't nobody gonna make me stop!

The audience erupted too. Obviously Miki was very popular. Jake wondered whether an inexperienced hick such as himself could really have a chance with a girl like Miss Cherry Blossom.

There were a couple more acts, a fat drag queen who was so funny that Jake nearly shot his four-dollar club soda out his nose more than once, then the black queen again. She was Josephine Baker now, complete with a little skirt made from bananas. When she was done, the lights dimmed and the staccato beat and wailing intro of Peking Opera filled the darkened club. *"And now, the moment you've all been waiting for, welcome back Miss Cherry Blossom as White Snake!"*

When the music came to a sharp, twangy stop, light flooded the stage and there was Miki. His face was painted white with cherry lips and wide black-lined eyes. He wore a long brocade robe and a huge headdress covered with tassels and rich embroidery. His toy pistols had been replaced by a pair of very real-looking swords. He crossed the blades before his face and struck a pose of delicate, liquid tension.

Jake watched with his mouth half-open as a techno beat insinuated itself through the Chinese music and Miki began an astonishing display of poise and grace, his body and his swords moving in snakelike tandem. His acrobatic maneuvers seemed more like martial arts than like any sort of traditional dance. Jake gasped as Miki threw the swords into the air and spun around, heavy robe falling away like a silvery whirlwind. He caught the flashing weapons and struck another flawless pose as the music stopped again. He was naked now except for silver pasties over his flat, boyish nipples and a tiny silver g-string.

The audience went wild, but Jake barely heard them. He could not take his eyes off Miki, his lean, muscled legs, his narrow hips and taut belly, his muscular chest and graceful arms all topped with that immaculate painted face. And on the stage Miki caught his gaze and threw it back with unabashed heat. No joking now, only desire. Jake knew there was no going back from here.

After the show, he found Miki in a tiny dressing room behind the kitchen. Wrapped in a plain white kimono, Miki was wiping greasepaint off his face. The black drag queen was there too, but as soon as she saw Jake she pulled her marabou feather robe around herself and hustled out. "My goodness," she threw over her shoulder, "I think I need to change my tampon."

Jake smiled. "That was incredible, Miki. I had no idea you were a martial artist too."

"Well, Jet Li doesn't need to look for a day job or anything." Miki stood and turned to Jake. "My father's side of the family, the Chinese side, are all Peking Opera actors. I guess it's genetic."

"Really?" Jake stuck his hands in the pockets of his jeans. "They took me to see Peking Opera while I was shooting in Hong Kong. It was much more...I don't know, more static."

"Well, I bet nobody whipped their clothes off at the end."

Jake shook his head, laughing softly. He realized that for the first time he really felt totally comfortable with Miki. All his nervousness was gone.

"And that singing." Jake wrinkled his nose. "God, it was awful. Like cats being tortured."

Miki stood, threw his arms wide, and began to sing just like the Hong Kong actors.

"Please," Jake begged, covering his ears. "Please have mercy!"

Triads

Miki continued, placing his hands beside his face with his fingers elaborately posed. His eyes glowed with mischief.

"Stop stop stop." Jake reached out and grabbed Miki. Miki tried to squirm away and Jake held him tighter, covering his mouth with one hand. Miki looked up into Jake's eyes and stopped fighting. Jake could feel Miki's breath against his palm and a fierce shiver skittered down his spine. The whole length of Miki's body pressed against him and Jake could feel that Miki was naked underneath the white silk.

Jake removed his hand slowly from Miki's mouth, letting his fingertips trail across Miki's lips. Miki's head tipped back and he closed his eyes.

Jake was so hard under the crushing confines of his jeans that he felt sure the denim would tear. He wanted to kiss that mouth more than he had ever wanted anything in his life, but he was also afraid of doing a bad job of it, terrified that he would come off like a fumbling bumpkin. "Miki," Jake managed to say. His voice was rough in his too-tight throat.

Miki opened his eyes, that little smile tugging at the corner of his mouth. "What, baby?"

"I…" Jake looked down into Miki's dark eyes. "I haven't done this very many times. I want to do a good job."

Miki's smile widened and he touched Jake's hot face. "Come on now, it's not just a job." Miki paused, eyes glittering. "It's an adventure!"

Jake burst out laughing, anxiety rushing out of him like a held breath.

"Baby, how old are you?"

Jake swallowed hard. "I'm twenty-two," he said.

"Well, I'm gonna tell you something." Miki put his lips right against Jake's ear. "*This is not an audition.* The part was yours since the day we met. Besides…" Miki trailed his fingers over the trapped shape of Jake's aching hard-on. "You're twenty-two. If you don't get it right the first time, we can try again. And again."

Jake kissed Miki then, and it was even better than he ever could have imagined. Miki finally broke the kiss. His face was flushed, his cock standing out comically beneath the kimono. "C'mon," he said. "Let's get out of here."

Miki lived in a sprawling terra-cotta-colored house up in the hills above West Hollywood, hidden away from the narrow, curvy street by an imposing wrought-iron fence entwined with leafy vines. He led Jake around to a side door and down a long, dimly lit hall, giggling like a kid sneaking through his parents' house.

They kissed, leaning against the door to Miki's room. Jake could not resist slipping his hands up under Miki's shirt. Miki laughed into his mouth, whispering *hold on hold on hold on* while fumbling to open the door without turning away from Jake. The door finally gave way and they tumbled in together.

The smell of Miki's room was like the smell of his body, chocolaty-sweet and spicy combined with the smell of clean laundry and expensive hair products. The walls were painted a deep midnight purple and the single tiny lamp made the wide disheveled bed seem like a cozy yellow island in a dark sea.

Miki pulled away from Jake and bent to touch a lighter to a row of candles in glass tubes decoupaged with pictures of Chinese women in old-fashioned clothes. As Miki fooled with the stereo, Jake's eyes began to adjust to the dimness. He saw that one whole wall was covered with cut-out pictures from magazines. Mostly women's faces, but also some funny things like monsters, fighting robots, bizarre Japanese ads for incomprehensible products. There were also a fair number of nude and semi-nude male models, all Caucasian, almost all with dark hair and blue eyes like Jake's. Curious toys cluttered every available surface: a collection of Asian Barbie dolls wielding tiny automatic weapons, Japanese anime figures, weird stuffed animals, a large rubber Godzilla with silvery false eyelashes. A big yellow sign above the bed read "Danger: RADIATION!" in several languages.

Low, throbbing electronic music slithered suddenly from hidden speakers. Jake turned back to see Miki lying on the bed smiling, one hand behind his head, the other resting on his stomach with the thumb hooked under the waistband of his jeans. "Take off your clothes," he said.

Feeling a little self-conscious, Jake pulled his T-shirt over his head and began to undo his jeans, looking down at the purple leopard-spotted rug. He toed off his sneakers and awkwardly pulled his socks off one by one before finally letting his jeans drop. When he looked up at Miki, the look on Miki's face erased any shyness.

"Damn," Miki said, "I can't imagine what I did to deserve this. You are amazing." He sat up and held his hand out to Jake. "Come here."

Jake came forward and let Miki pull him down onto the bed. They kissed and then Miki put his palm in the center of Jake's chest and pushed him back until he was prone. Before Jake knew what was happening, Miki had Jake's dick in his mouth, deep into his throat and he was doing something fantastic, something that felt almost like a fist rhythmically squeezing him. Jake put his hands on Miki's shoulders, gasping.

"Miki, wait, I...aw fuck!"

Jake gave in and came, shuddering and shaking his head. Miki sat up and licked his lips with a cat smile. "Sorry," Jake said sheepishly.

"Don't be," Miki said. "Now that we got that over with, we can just play."

Miki kissed Jake, letting Jake undress him slowly, responding with soft wordless encouragement as Jake's hands and mouth explored his body for what seemed like a lifetime. Jake felt his own cock stirring again as he slid his tongue down the smooth, hairless crack of Miki's ass, loving the sounds Miki was making and the way he arched his back.

"Baby," Miki whispered breathlessly, "I want you to fuck me. I can't wait another second."

He pressed a condom into Jake's hand. His cheeks were flushed, dark eyes glittering in the dim light.

"OK," Jake said, immediately wishing he had said something smoother, something sexier. He covered his embarrassment by concentrating on getting the condom unrolled onto his dick and slicking it with thin, clear lube.

Miki stretched out on his back and held up his arms to Jake. Jake had never fucked anyone face to face before, wasn't even sure how to do it, but he let Miki pull him down. There was a moment of tension where it seemed almost like it wasn't going to work, like it wasn't going to go in at all, but then suddenly it did, all the way, and they gasped into each other's mouths.

As he moved inside Miki, Jake started to feel in control of what was happening. Sex for him had always felt something like falling down a hill. Now, suddenly, it seemed more like...like skiing, still fast and exhilarating but he was able to turn, to bank, to slow down or speed up.

When Miki came, Jake gave up trying to hold back. The feeling of Miki's ass contracting around his cock was more than he could stand and he said Miki's name out loud, finally, as he let his orgasm wash over him.

In the warm aftermath, a string of snapshots, little emotional connections and a headlong rush to know everything about each other.

"My mom was born in Hiroshima." Miki spoke against the back of Jake's neck. "She was just a baby when they dropped the bomb. I like to tell everyone I'm a nuclear mutant, even though I wasn't born until twenty-five years later."

"My mom's a pediatrician," said Jake, stroking the back of Miki's hand with his thumb. "My dad died when I was five. I was the oldest, the only boy."

"I used to play in my father's greasepaint when I was little. I knew how to do every face in Peking Opera before I knew how to write." Miki kissed the tip of each of Jake's fingers. "My mom's makeup kit was next. You should have seen me, eight years old and all made up like Marilyn Monroe singing 'Happy Birthday Mr. President' in the bathroom mirror. I looked like an anorexic Connie Chung after a two-week bender."

"I started tae kwon do when I was six." Jake wrapped his hand around Miki's hipbone and bent to kiss his shoulder. "It's so hard to describe, but it's like...like how a musician picks up an instrument and it just feels right in his hand. Martial arts feel right to me. Like breathing. I don't think about it, it just flows through me."

"I used to get beat up every day in high school." Miki leaned his cheek against Jake's chest. "It hurt physically, but even if I got my face ground in the dirt, it was all worth it if I could get off one really devastating line on the way down."

"His name was Ronald." Jake closed his eyes and let Miki stroke the back of his head. "I've never forgiven myself for the way I treated him. I was just so scared of getting caught. I wonder whatever happened to him."

On and on like that. Sometimes quiet, sometimes exchanging hot whispers, sometimes falling back into fucking and never wanting it to end. Finally Jake drifted off, his belly against Miki's back, breathing the smells of sweat and sex and the lingering aroma of blown-out candles.

He woke hours later, amazed at the warm flesh pressed up against him, wanting to wake Miki up and start again right away.

Instead he pulled on his jeans and crept out of the bedroom, down the hall to a huge sweet-smelling bathroom. After an endless piss, he let himself out into a yard where two Siamese cats lounged on a low rock wall covered in passionflower vines. On a soft square of grass, Jake stood looking east at the pink horizon and began his t'ai chi warm up. The cats watched him bemusedly with crossed blue eyes. He was halfway through when a very deep voice spoke up behind him.

"Mind if I join you?"

It was an older man with a silver crewcut, a deep tan and a hugely muscular physique. He wore loose unbleached cotton drawstring pants and his feet were bare. He smiled. "You must be Jake."

"Yes sir."

The man's grin widened. "I'm Kenner," he said, offering a firm handshake. "Miki's told us all about you."

"Pleased to meet you," Jake replied. "All good I hope."

"Better than good. And he was right. You have a great upper body, really well-balanced. Where do you work out?"

Jake fell into easy conversation with the older man as the sun crept higher in the big clear sky. Kenner owned a gym and a fitness supplement company and was full of great advice on nutrition. He even offered to give Jake some sample shakes he could bring to the set to offset the horror of craft services. The two of them were laughing and stretching together when a new voice called out to them, "Come and get it, men."

A man in a silk brocade robe stood in the open doorway stirring the contents of a large blue bowl with a wooden spoon. He was in his early forties with thinning reddish hair and an indulgent smile. "That's Michael," said Kenner. "My husband. He's a wonderful cook."

In a dining room that looked like something out of "Lifestyles of the Rich and Famous," the red-haired man laid out an unbelievably wonderful breakfast of fresh fruit, herbed egg white omelettes, and sliced chicken breasts marinated in lemon and spices. There was tons of fresh juice, orange, mango and carrot. Jake felt as if he were eating in a fancy restaurant.

One by one the other roommates appeared: first the black drag queen, Caramel, all glamour in gold satin pajamas, fluffy high heeled slippers, and a Gucci scarf tied tight around her head; then the fat one, Fanny, no makeup and shaved head and a really atrocious pink night shirt with appliqued hearts on the front. Miki came last, blinking like a child in Hello Kitty pajama bottoms and nothing else.

"Good morning, beautiful," Miki said, coming around to sit on Jake's knee.

Jake put his arms around Miki's waist. He could still smell last night on Miki's skin. He held up a piece of melon on his fork, but Miki scrunched up his face. "Don't give me that healthy shit. I want Cocoa Pebbles."

"Come on now," Jake said, waving the fork. "You can't eat that kind of garbage. You need to take care of this body, if not for your sake, then for mine."

Miki's cheeks pinked up and he cracked a smile, coiled his tongue around the melon, and sucked it off the fork.

"Oh my lord!" Caramel put a dramatic hand to her forehead. "Can it be that little miss eat-all-the-junk-food-she-wants-and-never-gain-weight has actually put something healthy in her mouth? Alert the media!"

"I wouldn't mind getting something that healthy into *my* mouth," said Fanny, pinching the underside of Jake's triceps.

Triads

The amazing breakfast continued with homemade muffins ("Low-fat, of course," Michael assured him) and coffee for "the girls." The gentle, funny bickering that underscored it all made Jake feel truly at home for the first time in months. This was like eating breakfast with a quirkier version of his own family.

He was accepted into this odd little tribe without a second thought, everyone asking him about himself, about Hong Kong and his current project, telling him all about themselves. Michael was an interior designer from New York who also did theatrical set design. Caramel was a wigmaker who crafted huge, bizarre hair sculptures with flowers, fake birds, and Barbie dolls. She told Jake she was saving up for what she referred to as her "corrective surgery." Fanny was an actor and stand-up comic, smart as a whip, dealing out one-liners so fast that Jake could barely keep up. And at the center of this happy chaos, Miki, touching his leg, smiling at him. It was all Jake could do to let him finish his coffee before dragging him back into bed.

■ ■ ■

Later, as the clock by Miki's bed eased towards midnight, Jake felt the inevitable creeping up on him like slow poison. Finally he pressed his lips to Miki's forehead and said softly, "I better go."

Miki looked up at him and frowned. "C'mon, baby. You don't want to go back to that empty flat." He curled his fingers around Jake's arm. "Besides, we can be all environmentally conscious by carpooling to work."

Jake closed his eyes and took a deep breath. "I need to be back at my own place when the driver shows up tomorrow morning."

"But I've got the transportation number right here." Miki reached for his notebook on the bedside table. "We can call them and let them know to get us both here."

Jake said nothing. Miki's smile faded and then rebounded into a sharp smirk.

"Right, of course, how stupid of me. Mr. Straight Action Hero can't be seen at the WeHo House of Sodom."

Jake winced. He wanted nothing more than to spend tonight and every night here in Miki's bed, in Miki's arms, but it just wasn't possible. "I'm sorry," he began.

"Yeah, I know you are." Miki stood and started yanking on his crumpled clothes. "They always are. It doesn't matter. We both got off and now it's time to move on. Right?"

Jake frowned, incredulous. "Christ, Miki, it's not like that. It's…"

"What?" Miki turned to him, furious dark eyes burning. "What exactly is it like?"

Jake tried to speak, but his voice had dried up.

"Look," Miki spat. "I've been with enough closeted toddlers like you to know how this movie turns out. I let myself imagine you might be special somehow, but in the end it's just same shit, different dick, and I'm getting too old for it."

Miki left, slamming the door behind him. Jake stood there stupid for nearly a minute before gathering up his things and slinking out.

He sat behind the wheel of his parked car for nearly forty-five minutes, trying to find the courage to go back inside. The house was still lit up and cheery in the dark night, and Jake could hear laughter from the backyard. He felt more alone than ever. Did he dare? No, of course he didn't. Mr. Straight Action Hero didn't have the balls to admit what he really liked. Besides, they probably all hated him now.

When he finally cranked the key and drove away, he found himself speeding down Sunset Boulevard., gaudy lights nothing but a colored blur through his tears. He missed the turn for his street but didn't care, blowing through yellow lights, wishing childishly for an accident that would take away his pain. When he eventually turned off Sunset and pulled over to figure out where the hell he was, he found himself in front of a hospital. *Queen of Angels*, the sign read.

It had to be way past visiting hours, but Jake was able to slip past the guards and up to the third floor. He couldn't remember the room number Blake had given him, so he poked his head into several rooms until he saw an ancient, shrunken skeleton of a man whose body barely made a rise in the sheet. The chart at the foot of the bed confirmed that this living corpse was Jimmy Lee. He had no hair left at all, and his toothless mouth hung slackly open. There was a tube up his nose and more tubes snaking out from under the blanket. He smelled like medicine and unwashed clothes. The only thing that looked familiar was his large, prominent ears. Jake leaned over the old man and took one fleshless hand in both of his own.

"Hello, Jimmy," he whispered.

Then Jake found himself spilling everything, telling this extremely captive audience about the silk-covered diaries and the man in the dark suit, about his homesickness and career doubts and every detail of what had happened with Miki. "I love him," Jake finished. "I really do, and now I'm afraid I've ruined it forever."

Silence in the dimly lit room, just the soft sounds of the various machines. Jake still held the old man's hand. He heard rubber-soled footsteps out in the hall, and he barely breathed until they passed. When he looked up, the silhouette of a man was backlit against the window. As a car passed on the street, pale headlights washed across the walls and ceiling. The figure's face was illuminated for a choppy series of seconds: the man in the dark suit.

"Jimmy?" he whispered, turning to face the man in the suit. "It's you, isn't it?"

He stood, letting the old man's hand drop back on the bed. As it fell, the man at the window disappeared, or more precisely seemed to follow the splash of headlights up across the wall and away into the night.

Jake blinked incredulously and started backing away from the bed. All at once it was too weird, more than he could handle. He turned and ran without looking back.

■ ■ ■

Jake couldn't sleep. He lay curled in his sleeping bag, wanting Miki so badly he could hardly breathe, dreading seeing him on the set in the morning. How could he go on with the stupid, pointless movie as if nothing had happened? Finally the sun began to rise. Jake gave up on sleep and decided to get in an extra-heavy workout before the driver arrived.

He was mixing up one of his free shake samples, trying not to think about Kenner and subsequently about Miki, when he noticed the flashing light on his answering machine. Even though he was sure he hadn't given Miki his number, his heart still clenched, convinced it could be no one else.

It wasn't Miki. It was Rhonda, his agent.

"Jake, Rhonda." Jake could hear the quick inhale of a cigarette. "Are you trying to break my heart? Why not just drive over to my house and take food out of my children's mouths? My assistant saw you at the Horn of fucking Plenty Saturday night. Jake, we can't afford to have you gallivanting around fag bars at this point in your career." A pause, another inhale. "Look, I'm having a little get together over at my place this weekend. Sophie Janzen from E! will be there. She's a very nice girl, very pretty. Into fitness. I think you'll find you have a lot in common. Call me."

The machine beeped and Jake slammed his fist into the cabinet door, splintering it and sending the larger pieces flying across the room. Fucking Rhonda. She was right, of course. Rhonda was always right. Rhonda, who had approached him at the Pasadena tournament and asked if he'd ever considered acting. Rhonda, who had changed his life as easily as she had changed his name.

"Comedians are Jewish," she'd told him. "Agents are Jewish. Action heroes are not Jewish. Ryan Jacob Katz just isn't gonna work. Trust me on this."

Picturing himself on a photo-op date with blonde, useless Sophie Janzen, trying to smile at her while Miki was out there laughing and talking and fucking some other guy who was man enough to admit how he really felt, made Jake want to smash everything in the house. Instead, he went into the backyard and started a series of tough, punishing forms.

When he heard the driver's horn out front he stopped and pressed his forehead to his knees, wrapping his arms around his thighs and pulling a deep breath in through his nose and out through his mouth.

"You're an actor," he told himself. "You can do this."

He went to work.

Triads

Of course seeing Miki was like a punch in the stomach. Miki looked tired and pale, with faint bluish circles under his eyes. His usual banter seemed meaner, more pointed. Jake could not bear to look at him, but couldn't seem to stop himself either. No matter where he was or what he was doing, Miki always seemed to be there, like a splinter driven in deeper with every move. It was harder than ever to concentrate on the inane dialog and lame fight scenes.

At ten P.M. they had finished fewer than half of the scenes scheduled for that day. All the things that had seemed funny when Miki was whispering catty remarks now just seemed unendurably depressing. Jake sprawled on the floor, clenching his plastic pistol so hard his knucklebones stood out like a white mountain range under his scarred skin. A burly alien stood over him scratching under his mask with a wire hanger. They were waiting again—Jake didn't know or care what for. A small knot of pyro guys stood around some kind of ugly homemade-looking device. They poked at it and rubbed their chins, but nothing happened for an excruciating amount of time.

Then, suddenly the awkward lump of plastic and duct tape burst into fierce, nearly transparent blue flame. Seconds later, as everyone ran around shouting for extinguishers, a smoky explosion blasted though the set. Cast and crew went sprawling. A nearby litter of half-demolished Styrofoam spaceship parts caught fire, spouting huge colored flames. Chemical fumes began to fill the air.

Jake sucked in a lungful of smoke and began to crawl like a Marine recruit toward the spot where he'd last seen Miki. In that moment, nothing mattered to him but finding Miki and getting them both out of there. People were shouting and coughing and the smoke was so thick Jake could barely see. He knocked over the director's chair and scattered script pages that promptly began to singe around the edges. He saw a half-melted alien mask, and a smashed camera, a big light with its foil-wrapped head in flames. When he finally hit what felt like an outside wall, he started to follow the length of it, yelling Miki's name into the heat.

He came to a door, but the knob was as hot as an iron and would not turn. He was starting to feel dizzy from lack of oxygen and had to stop more and more often as coughing fits wracked his body. He found himself thinking of Jimmy—of Ji Fung—searching for Lin Bai in the wreckage of the department store after the bombs fell on Shanghai, and suddenly it became more important than ever to find Miki. Jake silently swore that if he and Miki got out of this alive, he would wrap Miki up in his arms and never let him go. He would get down on his knees and beg Miki's forgiveness if that was what it took to get him back. As for Rhonda, she could go fuck Sophie Janzen herself for all he cared. There were other agents, and even if he never made another movie as long as he lived, he suddenly knew he would rather die right here than lose Miki.

In the haze up ahead he saw shoes, old-fashioned black and white wingtips. A strong hand reached down and encircled his wrist. The man in the dark suit, and for once Jake wasn't surprised to see him. The man pulled Jake to his feet and placed Jake's hand on a cool metal doorknob. Jake shut his eyes and pushed the door open.

On the other side of the door was a narrow corridor that led to another, wider door. Above that door, a pair of bright emergency lights and a glowing green sign that read EXIT. In a crumpled heap ten feet from the door lay Miki.

Jake staggered forward and skidded to his knees beside Miki. Miki's eyes were rolled up to silvery slits. Black gunk crusted around his mouth and nose. Jake put his ear to Miki's mouth, heard nothing.

He lifted Miki and ran, hitting the door with his shoulder, bursting it open and stumbling out into the cool night. Smoke billowed behind him, but Jake saw only Miki's slack bluish face. He laid Miki on the asphalt and began CPR.

"Please, Miki, please," he whispered, counting one two three as he pressed repeatedly on a spot just below Miki's sternum. "I'm so sorry, Miki, please..."

Jake breathed into Miki's sooty mouth, remembering his kisses and his anger. He continued the CPR for another minute until paramedics arrived and took over. Jake watched with his heart between his teeth, feeling absurdly jealous of the beefy Mexican paramedic who bent to administer rescue breaths. Miki coughed and sputtered, black snot shooting out of his nose. He turned his head, spat, grimaced.

Jake pushed through the paramedics and took Miki's hand, beyond caring if anyone was watching, caring only that Miki was alive. "I love you," he said.

The paramedics put Miki on an expanding stretcher and hustled him into a waiting ambulance. "You coming?" asked the Mexican paramedic, holding the ambulance's back door open.

Jake looked around him. The street was filled with people. Some of them were watching him, but he didn't care.

"Hell, yeah," he said, taking the paramedic's hand and hopping up into the ambulance.

■ ■ ■

Jake came into Miki's room at Queen of Angels with a large bouquet of roses.

"Damn, baby," Miki said, smiling. "I'm not dead." He gestured around the room at all the other flowers that crowded every horizontal surface. "You brought me so many already it's like a funeral parlor in here."

"These aren't for you."

"What?" Miki pressed a hand to his chest in mock indignation. "You bringing roses to some other bitch, I swear I'll kill you both."

"No, listen. Come with me," Jake said, taking Miki's hand and helping him to his feet. Miki looked very small and defenseless in the hospital gown. If you didn't know him, you'd never guess how tough he really was.

"What's going on?" Miki asked, stuffing his feet into a pair of pink paper slippers. Jake pressed a finger to his lips and led him out into the hallway.

"Are you nuts?" Miki whispered as they snuck up a back stairwell. "They're supposed to discharge me today."

"I know." Jake led Miki down a long silent corridor. He stopped before a closed door at the far end. "I just wanted to introduce you to someone."

He pushed the door open. On the single bed, Jimmy Lee lay thin and silent as before. Jake put his arm around Miki's shoulders.

"This is him, Jimmy," Jake said. "This is Miki. This is the man I love."

Jake was putting the flowers into a plastic juice bottle on the windowsill when he heard Miki gasp sharply. When he turned back, the man in the dark suit was standing by the oxygen monitor on the far side of the bed. Miki backed into Jake.

"What the fuck is going on?" said Miki. "Who is that?"

Jake put his arms around Miki. He could feel Miki's heart beating too fast through the thin hospital gown. "It's OK," he said. "That's my friend Jimmy."

Now the man in the suit was suddenly on the near side of the bed, and Miki pressed into Jake as if trying to melt right through him. "I thought the old guy was Jimmy."

"It's OK," Jake said again, reaching his hand out toward the man in the suit. "Trust me, it's finally really OK."

The man reached out to take Jake's offered hand. He was smiling, but as his hand touched Jake's he began to lose form, fading back into the dappled shadows across the hospital blanket. The room's silence was split by a sound straight out of every bad hospital drama ever made: the long, drawn-out tone of a heart monitor that had ceased to register a beat.

Nurses burst into the room and surrounded Jimmy. "I need you both to step outside," said a stern-faced Filipina.

Jake and Miki stood in the hallway. After a while, a doctor came to them with his glasses in his hand. "I'm sorry," the doctor said to Miki. "We did everything we could for your...grandfather?"

Jake felt tears threatening as Miki put his hand on Jake's arm. He wanted to say something about the doctor's casual assumption that Miki and Jimmy were related, but he held his tongue, knowing it would make no difference. Perhaps the doctor was right somehow; perhaps they were really related, all of them, in a way that went far deeper than blood.

He could see the nurses pulling a curtain closed around the bed and wondered what would happen to Jimmy's body. He had no family and probably no money. But in a strange way Jimmy's dying now seemed weirdly right, as if some circuit had been broken when Jimmy lost Lin Bai, failed to reconnect when Jimmy met sad, scary

Victor See, but was now somehow reconnected between Jake and Miki nearly sixty years later.

"Come on," Miki said. "Let's go home."

■ ■ ■

Jake stood with Miki on the porch of the guesthouse behind his apartment. A kind of nervous excitement coiled inside his belly and Miki poked him, giggling softly behind his hand. Jake knocked. Blake peered out at them through the small window in the door, then opened it.

"Help you?" she said gruffly. As recently as a few weeks ago, this would have intimidated Jake, but now he knew it was just her way of facing the world. Everybody needed some kind of armor. Blake acted tougher than she really was; Jimmy Lee had refused to feel anything; Miki used his wry humor. Jake had his own armor, and probably always would, but he was ready to take off some of it.

"Evening," he said. "Can I talk to you for a minute?"

"Christ, Blake," Ms. Farburg said over Blake's shoulder. "Invite them in already." She stepped forward and smiled. "Come on in, boys."

"All right all right," Blake stepped aside. "Just for a minute."

The inside of the little guesthouse was neat and cozy. Every wall was crowded with bookshelves. On a scarred old desk in one corner, an ancient-looking typewriter crouched amid a clutter of crossed-out, marked-up pages.

"Would you like anything?" asked Ms. Farburg. "A little snack, some tea?"

"No thanks," Jake said.

"Sure," Miki said. "What do you have?"

Ms. Farburg laughed. "No health food, I'll tell you that."

"Great!" Miki said, twisting away from Jake's attempt to pinch him.

"Come back to the kitchen," Ms. Farburg said, taking Miki's arm. "We'll find something for you. You're such a skinny little thing."

Blake sat down in a sagging old leather chair. Jake scuffed his foot and looked around, unsure. He noticed that several of the bookshelves surrounding the desk were filled with lurid pulp paperbacks sporting the byline "Blake Blackline."

"Did you write all those books?" he asked.

"Yup," she said, glancing at the colorful spines. "Crap, mostly. Though all these college gals have been coming around lately trying to tell me I was some kind of dyke pioneer. I don't know about that. I was just trying to make money." Blake lit a cigarette. "So anyway, to what do we owe this unexpected visit?" She gestured at the pale yellow sofa. "Sit down, will ya?"

"Well," Jake said as he sat. "I want Miki to move in with me."

"Oh yeah?" Blake took a deep drag. "It's like that, is it?"

Jake smiled sheepishly. "Yeah, it is."

"He's not a tapdancer or an arsonist?"

Jake shook his head.

"Does he own bagpipes or a pet rhinoceros?"

Jake laughed. "Nope."

"OK, then," Blake said. "Not a problem. Move him on in."

Miki and Ms. Farburg came back from the kitchen at that moment. Miki was eating the largest chocolate cupcake Jake had ever seen. "I understand Miki is going to be our new tenant," said Ms. Farburg, touching Miki's bulging cheek in a grandmotherly gesture.

"Yes ma'am," Jake said.

"Swell," Blake grunted. "Now maybe you can go out and buy yourself some furniture. Or at least a bed."

"You bet," Jake said, cracking a dumb, happy smile. Miki came around and pressed a chocolaty kiss to Jake's cheek. Jake stood and they turned to go.

"You made the right choice, kid," Blake said. Jake turned back, curious. Blake nodded and stubbed out her cigarette. "No doubt about it. Jimmy would be proud."

Jake knew she was right.